# THE REUNION 2

The Secrets Behind The Reunion

Graham Avery

Copyright © 2020 Graham Avery

All rights reserved

The characters and events portrayed in this book are fictitious. Any similarity to real persons, living or dead, is coincidental and not intended by the author.

No part of this book may be reproduced, or stored in a retrieval system, or transmitted in any form or by any means, electronic, mechanical, photocopying, recording, or otherwise, without express written permission of the publisher.

ISBN-13: 9798675049646

Cover design by: Art Painter
Library of Congress Control Number: 2018675309
Printed in the United States of America

*To Judith, Becca and Ian for being proper critics.
Also to mum for being the best mother in the world and to my dad who is probably still wondering why i was never good at carpentry as he looks down on me
And to Nicky - my favourite sister even if she is the only one.*

# CONTENTS

| | |
|---|---|
| Title Page | 1 |
| Copyright | 2 |
| Dedication | 3 |
| PREFACE | 7 |
| PRESENT DAY | 10 |
| THE HOSPITAL | 18 |
| GILLIAN'S MEAL | 23 |
| THE VISIT TO CHRISTOPHER DUNCAN | 30 |
| THE HOSPITAL REUNION | 40 |
| 2018 | 47 |
| PRESENT - VISITING DIANA KING | 54 |
| 2018 PART TWO | 64 |
| PRESENT - CHRIS DUNCAN'S REARREST | 70 |
| BOOK TWO | 76 |
| THE AFTERMATH OF THE SHOCK NEWS. | 77 |
| ARRANGING A FUNERAL AND ATTENDING THREE OTHERS | 85 |
| FUNERAL CAT FIGHT | 96 |
| 2018 PART THREE | 104 |
| BOOK THREE | 107 |
| PRESENT DAY | 108 |

| | |
|---|---|
| GRAHAM LONGMUIR'S FUNERAL | 111 |
| THE AFFAIR? | 122 |
| ANOTHER INVESTIGATION BEGINS. | 130 |
| SUSAN BLACKMORE/DIANA KING POSSESSIONS | 136 |
| REHEARSALS AND AMERICA | 143 |
| THE AMERICAN INVESTIGATION CONTINUES | 153 |
| THE FINAL TWO DAYS IN AMERICA | 165 |
| TONY'S FIRST MARRIAGE | 174 |
| ANOTHER SECRET SOLVED? | 186 |
| THE FINAL SECRETS | 197 |
| THE GRAHAM LONGMUIR MEMORIAL CONCERT SOUND CHECKS | 208 |
| THE MEMORIAL CONCERT PART ONE | 218 |
| THE MEMORIAL CONCERT PART TWO | 228 |
| THE MEMORIAL CONCERT PART THREE | 239 |
| EPILOGUE | 249 |
| Acknowledgement | 255 |
| About The Author | 257 |
| Praise For Author | 259 |
| Books By This Author | 261 |

# PREFACE

There was only about three months separating their birthdays, they were both eight, so it was no surprise that the two young "patients" had become friends. They had become incarcerated within weeks of each other which had left one of them quite tearful. The younger girl was not. She came across as being just strange and never saying a word. She had heard that someone around her age was "staying" in the house; and this is what the young girl thought it was, just a normal house for her to live in. As long as she did what she was told - and she usually did, except for one thing and that was speaking - then, basically, the people wearing the funny uniforms tended to leave her alone. But she wanted someone to play with her. Most of the other people there were older than she was and did not want to play the games that she wanted to play. They even became cruel and called her "dumb" for not being able to speak. Little did they know that she could speak but she didn't want to. If she did talk then that would get her into trouble with HIM. And she did not want to upset HIM.

She found the girl a couple of days later, on the other side of the house. She had walked by this room and had looked in. She saw the girl, standing with her back towards her, staring out the window. One of the "staff" had passed by.

'She's been standing there, like that, for nearly three hours,' she had said. The girl had read the name badge on the uniform of the young woman who couldn't have been much older than school leaving age; "Amy Dunne" it said. She was one of the better ones and had always been nice to her. 'Perhaps you two could be friends?'

The young girl thought this too. She knocked on the door but got no reply. Plucking up courage she walked into the room and stood next to the girl and stared out of the window.

There was not much to see on this side of the house. Just a high breeze-block wall. She wondered what the other girl was looking at.

'My mum will be here to pick me up soon,' the shaky voice startled the young girl. She looked at the other girl. She could tell that she was a little bit taller than her but, other than that, they had the same build, skin tone and hair colour. Hell, they could have been twins. 'I asked if your mum will be here to pick you up soon?'

She hadn't heard the girl speak but she shook her head.

'What's the matter with you? Has the cat got your tongue?'

Again she shook her head. Stupid question; there weren't any cats here. The girl turned to look at her. It was like looking in a mirror. 'Something must have happened to make you not speak?' It was a rhetorical question but she nodded anyway. 'Would you like to be my friend?' This time she nodded eagerly.

The two young girls became inseparable. The one who was crying was called Diana and it took a little while for her to work out the other one was called Susan. They spent most of their waking day together; mainly in education but a vast quantity in play. They started to get the nickname "Twins" which they quite liked.

It was about a year and a half after the two first met that Susan spoke her first words to Diana. Diana was stood behind Susan, who was sat in a chair, brushing her hair when she said, 'Something serious must have happened to have made you stop talking.'

'I've got a secret,' Susan said barely audibly.

It was so quiet that Diana nearly missed it. Instead she walked around and crouched down so that she could look the girl in the eyes. 'You've got a secret? Do you want to share it?'

Susan shook her head. 'Not yet,' she said, this time at normal speech volume.

They kept it a secret that Susan could speak. This was to be their secret. Eventually they found something more exciting to entertain themselves - Dance. Although they were both pretty good at it, it soon became obvious that Susan was the more skilled. She would choreograph routines for them both to perform in front of the other "patients" and staff. They became the celebrities at The Moorland.

One day Diana was looking through Susan's wardrobe. It was so much tidier than hers.

'You have some wonderful things,' she observed.

Susan checked to make sure no one was watching before closing her door. 'Why don't you try something on?' She encouraged.

Diana took a pink with yellow flower petals dress from off its hanger and laid it neatly on the bed. She unbuttoned her cotton blouse and took it off, placing it on the bed next to the dress. She picked up Susan's garment and, making sure she had it the correct way, put it on over her head. Susan helped to zip her up. As there were no mirrors in the room, she could only She how the front looked.

'What do you think?' She asked Susan.

'I think it suits you,' Susan replied. 'Go on, give us a twirl.'

As Diana swirled around, Susan started smiling. A plan was formulating in her head but the time was not quite ready to carry it out. In fact it would take quite a few years before it was ready. But she knew that time would come and that kept her going.

# PRESENT DAY

The voice from my phone informed me that I had received an email. I picked up my phone and looked at it. The writing informed me that it had been sent by Diana King. Well, I'm sorry, Diana, but I really don't feel up to playing Go Fish at the moment. I pressed delete.

My mind played back the recent events. When it did everything was in slow motion. The look on everyone's face when Sue entered the room carrying the gun. The noise it made when she fired it. I tried not to picture her killing herself but it's an image I'll take to my grave.

Tony had been arrested. Luigi and Tracey were dead. Samantha was wounded but had been released from hospital. Graham was currently fighting for his life in that very same hospital. Everyone had been question. Thankfully I had kept DCI Martin in the loop with all my information and he had been on his way to Graham and Parveen's house. The scene that greeted him was one of carnage. But he soon began to organise things. The press, unfortunately, had gotten hold of the story quite quickly. My boss phoned me and was furious that I hadn't given the headlines to him first so I quit on the spot, venting all my fury on him that should have been aimed at Susan. He had tried to call me earlier but I had ignored him. He had left a voicemail but I just couldn't be bothered to listen to it. In fact my phone had received many calls over the last forty eight hours but I had rejected them all. I really just wanted to be by myself.

My laptop was opened, on the desk, in front of me. The cursor was flickering on the empty space after the sentence I had completed a few days ago. I stared at the screen but there was no way that Danny Williams and the Virus Chasers was going to be added to today...or for the foreseeable future.

Judith, my wife, came in carrying two cups of coffee. She reached over and placed one on the coaster next to my laptop and kept hold of hers whilst she sat in the chair opposite me. We looked at each other. I just thank God that nothing had happened to her.

'You're not to blame, you know,' she said.

Damn! She knew me too well. 'If I hadn't have gone looking for her then none of this would have happened.'

'And IF the cow hadn't jumped over the moon then the little dog wouldn't have laughed but the dish may still have ran away with the spoon,' Jude replied. My wife came up with some real random comments but I could see what she was trying to say. 'They all gave you their blessing to search for Susan. No one knew that she was right under their noses.'

'That must have been a shock,' I agreed. 'Gillian must be devastated.'

'Have you spoken to her?'

I shook my head. 'No,' I admitted.

'Have you spoken to anyone?' I lowered my gaze and reached for my drink. This time I just shook my head. 'So you think locking yourself away in your office is going to help?'

'I don't think I can face anyone just yet,' I replied.

I could sense the anger building up in Judith. 'And you think that Gillian, Samantha, Parveen, me and the others don't give a toss about it?'

'That's not what I said,' I argued.

'Yes, it was,' Jude threw back. 'You can't face anyone just yet. Well, just you remember, Mr Big Shot, that I encouraged you to go and look for Susan. A couple of times you were going to quit but I made you continue. So, does that make me more to blame than you?'

I looked at her as though she had just grown a pair of horns. 'Of course it doesn't,' I said.

'So why am I still speaking to our friends and you're not?' She said sternly. 'Do you even care how Graham is? Or how Parveen is coping?'

'That's not fair, Jude,' I said. 'Of course I care.'

'But you would rather remain in here, wallowing in self pity,' Judith shot back. 'Call Parveen. Call her right now.'

I looked apprehensively at my phone before picking it up. I instructed it to call Parveen. After about three rings Parveen answered.

'Hello, Graham.' She sounded hollow.

'Hi, Parveen,' I said. 'How's Graham?'

'Not good,' she replied truthfully. 'He's on a machine that's breathing for him. The next seventy-two to one hundred and twenty hours are critical. You must come in, Graham. I know he would like you to visit.'

'I promise I will,' I said. 'How are you coping?' It felt like a stupid question as soon as I asked it. But what else do you say at a time like this?

'Not good,' she replied. 'I just want him to wake up and come home.'

'Is there anything we can do for you? Anything at all?'

'Just come in and talk to him,' Parveen replied. 'I've been told that they can hear your voice but I'm not so sure. Anyway, he's probably fed up with me prattling on. It would be a nice change for him.'

'Have his mum and dad been there?' I asked. 'Maybe I could give them a lift.'

'They've been in, Graham,' she said. 'I told them that I will contact them if there is any change. Oh, and one more thing you can do for us.'

'Name it.'

'Find out why this happened,' she begged. 'For me.'

'I will. I promise,' I almost began to cry. 'I'll visit tomorrow.'

We said our goodbyes and I disconnected the call. I stared at my phone.

'How is she?' Jude asked.

'Not good,' I replied. 'Graham is on a ventilator being kept alive. The next few days are going to be critical. You'll come with me to the hospital?'

'Of course I will,' Jude replied.

'She wants me to find out why this happened.' I thought I had said it to myself but then Jude replied.

'Well, something doesn't ring true about it. There was no reason for her to shoot anyone. She was just required to be a witness for her brother, Chris. And one things for sure, Tony is innocent.'

'Well, we certainly agree on that,' I nodded. 'I guess they are still holding him?'

'You've got your phone,' she said.

Before I could do anything, it started ringing. The caller ID informed me it was Tony.

'Hello, Tony,' I said. My wife looked at me surprised. 'Are your ears burning?'

'What?' asked Tony.

'Jude and myself were just talking about you. Wondering if you had been released yet.'

'I've just been let out on police bail pending further enquiries,' Tony explained. 'Do you think I can come 'round to yours. I don't feel like going home.'

'Of course you can, Tony,' I explained. 'What about the children?'

'Tracey's....Tracey...Tracey's Mum is looking after them at the moment.' It was heart wrenching listening to him say Tracey's name. The news probably hadn't hit him fully at the moment. But it would do.

'A coffee will be waiting for you when you arrive,' I said.

'Thanks, Graham,' said Tony. 'I'll see you in a bit.'

Tony arrived approximately thirty five minutes later. He looked a wreck. I let him in as Judith made the drinks. She had offered to leave us to it but Tony wanted her to be there. We took our drinks into the lounge. Tony sat in the armchair and Jude and myself sat on the three seater sofa. It was a room that we rarely frequented. Jude had her own study for work purposes and I had mine. Our children never came in here preferring their bedrooms and the kitchen or their boyfriend/girlfriend houses. That was the main reason it looked immaculate. Jude had designed it herself. She did that as a job and a hobby and she was damn good at it.

'I can't believe she's dead,' Tony said.

'Nor can we,' Jude said. 'When did they tell you?'

'Right away,' Tony admitted. 'I was taken to the hospital by the police. They let me see her. She looked at peace. The doctor said that she would have died instantly. I knew she was taken from me before the police and paramedics arrived. I couldn't feel any pulse.'

He went quiet and took a sip of his drink. We all did.

'What happened at the police station?' I asked.

'I haven't been charged with anything...yet,' Tony began. 'Like I said, I've been released on bail pending further enquiries. The statement that I gave back in two thousand and twelve, regarding the Susan Adams's disappearance, has all but ruled me out of her murder.'

'How so?' my journalistic mind was taking over.

'I was with my family in Italy,' Tony explained. 'My father had temporarily transferred over there to improve the results of the business he was working for. Also, they could not find any of my DNA at any of the sites. I guess that as I had been Susan's boyfriend, then I had to be a suspect.'

'So are their enquiries based on seeing if you had somehow managed to sneak back from Italy?' Jude asked.

'I guess they will look into that but, no, that is not the main reason for further investigations,' Tony continued. 'That focuses on the death of my first wife and the waiter who I found in bed with Gillian that night.'

Jude and myself looked at each other before turning our attention back to Tony. 'They think they died in suspicious circumstances now?' Jude said incredulously.

'Remember what Sue said before she started firing that gun

indiscriminately?' Tony asked.

'She wanted me to investigate the deaths of your first wife and the waiter.' Her words came back to me as soon as Tony had finished his sentence.

'And I want you to, as well,' said Tony.

I took a sip of my drink and looked at him before asking, 'and did you kill them?'

I felt Jude stare at me. 'No, I didn't, Tony replied.

It all went quiet. 'Why Tracey?' Tony suddenly asked. 'She wouldn't hurt anyone.'

'Do you want the to stay here tonight, Tony?' Jude asked.

'If you don't mind,' Tony replied. 'I can't face going back home at the moment.'

'You know that you're going to have to go back sooner or later, for the sake of the children?' Jude pointed out.

'I know,' Tony admitted. 'I'm just not ready for it tonight.' We all took a sip of our drinks. 'What the bloody well happened a couple of nights ago?'

I don't know if he meant it as a rhetorical question or one that required an answer, but I chose to respond anyway. 'It doesn't make any sense. There was no reason for Sue to react in the way she did. All she was needed for was to be a witness for her brother.'

'Half-brother,' Judith corrected.

'Half-brother,' I corrected. 'I honestly didn't know she was going to do what she did.'

'Of course you didn't,' Tony nodded. 'How could you have? I wonder how Gillian is? I mean, she's lost someone she loved, as well.'

'Graham was going to give her a call, weren't you, Graham?' My wife said. I shot her a look but she just smiled at me.

I lifted my phone, searched for Gillian's number, and selected call. She answered on the third ring. 'Hello, Graham,' She said. You could tell instantly that she had been crying.

'Hi, Gillian,' I replied. 'Stupid question alert...' I actually heard her chuckle, '...how are you feeling?'

'I've been better,' she admitted. 'I keep getting images of Sue putting the gun in her mouth...' the rest of the sentence did not need to be finished.

'I can understand what you mean,' I said. 'I've got Tony and Judith sitting here with me. I'll put you on speakerphone.'

'Hi, Tony. Hi, Jude,' she said.

'Hello, Gillian,' they replied in unison.

'They saw sense and released you then, Tone?'

'Pending further enquiries,' said Tony. 'Although, probably not in the Graham's sister's death.'

'Then what?'

'The death of my first wife and that waiter in America that you...' he stopped himself from completing the sentence.

'Oh. Right.'

'Sorry about your loss,' said Tony.

'You've got nothing to apologise for, Tony,' Gillian said. 'If anything, I should be apologising to you for your sad loss.'

It went quiet for a few moments.

'You had no way of knowing what Sue was about to do,' Jude pointed out.

'I'm starting to think I didn't know that woman at all,' said Gillian.

'Don't beat yourself up over it, Gill,' Tony sympathised. 'You're not to blame for any of this.'

It went quiet Gill's end so I said, 'why don't we meet up tomorrow? All of us. I'll contact Samantha.'

'Where to?' Gill asked.

'I'm going to the hospital to see Graham, so where would be best for you both?'

'Why don't you come here?' Gill asked. 'I could cook us a meal.'

'Are you sure it's not too much trouble, Gillian?' Tony queried.

'It's better that I keep myself preoccupied at the moment, Tony,' Gillian responded. 'I'm sure that you feel exactly the same way.'

'I've been cooped up in the police station for over twenty four hours, answering questions. So I guess you're right,' said Tony.

'Will you be joining us, Judith?' Gillian asked.

'Unfortunately, I have a business meeting tomorrow so will not be able to make it,' Jude apologised.

'What time are you going in to see Graham, Graham?'

'About two-ish,' I replied.

'So you should get to mine around six?' Gillian said.

'Should do,' I answered. 'Does that work for you, Tony?'

'Fine with me,' he replied.

We said our goodbyes to Gillian before I dialled Samantha. Again, you could tell that she was still very upset. I knew how I felt when I thought I had come near to losing Judith, but these three had actually lost their love ones. Samantha agreed to meet us at Gillian's.

Although I knew it would be difficult at Gillian's, it would all work out for the best. What I was not looking forward to was visiting Graham in the hospital.

# THE HOSPITAL

I hated hospitals. Always have and always will. I think it's the smell of disinfectant that does it. To me it is to mask the stench of death. Don't get me wrong, I know many great things happen in hospitals. Although home births have increased dramatically since the turn of the century, hospitals are still the safest place for bringing a new life into this world. They also do wonders at healing people who are very sick and finding cures for the many diseases that roam this Earth. But to me, it's where many people go to die.

The hospital looked very dated now disputed being modernised in the early twenty-thirties. It was built circa 1844 with new wings added over the course of its history. The "new" Intensive Care ward was opened in two thousand and seventeen and was further modernised about six years ago with new technology.

Parveen was waiting for me in the seated area. She looked dreadful, like she hadn't eaten or slept in days which, in all honesty, she probably hadn't. We hugged and kissed each other's cheek.

'Thank you for coming,' she said.

'It's my fault that he's in there,' I nodded towards the private room. 'If I hadn't have gone looking for Sue...'

'Now you can stop that kind of talk straight away,' Parveen ordered. 'Or I'll ban you from coming.'

'Fair enough,' I smiled. 'How is he?'

'No change,' she replied. 'At present the ventilator is breathing for him. The next three to four days are critical, the experts are saying.'

'Oh,' was all I could find to say. We both went silent for a few moments.

'How are the others? Gillian? Samantha? Tony?' Parveen asked.

'Tony has been released on police bail pending further investigations,' I replied.

'They can't be definite then that he killed Susan,' she noted.
'Good. Because I don't think he was involved either. I've got no idea how Sue thought it was Tony.'

'It goes without saying that he's devastated about Tracey,' I continued. 'Gillian can't comprehend what happened. She seems to think that she's at fault. Samantha just sounds lost. We are, though, all meeting up at Gillian's tomorrow.'

'I'm glad to hear it,' she smiled. 'It will take a long time to get back to some sort of normality.' We both went quiet for a few seconds lost in our own thoughts. 'Did you hear me?' I heard Parveen say. I obviously hadn't and asked her to repeat it. 'I still want you to investigate why this happened, like I said on the phone.' I nodded but didn't say a word. 'We trust you to find out the truth.'

I looked at Parveen. 'I wouldn't know where to begin,' I confessed.

'Maybe not in your present state of mind,' Parveen agreed. 'But give it a couple of days and I'm sure you'll remember some tiny clue. I need you to do this, Graham. I don't want Tracey and Luigi to have died for no reason at all.'

I could see the tears trying their hardest to form in her eyes. But give her credit, this girl had grit. 'Okay,' I finally agreed. 'I'll look into it.'

She looked at me and smiled. 'Thank you,' She said. 'Now, lets get you in to speak with Graham.'

I knew that we couldn't put it off much longer but I was dreading it. Before we entered the room, Parveen warned me on what I would see. It seems strange with all these advances in technology, I mean I can switch me kettle on from my phone, but they have yet to come up with something to replace the tubes that assist you to breathe when you're in a coma.

For some strange reason I was expecting the room to be dark but it was quite light. I'm glad that Parveen had warned me but it was still quite a shock to see all of the tubes coming out of Graham. And the beep of the machine indicating that it was still working. I stood there and looked at him whilst his wife went right up to him and kissed him on the lips.

'A friend of ours has dropped in to pay you a visit,' she said. She coaxed me over.

'Hello, Graham,' I said. 'Guess who.'

Parveen went and sat on the chair that was positioned on the other side of the bed which left me to sit on the nearest one.

'What do you think of the room?' Parveen asked.

'It's a lot larger than I imagined,' I replied. And it was. There was a couch on the far wall, opposite the bed which, Parveen informed me, doubled up as a sofa bed. There was a 50" television that was fixed to bracket on the right hand wall as I looked at it. There was a wardrobe and chest of drawers. All that was missing was a carpet but, I guess, that had something to do with sterilisation of the room. 'Where are the staff?'

'They are very close by,' replied Parveen. 'And be careful what you say. They can hear every word.'

I looked at Graham. Possibly one of the most famous and admired men on this planet, it was not right that he was lying here on this hospital bed. 'Has he moved at all since he's been in?' I asked.

'No,' parveen replied. 'They want to keep him still in case there are any internal injuries that they haven't been able to diagnose yet.'

I nodded like I knew what she was talking about. I knew that Parveen wanted me to talk to Graham but I knew that I was going to feel stupid. However, I didn't want to let her down.

'Tony was released on police bail yesterday evening,' I said. I felt Parveen looking at me encouragingly. 'It doesn't sound like they are linking him to Susan's death as the records show that he was with his family, in Italy, at the time of the murder. Unfortunately, though, because someone told the police what Sue said, they are investigating the death of his first wife and the waiter in America which caused the split up of the group. Personally, I think they're clutching at straws. Chris's solicitor has somehow been informed so she is pushing for the release of her client.'

'Do you think she'll be successful?' Parveen asked.

'It wouldn't surprise me,' I shrugged. 'If there is an element of doubt then he probably will get out pending further investigations.'

'But what about all the evidence that tied Chris to the murder?'

'The solicitor will cite new evidence and we may all be called as witnesses to what Sue said,' I replied. 'Sorry, Graham. I guess you didn't want to really hear that.' I tried to think of something else to say. 'Samantha, Gillian, Tony and myself are meeting up later. Gillian's cooking us a meal so we could be joining you in here later. Obviously I've spoken to them since the other night. It's not surprising that they are all in a state of shock.'

'Hey, darling,' Parveen began. 'You know that thing we discussed? Well, Graham has agreed to investigate it for us.'

I had to remember what it was. 'You both want me to look for clues and evidence as to why Sue went...mad...for want of a better word, the other night. I'll certainly look into it. I owe you both that much.'

All of a sudden one of the machines started to make an alarm noise. Three members of staff appeared virtually out of nowhere. Everything started to move in slow motion. I looked across at Parveen who was now ashen faced. She started screaming but, to me, it appeared to just blend in with the noise of the machine. I bolted out of my chair and virtually ran around the bed, avoiding machines and staff, to get to her. I pulled her close as they started to wheel the bed through a connecting door which must have lead to an operating theatre. Another member of staff showed us to the waiting area. But Parveen was trying to pull away and be with her husband. It took much of my strength to stop her. She was crying and screaming. It was heart-wrenching. I made her sit down. The nurse was trying to explain what was happening. I kept hearing words like 'precaution' and 'he's in safe hands' but nothing was really going in for me or Parveen.

We must have been in the room about an hour. I think Parveen was getting fed up with drinking coffee and, I admit, I could not drink another drop of it. The door opened and Mrs Adams entered. Parveen stood up and ran to them. They stood hugging each other for quite a while. I glanced at the clock on the wall and saw that it was almost quarter to four. I knew I should phone Gillian and cancel. But just as I was about to excuse myself to make the call, Parveen called me over.

'You'd better think about making a move,' she said. 'Can't have you being late.'

'I was just about to cancel,' I replied.

'Don't you dare,' she said. 'There's nothing you can do here. I promise that I'll keep you posted with any news on Graham.'

I looked at her but knew that she was right. I said my goodbyes and made a move.

# GILLIAN'S MEAL

I went home and changed first. I spoke with Jude on the journey back to tell her the news. It upset her, I knew it would. She made me promise to tell her when I heard something. She was going to be home late. I told her that I would go into my study and work on my book.

I arrived at Gillian's at ten to six. She opened the the door and greeted me with a peck on the cheek. I offered her the bottle of wine that I had brought with me. She showed me into the lounge and the others were there. It was all very subdued, which wasn't surprising, as everyone apart from me in that room had lost someone close to them a few nights ago. However, the aromas coming from the kitchen were astounding. She asked me what I wanted to drink and, seeing as I was driving, I decided to just have a lime and lemonade

'How's Graham?' Samantha asked.

'Not good,' I replied. This got the others attention. 'Whilst I was visiting he took a turn for the worst and was rushed into theatre. Parveen said that she would contact me if she had any news.

'That doesn't sound good,' Gillian said as she handed me the drink.

'Have you been in to see him?' I asked.

They all, sadly, shook their heads. I wasn't surprised, though. They had more important things on their mind. 'How have you been keeping, Sam?'

'It's tough, Graham,' she replied. 'I miss him so much. But it's hit the children a lot harder.' I nodded but didn't say anything. 'I keep on asking myself why did Sue shoot my Luigi? I'm sure Tony's saying the same about Tracey.'

'I am that, Sam,' he said. 'I am that.'

'The funeral is going to be in Italy,' Samantha explained. 'It's a week tomorrow. It's what Luigi wanted. At least I can give him that wish.'

'Unfortunately, because I was pulled in for questioning, Daphne, Tracey's mum, has had to make arrangements for the funeral,' Tony said. He went quiet. I could just see his eyes starting to moisten. It was heartbreaking.

'Did you go home today?' I asked.

Tony nodded. 'Daphne brought the kids back and explained everything that had happened. She was shocked that the television news picked up on it so quickly. Fortunately the police arranged for me to released without the reporters knowing.'

'I guess this means that they'll keep Chris locked up,' Samantha said.

'Doubtful,' I replied. 'His defence team will probably want him released pending further investigations. I wouldn't be surprised if he's released on bail soon.'

'He's already out,' Gillian said. We all looked at her. 'I got information today that he visited Sue's body.'

'That can't be,' Samantha gasped. 'It was only three or four days ago.'

'He had the best defence that money could buy,' I reiterated. 'And he would have had the money to post bail. But I would have thought the Detective Inspector Martin would have contacted one of...' I checked my phone. Sure enough, his number was there with the countless others I had chosen to ignore. 'Oh, guys. I am so sorry.'

'You've had other things on your mind, Graham,' Samantha sympathised.

I pressed reply on my phone. 'Detective Inspector Martin,' the deep voice greeted me.

'It's Graham Avery,' I explained. 'Sorry I missed your call.'

'Hello, Graham,' he replied. 'I was phoning to tell you that Christopher Duncan has been bailed. But you've probably heard about it by now.'

'Uh huh,' I answered. 'That was quick.'

'His solicitor is like a piranha on an injured fish,' DI Martin said. 'When she sinks her teeth in she won't let go until all the flesh has gone. She'll be seeking a retrial or, possibly, a pardon.'

'Chances?' I asked.

'Not very good,' came the reply. 'I can't comment on ongoing investigations but the evidence still points to Chris being the murderer. Unfortunately, he has had to be bailed because of new information gathered which puts an element of doubt on his guilty verdict until it can be properly investigated.'

'So, how long will he be out for?' I asked.

'All depends on how long it takes us to investigate the new information,' DI Martin responded. 'We want to do a thorough investigation on this new evidence so that his defence can not blow it out of the water.'

'Agreed,' I replied. 'But Chris could fall in a barrel of horse manure and still come out smelling of roses. If anyone can find a damn loophole it will be him and his defence team. You make sure that doesn't happen.'

I must have said this vehemently as I felt the eyes of the other three people in the room turn to stare at me. 'I will, Graham,' DI Martin replied. 'You have my word.'

He said "goodbye" at that point and I reciprocated. I put my phone back in my pocket.

'I take it he's going to make sure that doesn't happen,' Gillian smiled and we all laughed for the first time in days.

'Something is sure smelling good, Gill,' Tony said.

'It's a vegetable curry,' Gillian said. 'After what happened recently, I don't feel up to eating meat.'

My phone made that funny noise again to tell me I had a new e-mail. I took my phone back out again and glanced at it. The message was from Diana King. I pressed delete. I was still not ready to go and play "Go Fish". The others looked at me quizzically. 'Diana King,' I shrugged.

'You're really going to have to go and play that card game with her, Graham,' Samantha said. 'You've made a friend for life there.'

'I will go and see her,' I relented. 'Just not yet.'

Gillian went to check on the meal whilst Samantha, Tony and me discussed the biography. I had finished it and Judith, the greatest critic I have ever had, was currently proofreading it. I discussed postponing it but the others did not want the charity to suffer it. Gillian announced that the meal was ready. We made our way to the dining room and sat down.

The table was neatly laid with a yellow tablecloth and matching napkins. Silver cutlery stood proud next to yellow placemats. Crystal wine goblets waiting to be filled, we're standing to attention on yellow coasters. The table decorations matched the room decor and we all knew that Gillian and Sue had named this room "The Yellow Room". Gillian started ladling the curry from a tureen onto plates.

'Tony?' She said. 'Would you pour the wine for me?'

It wasn't the bottle I had brought with me and this one must have been chilling a little while. It was still in its ice bucket on a serving table just to the left of Gillian. Tony stood and did as he was asked.

The meal was fantastic. I'm not a curry lover myself but this tasted great. The wine may have helped me. After the events of a few days ago, it was enjoyable being relaxed. We discussed quite a few things. We talked about Sue; toasted Luigi and Tracey. Gillian also gave her opinion that the biography should be released.

After a couple of hours my phone started ringing. I took it out of my pocket. 'It's Parveen,' I announced to the others. I put her on speakerphone. 'I'm still at Gillian's with everyone listening. How is he?'

'Well, he's out of theatre.' Her voice sounded very strained. My heart went out to her. 'They're saying...actually, I've no idea what they're saying. It's all a blur. I'm sure that it had something to do with a blood clot and it travelling near to his brain.'

I looked at the faces of the others seated in the room. They were ashen.

'Are there any long term side effects to this?' I asked.

'It's to early to say,' Parveen replied. 'Although they are monitoring Graham closely, they have said that this can happen again.'

'But he's going to pull through though?, Samantha almost whispered her question.

'Again, it's too early to say,' Parveen replied and I could hear her desperately trying to stop the tears.

'Are we allowed to visit him tomorrow?' Tony asked.

'I'm sure he would like that,' Parveen responded. 'I know I would.' She sounded relieved that Tony had suggested it.

At that precise moment, Gillian's, Tony's, Samantha's and my phone made that irritating noise that indicated that we had all received an email. 'Oh, hang on a mo,' Parveen was saying, 'Graham's phone has just gone off.'

'Is this some kind of sick joke?' Tony said.

'What is it?' I asked.

Tony pointed the display on his phone my way. "I KNOW YOUR SECRET" it read. Gill showed me her phone. It carried exactly the same message. Samantha went to show me her phone but she was shaking so much that I had to steady her hand with mine. I knew what would be on the screen and, sure enough, those four same words jumped out at me.

'What the hell is this?' I heard Parveen saying.

'What is it?' Gillian asked.

'Graham has just received a message that says "I know your secret". Hang on a moment.' I heard her fumbling for something which I assumed was her phone. 'I've received exactly the same message. What the hell is that all about?' Parveen almost shouted.

'We've received exactly the same message,' Gillian responded. 'Does it say who it's from?'

'No,' Parveen answered. 'It doesn't.'

'Neither do ours,' Samantha said.

'I thought there was legislation and software that was meant to stop these unsolicited messages from happening,' said Tony.

'But, like anything, if someone can find there way around it...' I left the rest unfinished as I read the message I had received.

'You have got to investigate this, Graham,' Samantha said.

'I think someone wants me to,' I said and I laid my phone so that they could read it.

'OMG,' Gillian whispered.

'What does it say?' Parveen demanded. 'What does it say?'

'YOU WILL NO DOUBT BE AWARE, MR AVERY, THAT YOUR FRIENDS HAVE ALL RECEIVED A MESSAGE TELLING THEM THAT I KNOW THEIR SECRETS. YOU HAVE 7 DAYS TO FIND OUT WHAT THEIR SECRETS ARE. ALL THE CLUES ARE THERE. ALL YOU HAVE TO DO IS LOOK FOR THEM. IF YOU DO NOT DISCOVER THEIR SECRETS THEN MY INFORMATION WILL BECOME PUBLIC KNOWLEDGE. TRUST ME, THEY WILL NOT WANT THAT TO HAPPEN,' I read the contents to her.

It went quiet. Deathly quiet. We all stared at our phones. Each of us trying to let the message sink in.

'It's got to be Chris,' Tony said.

'Of course,' Gillian agreed. 'He's just been released from prison and suddenly we start getting messages like these. What do you think, Graham?'

Actually, to me, this did not sound like the work of Chris Duncan. He wouldn't be so stupid. 'I've got a contact who might be able to trace whoever sent this,' I replied, carefully avoiding answering whether I thought it was Chris or not. 'If they can get a name, then we'll know how to handle it.'

'Well, you're the investigative journalist, Graham. 'I had almost forgotten that Parveen was still on the phone. 'I guess we'll just have to leave it your capable hands.'

Samantha, Gillian and Tony also gave their consent. This was a huge responsibility on my shoulders. After the last time, we'll, we all know how that ended. I looked at the others. The look on their faces were for me to help them. I'm guessing Parveen was looking exactly the same way.

'Okay,' I agreed. 'I'll look into it for you. The first port of call will be Christopher Duncan.'

# THE VISIT TO CHRISTOPHER DUNCAN

I told Judith all about the events that happened at Gillian's when she got home late that night. I showed her the message that I had received. She was gobsmacked. She thought it strange that I should receive a message exactly the same time as the others. She thought that it certainly sounded like someone was trying to goad me. Only trouble is, apart from Chris, I couldn't think of anyone else. And neither could Jude. I went to bed with an uneasy feeling.

In the morning I woke to the smell of bacon and sausages being cooked. I know that was a lot of fuss made about healthy eating in the early part of the millennium but both Judith and myself were of the opinion that you're going to die one day so you might as well die happy. I got dressed and went downstairs.

Sure enough, as I entered the kitchen, Jude was just dishing up the fried breakfast. I gave her a kiss before sitting down at the table. She put the plate in front of me and sat down to tuck into hers.

'I thought I would make you this to try and cheer you up,' she said.

'Thanks,' I said with a mouthful of food.

'I know you didn't sleep too well,, she said completely ignoring my bad manners. 'You were tossing and turning.'

'I just can't figure it out why anyone would send the same message to Samantha, Gillian, Parveen, Graham and Tony. And then that one to me,' I replied.

'So, what are you going to do?' Judith asked.

'I'm going to pop in and see Mark to see if he can trace the sender,' I answered. 'And then I thought I might pay Chris Duncan a visit.'

She nodded her head. 'Good idea,' she said. 'Although, judging by the sound of your voice, you don't think he's got anything to do with it.'

'It just doesn't seem like something he would do,' I said taking another mouthful of that delicious food.

'Seems strange that it's just started happening after he got out of prison,' Jude pointed out.

I nodded begrudgingly and finished what I was devouring. 'But that's my reason for it not to be him. It just seems too convenient for it to be him.'

Jude took a sip of her drink. 'As an investigative journalist, it's your responsibility to delve deep,' she said. 'But sometimes, darling, the answer does turn out to be the most obvious one.'

And that is what I love about my fantastic wife. She makes sure that I look at every angle.

It was only a short drive to Mark's. He lives in a three up three down, Victorian terraced property near the town centre. He purchased it as a project about five years ago and, to be honest, he hasn't actually done much to the place. To be fair to Mark, he is a busy guy and everyone is trying to get a slice of him - individuals, companies, major companies, governments, the forces etc etc. His knowledge of cyber attacks is second to none. He has hacked in to many computers to show them how easy it is and then advise them on how to fight this war. It's an ongoing task as the criminals become more and more sophisticated in their attacks. It wasn't that long ago the attack on all the major airports in Britain and Europe. And people still remember the incident involving the NHS back in 2017. Gillian and Tony even wrote a song about it called "What If...?" which appeared on the "Tell It Like It Is" album.

You've probably gathered that modern technology is a no go for me. I use a good old laptop for writing...well, everything really. Is it protected? It is now, thanks to Mark. When he showed me how easy it was for someone to access my files and steal all my manuscripts, I just could not believe it.

Mark showed me into his "study". It really could have been the dining room but it's set up with all his equipment. And, no doubt, the latest holographic game. It's the latest rage at the moment. It started off quite shaky about seven years ago. I likened it to when R2D2 accidentally played the Princess Leia clip to Luke Skywalker in the original Star Wars movie before it was digitally enhanced. But these days they are very sophisticated. Unfortunately, I just don't get it. Usually I'm waiting for all the epic graphics to finish and waiting for the start when "GAME OVER" appears.

'It sounded quite intriguing over the phone, what you were saying,' Mark said.

He stood at about 6ft 5inches which is two inches off being a foot taller than me. I was glad when he sat down. I chose to sit in the chair opposite.

'I bet it did sound intriguing,' I said. 'Because it is.'

We looked at each other for what was only, probably, seconds but seemed a lot longer.

'You're going to have to give me some sort of clue, Graham,' said Mark. 'I have a lot of technical equipment here but I have absolutely nothing that can read minds.'

'I'm surprised that you haven't,' I chuckled. I took my phone out, got the message I had received the previous evening and handed it over to him. 'I need to find out who sent this, Mark.'

Mark took the phone and looked at it. 'Interesting. Very interesting,' he said. He reached for a wire which looked like one of those old chargers from around 2010-2020. This connected my phone to his computer. Mark tapped a few keys on the screen (touch screen is still all the rage). And then he waited.

'Is it doing anything?' I asked.

Mark looked at me as though I had grown another head. 'Of course it's doing something, Graham,' he said incredulously. 'This is a very sophisticated piece of machinery. This computer can trawl through trillions and trillions of data in minutes. It will tell me how many IP addresses this message has gone through...if any...to conceal the identity of the sender.'

'You lost me at sophisticated,' I murmured.

'Not surprising for someone who will still not use fingerprint reader, voice recognition or eye recognition for their security as I recommended.'

'I'll get around to it,' I said. He stared at me. 'I swear. Anyway it's password protected.'

'It'll be your wedding anniversary, Graham,' Mark said.

'Looks like I'll have to change it, then,' I replied.

Mark went back to looking at his monitor. 'Do you fancy a cup of tea?'

'Sure,' I answered.

Mark want out to make the drink. I stood up and went to have a look at how the download, or whatever it was he was doing, was going. I could tell it was doing something. It looked like the computer section out of "The Matrix" to be honest. I was expecting to see something that said "23% complete" or whatever. But there wasn't anything like that on the screen. I just shrugged and went and sat back down again.

Mark comeback in and handed me the tea. I took a sip. Damn! Why do I do that every single time? Mark set his down on the table next to his computer.

'Anything else you can tell me about the message?' He asked.

'I received it at exactly the same time as Samantha, Gillian, Tony and Graham receiving one,' I responded.

'So it's not a one-off or coincidence, then,' said Mark.

'Wouldn't appear to be,' I agreed.

'Any suspects?'

'Probably loads,' I laughed. 'But the most likely candidate is Chris Duncan.'

'Duncan?' Mark questioned. 'Wasn't he the bastard convicted of killing Graham Longmuir's sister?' I confirmed with a nod. 'Thought he was in prison.'

'For a computer geek, Mark, you sure don't keep up to date with the latest news,' I said. For the next five minutes I filled him in on recent events. His eyes went wide.

'Wow!' He exclaimed. 'I miss all the fun.'

'Well, I wouldn't really call it fun, Mark.'

'No,' he said embarrassedly. 'Apologies.'

My phone beeped. 'Is that it? Is it completed?' I asked Perhaps a little too excitedly.

'No,' Mark said peering at my screen. 'You've got mail.'

'Does it say who from?'

'It just says "GO FISH".

'Christ, I wish she'd stop pestering me,' I fumed. 'I'll delete it in a minute.'

His machine then made a funny noise. It sounded like a pig grunting. 'Now we're in business,' said Mark.

'You mean it's finished?' I asked and drank the last few remnants of my cup of tea.

'Yep,' Mark replied. 'Now let's find out who sent you that email. What the f...?'

'What is it?' I asked concerned.

'This can't be right. There has to be a glitch somewhere.'

Mark was losing his cool. I had never seen mark lose his cool before. 'What is it, Mark?'

He turned the screen around so that I could see it. 'It's saying that I sent the message to you.'

I looked from the screen to his face, which was ashen, and back to the screen again. 'I don't understand,' I said. 'What does this mean?'

'It bloody well means that someone has hacked into my computer,' Mark replied shaking his head in disbelief.

'But no one can hack your computer, Mark,' I pointed out.

'Precisely.'

I left Mark's in a state of shock. But not as much of a shock that Mark was in. He was livid. He was mumbling that it would take him hours, possibly days, may be even weeks or months to find out who had managed to penetrate his computer defences.

I had contacted Chris to ask him if I could pop around to see him. Chris agreed that I could and said that he would get the kettle on. It took me about twenty five minutes to drive to his Devon address. This was just the other side of Exeter. The property had a driveway which I drove up. I managed to park near his front door. Mine was the only car there.

Chris must have heard me approach as he had opened the door before I had even unclipped my seatbelt. 'Mr Avery,' he greeted proffering his hand.

'Mr Duncan,' I said shaking his hand.

'Come in,' said Chris moving slightly aside so that I could get by him. I was shown straight into the kitchen. As promised, the kettle was boiling. 'I must say that I wasn't expecting a visit from my most favourite novelist and investigative journalist.'

Chris began to make the drinks. 'I must admit,' I began, 'I wasn't expecting to pay you a visit.'

'I must thank you for finding my sister,' said Chris. I nodded but didn't say anything. 'It sounds like she certainly put the cat amongst the pigeons.'

'You could say that,' I agreed. 'In more ways than one. Sorry that you didn't get to spend any time with her.'

'She has got me released from prison,' Chris shrugged. 'I owe her everything.'

He placed the drink in front of me. I instinctively took a sip. Boy it was hot. 'It was quite an horrific end,' I said. 'But why did she have to kill Tracey and Luigi and injure Graham?'

'I've no idea,' Chris said. 'But this will probably shock you but I don't care. I'm just glad to be out of prison. Sure, it would have been better that no one died. But she has set me free.'

'I thought you had been released on licence pending a further police investigation?' I noted.

'A mere technicality, Graham,' Chris smiled. 'My defence team are currently working on getting my guilty verdict quashed. They think they have a pretty good chance. I mean Tony has been arrested for Susan's murder. You're one of the witnesses that heard Sue that she had seen him do it.'

He obviously had not heard that Tony had been released. I didn't know if I should break the news to him. But, then, I could always plead ignorance. 'True,' I nodded.

'But you still think I'm guilty,' Chris said appearing to know what was going through my mind.

'Where's Kathleen?' I asked.

'She's at a secret location,' Chris answered. 'We thought it wise that she keeps low until my release blows over. You must have seen the press outside when you pulled up?'

'I didn't see a soul,' I admitted.

'That's funny,' said Chris looking out the window. 'There were a few camped out there earlier. They must have gotten bored.'

'No doubt you are in negotiations with a couple of them to get your story across?' I said. It was a rhetorical question but Chris was always going to answer it.

'You know me too well, Graham,' he laughed. 'As it happens, I am in discussions with two papers at present. Both are very interested at getting my story across. And the fact that I have lost my dear sister. How did you find her by the way?'

I took a sip of my tea. It had cooled a little bit. 'I'm sure that you already know how I found her,' I replied. He looked at me blankly. Perhaps he did not know. 'I got in touch with the mental institute your mother put her in. They gave me access to one of the patients who had known your sister. She told me that Susan was married to Gillian.'

'Gillian?' Chris said in disbelief. 'The Gillian?'

'The very same,' I asked. It definitely sounded like he did not know but, if as he says, he's had journalists camped on his doorstep, then surely one of them would have broke the news to him, wouldn't they?

'How is Gillian?' He asked.

'How would you expect her to be?' I responded. 'I don't think she has a clue what happened or why it happened.' Chris nodded and took a sip of his drink. ' She's very upset. Not only has she lost her wife but she witnessed two friends get murdered and knows that Graham Longmuir is fighting for his life.'

'You can't blame me for that,' Chris reacted.

I stared at him but nodded. 'You're right, Chris,' I agreed. 'I've got no one to blame but myself. I really shouldn't have gone looking for your sister.'

'Then, why did you?' He asked.

I shrugged. 'The million dollar question,' I said. 'I guess my investigative side took over. No, that's not it. If there was a small inkling that you were innocent, then I don't think I would have rested knowing that I had helped put you in prison. That's why I had to find your sister.'

We both took a sip from our drinks. 'And yet, despite what you heard from Susan, you still think I'm guilty,' Chris pointed out. I didn't reply.

He had a point. His sister was the only one who could prove his innocence. She had pointed out the fact that Tony had murdered Graham's sister. But I knew that the police had ruled Tony out of the equation. And, therefore, that left one person who could have killed Susan, and he was standing in front of me. Unless - unless there was any way that Tony could have come back early from his holiday in Italy. Perhaps Tony was the the murderer after all. I shuddered at the thought. I knew that DI Martin was investigating the possibility.

'Let's just say that the jury's still out, Chris,' I finally said. 'We both know that the police are questioning Tony about his moves in two thousand and twelve. And Sue did appear to back your story. Unfortunately, for me, the evidence is strong against you. I can't say fairer than that.'

Chris seemed to digest this. He nodded. 'Fair enough,' he said. 'I'll just have to hope that the police get the breakthrough that will prove my innocence.'

We both took another sip of our drinks. 'Have you been to see Susan's body since you've been released?' I asked.

Chris actually pulled out a chair from under his breakfast bar. He sat down. 'Excuse my manners. Please sit,' he said. I remained standing. 'Yes, I have been to view Susan's body. Most of her head was covered by a shroud. But, I guess, if you put a gun in your mouth and pull the trigger, well, it's going to make an awful mess.'

'You can say that again,' I said. The images revolved around my head at the precise moment that Sue ended her life. It was so gruesome that those pictures will go with me to the grave.

'From what I could see of her, though,' he continued, 'she looked at peace.'

I nodded. 'After living with that secret and torment for most of her life, she deserves to be,' I replied.

We remained in silence for a few moments. We were probably both remembering Susan at different ends of her life spectrum. Chris was seeing her as though they were pre-teenagers and were messing about as any normal brother and sister would. While I was still trying to get those awful images out of my brain.

'So, Mr Avery, down to the nitty gritty,' Chris said breaking the silence. 'What have you really come to see me about?'

I took out my phone and pulled up the email I had received. I showed it to him. He read it and then looked at me, questioningly. 'Did you send it?' I asked.

'No,' he simply replied.

'I received it the same time as Samantha, Gillian, Tony and Graham, so Parveen said, received messages. What with you just being released from prison, well...'

"I'm the likely guilty party,' he smiled. For some reason he took out his own phone and pressed a few keys. He turned the screen to me. 'Did theirs read the same as this?'

"I KNOW YOUR SECRET" was emblazoned across the screen. 'You got the same message?' I said in disbelief.

'Hey, I get loads of these,' Chris said. 'Being the alleged murderer of Graham Longmuir's sister makes you pretty hated, you know.'

'I bet it does,' I replied. 'You obviously have no idea who sent it.'

'None at all,' Chris answered. 'My sister would have been the logical choice.'

'But she's dead.'

'Right. So it can't be her,' Chris said a little absentmindedly. 'Haven't you got a contact who can trace this sort of thing?'

'I've got someone looking into it but it's going to take them a while to get an answer,' I said. Something told me to keep it from Chris what had happened earlier. I don't think it would have really mattered if I had told him but, you know when you get that nagging doubt? I was certainly getting it at this point.

'You'll let me know if you find out?' Chris asked. He had actually started to look a bit worried.

'I will,' I said solemnly. 'I promise.'

# THE HOSPITAL REUNION

Whilst I was visiting Chris, Gillian, Tony and Samantha had gone to the hospital to see Graham. They weren't expecting much after the relapse he had had yesterday. But even something that we take for granted as visiting a loved one in hospital, takes some careful planning for a group of famous celebrities. Phone calls had to made so that the visit could be scheduled. Parking arrangements had to worked out. Entrances and security had to be planned.

Apparently when the three "Ladies and Gentlemen" members arrived at the hospital. There was a collection of staff all waiting to greet them. They had the cameras on their phones all ready and were taking pictures of the group as they were ushered in to the building.

The press and a group of die-hard fans had been camping at the hospital. They were expecting the group to turn up to visit the wounded friend and colleague. They were not disappointed. They probably all got their shots as Gillian, Samantha and Tony disembarked their lift. The paparazzi would certainly be keeping their editors happy. Speaking of which, mine was still trying to contact me but I was having nothing to do with him. The three band members waved appreciatively at their supporters as their names were screamed but their faces remained quite solemn.

Security and the hospital management team had thought it prudent that the celebrities entered the building a little way away from where patients were convalescing and required peace and quiet. They were then taken through a maze of corridors before finally being shown to the waiting area on the Intensive Care ward.

Parveen came out to join them. She had a huge grin on her face.

'You see. I told her that Parveen would be glad to see us,' Gillian laughed.

'I'm always pleased to see you guys,' Parveen laughed back.

'So why the big grin then, Parveen?' Samantha asked.

'You'll see,' she answered. 'You'll see.'

They had to go through the "counselling" of what to expect that I had to endure. The three nurses, I only had the one!, were probably more nervous than Samantha, Gillian or Tony. It soon became apparent that "Ladies and Gentlemen" was their favourite group of all time.

'I came and watched you at the racecourse in Newton on your opening night,' the first nurse gushed.

'Did you enjoy it?' Gillian asked.

'It was brilliant,' the nurse replied. 'That clip you showed of the original performance of "Teenage Dream" was sublime. I was devastated when you broke up but so ecstatic when it was announced that you were getting back together again.'

'And looking at you two,' said Tony, 'you probably won't remember us from the first time around?'

'My mum and dad brought me up on your music,' said the second nurse.

'I was about one and half when you split up in twenty-four,' the third nurse smiled.

'You can really go off people, can't you?' Gillian laughed. 'But don't build us up on a pedestal. It's people like you who, fortunately, like our music and us, that has made us what we are today. It's people like you that deserve all the credit. I don't think I could do what you three do day in day out.'

'Here's what we'll do,' Samantha said. 'We're going to give you and your partners VIP tickets for the next gig. Just as a thank you for what you do.'

'OMG,' said the first nurse. 'Thank you. Thank you ever so much.'

'And now I think it's time for you to come and sit with Graham,' said Parveen.

The followed Parveen into the room where Graham was being treated. They were surprised to find him propped up in bed with his eyes open.

'Hi, guys,' he said slowly.

'Are you sure it's Graham,' joked Tony. 'I mean it looks like him but it doesn't sound like him.'

'Hey, if you had been...shot in the head...and chest...then I'm...pretty sure...that you'd sound different,' said Graham.

'You may have a point there, Graham,' Tony laughed and everyone joined in with him.

'How are you all?' Graham asked.

'We're fine,' Samantha said.

'You all...escaped...without being wounded?' He questioned.

'Well, I had a slight graze,' Samantha admitted. 'But I was released from hospital virtually straight away.'

'I would have...hoped to have...seen Luigi and...Tracey,' Graham said.

The others looked at Parveen unsure on how to proceed with this conversation. She looked concerned but nodded her approval.

'Unfortunately, they were both killed in the attack,' Samantha said with tears forming in her eyes.

'I'm so...sssorrryy,' Graham responded and he began to cry.

'Group hug everyone,' said Gillian trying to lighten the atmosphere.

It was difficult with the tubes coming out of Graham to get close to him. Bit somehow they managed it.

When they finally broke apart their cheeks glistened from

the tears.

'How's the song...writing...coming along...without me?' Graham asked.

'Terrific,' said Tony. 'I think we've written, what? A big fat zero since Wednesday.'

'Well, promise me you will,' Graham replied. 'I've got something...for you to...work on.'

And he started to sing the following.

*Do you know what I despise?*
*There is no smile in his eyes*
*So I guess there's no surprise*
*When you fell for his lies*
*And I wish I could make you see*
*The man's a mediocrity*
*I know that you would be*
*Much better off with me.*

'Hang on a minute,' Tony said grabbing his phone from out of his pocket. 'Sing it again.'

*Do you know what I despise?*
*There is no smile in his eyes*
*So I guess there's no surprise*
*When you fell for his lies*
*And I wish that I could make you see*
*The man's a mediocrity*
*I know that you would be*
*Much better off with me*

'Did you get it, Tony?' Gillian asked.

'I did,' smiled Tony.

'Sure fire...number one...hit,' laughed Graham. 'Look...I want to say something...and it may take me...a little while...so bear with me. If anything...happens to me...'

'Graham!' Parveen admonished.

' This is...important...darling, so please...let me finish,' said Graham kindly. 'If anything...happens to me...then it is my...wish...that you continue...as the group. You know that we...have been videoing...the tour...so a projection...of me can be...shown on stage. Now I want you to promise...me.'

'You can tell that the bullet hit your speaking nonsense part of your brain,' said Gillian. 'What do you mean? If anything happens to you?'

'Just...humour me...Gillian,' Graham smiled. 'Now promise...me.'

Gillian, Toby and Samantha looked at each other before glancing at Parveen. Parveen just shrugged. The decision had to be theirs to make.

'I promise,' said Samantha.

'I promise,' Gillian followed.

'I promise,' Tony agreed.

'Good,' said Graham. 'I'm glad that's settled.' And he closed his eyes.

The three other band members looked at him concerned. Samantha turned to face Parveen. 'Is he...' she began.

'Don't panic,' Graham interrupted her. 'I'm not...dead...yet.'

Parveen burst out laughing and the others quickly joined in with her.

They reminisced about the old days. They discussed the tour and new material. But before long, Graham started to get tired. One of the nurses came in and informed them that they would have to leave for Graham to get his rest. They said their goodbyes.

When they got outside and before they could get into their car, the press and the crowd tried to propel forward. There were shouts of "how is Graham?" and "what's going to happen with the tour?". But they chose to ignore those comments and instead jumped into their ride.

I was driving back from Chris's when my phone went off. My

car information console informed me that it was Samantha. 'Hi, Sam,' I greeted.

'Hi, Graham.' I heard three voices responding enthusiastically to me.

'How is Mr Longmuir?' I asked expecting the worse.

'He was awake and talking,' Samantha replied.

'What?' I asked sceptically. 'I thought he was at deaths door yesterday.'

'He was certainly alive and kicking just a moment ago,' said Samantha.

'Well, that's great news,' I replied. 'I bet Parveen is over-the-moon.'

'I don't think anyone is going to be able to wipe the smile off her face any time soon,' Gillan joked.

'How's your day been? Tony asked. 'Did Mark have any luck tracing who sent the messages?'

'Er...yes and no,' I answered.

'Surely it's one or the other?' I heard Gillian say.

'No, we are none the wiser as to who sent it. But he did discover that it was sent from his computer,' I explained.

It went quiet. Very quiet. 'What do you mean it was sent from his computer?' Tony questioned.

'It appears that our most security conscious person has had his computer hacked,' I said. 'I've left him trying to figure out who had managed to crack his secure codes.'

'And what about Chris?' Samantha asked.

'He got a message at exactly the same time as we did,' I responded.

'What did he make of it?' Gillian said.

'Not much,' I admitted. 'He said that he was so used to receiving messages similar to this that he didn't think much of it.'

'Good. I'm glad he's receiving hate mail for what he's done,' Tony fumed.

I didn't bother to point out that Tony, himself, was still in the frame for Susan Adams's murder.

'But you don't think it was him that sent the emails?' Samantha said.

'Well, he could be hiding behind the fact that he received a message,' I responded. 'So he could have sent all of them. But, honestly? I don't think he sent them.'

'So who did, then?' Gillian asked.

'I promise that I'll find out,' I said.

# 2018

The two friends were watching the television in the younger girls room. It was the popular music show "THE NEXT CHART HITS". This basically was a tv series that predicted what would be in the charts the following day. The acts actually performed live. No lips syncing or miming was allowed. This really deciphered the good acts from the bad. It was a gamble. Artists wanted to appear on it because it could help sales and really launch their careers if they were good. However, if they were poor then their career could be ruined in seconds. The two friends, who were now both eighteen, styled themselves to look virtually the same that people were now mistaking them for the other.

Unbeknown to Diana, she was central to Susan's plan. Susan had even learnt to mimic Diana's voice and mannerisms. Every now and again they played each other, just to see what the staff would do. They mainly fell for it. Except for one. Amy Dunne seemed to always be able to tell them apart. This was really frustrating Susan. Amy Dunne could ruin her plan and she couldn't have that happening, now, could she?

Ladies and Gentlemen came on the television and began singing their new song "Teenage Dream". They were good. They were very good.

'They're brilliant,' Diana said.

'I know them,' Susan exclaimed. 'It's Samantha, Gillian, Graham and Tony. Graham lived down the road from us. They went to the same school as Chris, my brother. You're right, though. They are brilliant.'

'You KNOW them?' Diana shrieked.

'Well, I know Graham pretty well,' Susan replied.

'OMG,' gasped Diana. 'What's it like knowing someone famous?'

'They weren't famous when I knew them,' Susan said unsure of what her friend was getting at. 'Graham was just like a normal boy. He played football...' she gave it some thought at that point. '...no, he didn't, he was more of a rugby boy. He climbed trees. He fell out of trees. The girls liked him though.'

'Did you?'

Susan watched Graham performing on the television. 'Not really. He was just a friend to me. I liked Tony but he looked a lot like Chris.'

The two girls watched the rest of the performance.

'I quite liked the one playing the keyboard,' said Diana.

'That's Gillian,' Susan explained. 'She's quite funny.'

'I'm going to marry her one day,' Diana said determinedly.

'Good for you,' Susan enthused. 'But we need to come up with a plan to make sure that happens. But first we've got to get Amy Dunne on our side and I think I know a way we can do that. To do that, you've got to know me inside out and I've got to know you better than I know myself. Do you think you can do that?' Diana nodded.

And Susan began her story. 'Chris, my brother, murdered Susan Adams. She was Graham's sister. There was a wooded area behind where we used to live. All the kids used to play up there - well, the parents who would send their children outside to play instead of being on their computer games all day long. We would build dens and ride our bikes around a track up their. One day I went to see who was there to play with and I heard voices. My brother's was unmistakable but the female one was soft and it was difficult to hear her against the crying, as well...'

'I've told you before, Susan, we're finished,' said Chris.

'You can't finish with me, Chris,' Susan sobbed. 'We're good together. We belong together.'

'We don't belong together, Susan,' Chris sneered. 'We both had our fun but now it's over.'

'My younger brother warned me about you,' Susan shouted. 'He told me that if I let you have your way then you would move on to next unsuspecting conquest.'

'And I thought Graham was stupid,' Chris said contemptuously.

'No, I'm the stupid one,' Susan cried. 'I should never have let you have sex with me.'

'Quite a few times, Susan,' Chris bragged. 'You were a tough cookie to crack, but we got there in the end.'

'But I'll still give you what you want, Chris,' Susan said coyly. 'We don't have to break up.'

'You're letting yourself go, Susan,' said Chris. 'I mean, look at you, you're putting on weight.'

Well, Mr Big Shot, I'm glad you've finally noticed,' Susan said viciously. 'I'm pregnant and I'm going to tell everyone who the father is.'

'...Well, I could see the look in his eye. It was a look of hatred; of vengeance. He grabbed hold of Susan. I don't know if he knew the branch was there. I'm guessing he did. It was a long thick branch that came to a very sharp point. Chris grabbed hold of Susan spun her around and pushed her against this branch, her to it, with such force that I saw the branch protrude from her stomach. It was like watching that film "Alien' when the monster bursts through John Hurts stomach. She had probably died instantly but my brother took a knife from out of his pocket and started stabbing it with her. I must have screamed at that point because he stopped and looked directly at me. I held my breath as he walked over to me. His eyes were glazed over...'

'Did you witness that, little sister?' Chris asked.

Susan nodded dumbly. She didn't, no, couldn't take her eyes off the now dead body of her friend.

'If you say anything about this to anyone, I'll do exactly the same to you, do you hear me?' Chris threatened. Again Susan nodded dumbly. 'That's a good girl, Susan. I suggest you do as your doing now and don't speak for the rest of your life. Do you agree, Sis?' Susan nodded her head slowly. 'Good girl. Now you're going to have to help me clean this up. You get me some clean clothes and I'll get that old rug from the garage. And I'll tell you what, Susan. If anyone does ask you about this, then just say you saw Tony walking up this way. Okay?'

Susan managed to tear her gaze away from the now limp form of the other girl. She brought her eyes to look at Chris and, once again, she nodded.

'...And so we cleaned up the scene the best we could. I hadn't spoken from that day until I uttered those words to you six months after we first met. My mother's didn't know what to do with me so she got me institutionalised. Unfortunately for Chris, someone saw him dragging the rug up to the woods.'

'How do you know that?' Diana asked.

'Because I saw them following Chris,' Susan simply replied. 'I'm surprised that they haven't come forward yet. Okay. Your turn. Why are you in here?'

Diana took a deep breath. 'We were a happy family,' she began. ' Or so I thought. My dad became ill. Seriously ill. It was then that everything started to go wrong...'

*The young Diana was walking up the driveway. The door opened. Her uncle was standing there. He wasn't her real uncle. He was just a friend of the family. Well, a close friend of her mother's. Diana didn't trust him. No, correction, she hated him.*

'Your mother has had to go out so she's asked me to look after your father,' he said.

'Well, I'm here now, so if you want to go, I'll look after dad,' Diana said.

'Now I'm sure that your mother wouldn't want me to go. In fact, I know that she would like us to get to know each other better,' he said leering at her.

She stormed passed him but felt his hand touch her arm. She

recoiled as though she had been struck. 'I'm going upstairs to do my homework.'

'I'll be up to check on you,' he said sinisterly. 'I don't want to catch you playing games on your Xbox.'

'Yeah, like when do I ever get a chance to play on my Xbox,' Diana groaned.

She had been doing her history revision for about twenty minutes. It was all about the Tudors. She was reading up on Henry The Eighth and his six wives. She had read somewhere on the internet that the best way to remember what happened to the spouses was to remember this rhyme;

*Divorced, beheaded, died.*
*Divorced, beheaded, survived.*

Which was fine but it didn't help her to remember the names. She knew that Catherine of Aragon was the first wife. Anne Boleyn was always easy to recollect. Jane Seymour was third, and the one that Henry loved most of all; mainly because she bore him a heir. But who came next? Was Catherine Parr? Or Anne of Cleaves? Or Catherine Howard? One thing for sure was that Henry certainly liked his Catherines.

Then she heard the unmistakable footsteps of her "uncle" as he climbed the stairs. She groaned inwardly. The door opened.

'Good girl. Studying hard I see,' her uncle said.

'I said a would, didn't I?' She vehemently responded.

'Now, we really have to do something about your attitude, young lady,' he replied forcefully. He placed a hand on her thigh. She grabbed it away. 'You're going to have to learn, Diana, that you are going to have to do everything I want.'

'Never,' she shouted.

He smacked her hard around the face. It shocked her in to being obedient.

'...And then he made me perform a sex act on him,' Diana sobbed as the memory came back to haunt her.

'Oh, you poor love,' Susan consoled the other girl and hugged her. 'No child should have to suffer something like that.'

'It gets worse, Susan,' Diana sniffed back the tears. 'Much worse.'

'How can anything be worse than what you had already suffered?' Susan asked.

'Let me finish, Susan,' said Diana. 'After he had finished I had ran to the bathroom to be sick...'

*Her "uncle" was still in her room when she got back. She had hoped that he had gone but he obviously had something else in mind.*

*'Now that your starting to obey me,' he said, 'there's something me and your mum have been wanting to tell you for a little while.'*

*'What?' Diana almost whispered.*

*'You know that pathetic excuse of man who is laying in bed, dying, a couple of rooms away?' He said.*

*'You mean my dad,' Diana corrected.*

*'Well, that's just it, Hon,' he smiled in a jeering way. 'He's not your dad. You see I am.'*

*It took a little while for his words to sink in. Diana started shaking her head. 'No,' she said. 'No, You're lying.'*

*'Ask your mum when she gets home. She'll confirm it.'*

*'No. No. No,' Diana screamed. She ran out the room and ran downstairs. She heard her "uncle" running to try and catch her. She made it to the kitchen and she plucked out the carving knife from the wooden block which was near the oven. She swirled around just as he entered the room. 'You come any closer and I'll kill you.'*

*'No, you won't, love,' he smiled. You wouldn't want to kill your father now, would you?*

*He took a step closer with that lecherous look on his face.*

'...So I stabbed him,' Diana concluded. 'And that's what I'm doing in here. Not only for stabbing him but because if they let me out, I would try to kill him again.'

'Good for you, Diana,' Susan cheered. 'I would have done exactly the same thing. But I thought your mum would have supported you.'

'She had been completely taken in by him,' said Diana.

'And was it true what he said?'

'About him being my father?' Susan nodded. ' My mother confirmed it was true.'

'What was he called?' Susan asked.

'Richard Yeoman.'

# PRESENT - VISITING DIANA KING

Judith and myself were relaxing on one of our very few day offs together. The weather was not particularly good outside. It was blowing a gale and it was raining so hard that when the droplets hit the ground, it appeared as if they bounced back upwards again.

We were watching "THE MAGPIE" for the umpteenth time. I considered it to be the best adaptation that Heather had done of my work. Judith loved this movie and claims it to be her favourite film of all time. She was, however, still trying to spot my cameo appearance. Like Alfred Hitchcock, I have appeared in all the movies based on my books. I guess that this must have been the fifth time we had watched it and she had still to recognise me. For the other films, like the Nick Chicargo trilogy, she spotted me straight away. I had offered to tell her but she didn't want any clues.

'You never told me how it went with Mark and Chris yesterday,' Jude said.

'Chris didn't send the messages,' I answered. 'He had actually received one himself.'

'He could have arranged that so it didn't look suspicious,' Jude countered.

'He has only just been let out of prison so I don't think he would have access to anything that would make it virtually impossible to trace, especially in the timescale that he's had,' I replied.

'But surely Mark would be able to trace where the message was sent from?'

'Well, that's the thing,' I said. 'The messages were sent from Mark's account,'

'WHAT???' Jude shrieked almost spilling the glass of wine she had just picked up.

'His computer has been hacked,' I explained. 'He's trying to find out how at the moment.'

'But he's so anal about his techno security,' judith said. 'Isn't he always going on about it to you?'

'Yep,' I nodded. 'I'm sure he'll work it out and get back to me. On a completely different topic, the guys called me after their visit to Graham.'

'How is he?' She asked looking concerned.

'He was awake and talking them,' I replied.

'Really? Only he seemed on death's door when you went to visit him,' Jude remembered.

'Must be the affect I have on people,' I joked and my wife laughed. 'He was only awake for about forty-five minutes but in that time he had written another song.'

'How does he do it?' Jude wondered.

'I've no idea.'

'So, he's going to be okay then?'

'Well, they are saying that the next 48 hours are going to be critical,' I replied. 'But, fingers crossed, it does sound like he's going to pull through.'

'Parveen must be made up,' Jude said.

I nodded. My gaze returning to the film. A couple of moments later my phone began ringing. Jude looked at me knowing that our peaceful day was about to be shattered. I didn't recognise the number. I don't usually accept calls from numbers I don't know. But with everything going on at the moment, I decided to take it.

'Graham Avery.'

'Mr Avery. It's Stratford Institution here,' a mans voice introduced pleasantly. I groaned inwards. I knew what this meant.

'Hello,' I said.

'Hello,' came the reply. 'We are experiencing a problem with one of our patients...'

'Diana King?' I queried knowing what the answer would be.'

'Correct,' the response came hesitantly. 'She has become very agitated recently.'

'Since my last visit by any chance?' I pondered.

'Not really.' The reply surprised me. 'She was fine when you left. Better than we've seen her in a long time. It's been more since the news broke about that terrible incident involving the group Ladies and Gentlemen.'

He had managed to hook my interest. 'Go on,' I said.

'She keeps saying she needs to talk to you,' staid the man. 'She says that she has some information and she will tell it only to you.'

'Any clues?' I asked.

'You probably won't be surprised to hear that she hasn't let anything slip,' came the answer that I was expecting. 'I wouldn't normally ask this but is there any chance you can come and visit Diana tomorrow.'

'Well, what with the tragedy that you touched on a moment ago, I do have a lot on my plate,' I said but I knew I was being pushed into a corner.

'I appreciate that,' he responded. 'But its just that I know Diana would calm down if you paid her a visit.'

I looked at Jude. She nodded. 'Okay. I can be there for about one.'

'That's great,' he responded sounding quite pleased. 'I'll let Diana know. Thank you, Mr Avery. It's very kind of you.'

'Not at all,' I said. 'You're welcome.'

I hung up.

'I can do a bit of shopping in London tomorrow,' said Jude.

'Great,' I smiled.

We left the car in the large car park near to Reading train station. I never have or ever will drive in London. We caught the 11:02 train which got us into Paddington about half past eleven. We kissed as we headed for different tube trains. Jude took the Bakerloo line as she wanted to go to Oxford Circus for the shopping. I took the Central line to Stratford. Yes, I know that my wife could have taken the same one to Oxford Circus but she had a couple of things she needed to do first. I promised to phone her when I left the institution.

I arrived in Stratford before half past twelve so I decided to go and have a coffee. I found one of those vending machines that had sprung up in the Capital in the mid- thirties. You basically used contactless and your choice of drink was made for you. I went for a latte. I took a sip when I had received it. Fortunately it was not as hot as the drinks I make with the kettle but it still made my tongue tingle with the heat. I went a sat on one of the bar stools and watched the giant display screen which was showing Graham Longmuir's version of "Grease". A message popped up intermittently wishing him a speedy recovery which I thought was a nice touch.

I finished my latte and looked at my watch which informed me that it was quarter to one. The "hospital" was only a five minute walk and, by the time I got through security, I would be ready at exactly one o'clock.

Sure enough, the attendant, who I had met on my previous visit, showed me into the same room. I remembered not to sit in her chair. He left to fetch her.

Diana King was beaming when she entered the room. She had had her hair cut which, to me, resembled the 1960s Twiggy bob that I had seen whilst researching a character for one of my books. It suited her. In fact she looked stunning.

'Mr Avery,' she cooed. 'So nice of you to come back to see me'

'The pleasure is all mine Miss King,' I smiled. There was something about this lady that made you feel good.

'I've brought the game with me,' she said. I noticed the pack of cards in her left hand. I groaned inwards even though I knew that I was going to have to play 'I've got a sneaky feeling that you are going to beat me.'

'We shall see. We shall see,' I laughed.

She handed me the pack and sat down in her chair. I took the deck of cards out of packet, putting the empty carton on the table between us and began shuffling. After dealing the two hands I looked at Diana. She was still beaming. It wasn't a false look. The smile was in her eyes and al the way down to her mouth.

'How's your book coming along? Have you got any trout?' She asked.

'Go fish,' I answered. 'I'll be honest with you Diana, May I call you Diana?' She nodded. 'I haven't done anything on it since....well...since I last met you. Have you got any salmon?'

She handed me her card and giggled. 'Good start, Mr Avery. Good start.,

'Have you got any Carp?'

She laughed and clapped her hands. 'You're getting too good at this game.'

'Have you got any Bream?'

'Go fish.'

I picked up a card from the spare deck. It was a Bream. I showed it to her. She laughed merrily. Seeing her like this made me wonder what she was actually being kept in here for. She had been in here many, many years.

'How has your week been?' I asked.

'Same old. Same old,' she smiled. 'I did hear about that awful incident involving that group, Ladies and Gentlemen. You were working with them if I remember correctly.'

I briefly looked towards the orderly who nodded. 'Yes, I am,' I replied. 'I was there on that evening.' Her attention was now wholly on me. 'It was awful.'

'You must have been scared?'

'It all happened so fast,' I remembered. I really didn't know why I was opening up to her like this. I hadn't really discussed it with anyone. Not even Judith who went through it with me. Maybe it was because I thought she was cuckoo and wouldn't remember what I told her. 'But scared doesn't really cover how I was feeling. When I felt the bullet graze me, I thought I was dead and that, believe me, is not a pleasant experience and one I hope that I never have to go through again.'

'There were deaths though,' she said. 'I remember from the bulletin.'

'There were,' I confirmed. 'Samantha's husband, Luigi and Tony's wife, Tracey. A woman named Susan also died but she had killed the other two. She also wounded Samantha and Graham. You might remember Sue. You told me about her.'

She thought for a few moments, 'I did, didn't I? She witnessed a murder or something, didn't she?'

'Yes, she did.'

'Obviously drove her insane,' she said. 'But then, look at me?'

'What did you do, Diana? What's kept you in here?'

'I don't think they are suitable questions to be asking,' the orderly interrupted.

I immediately apologised.

'I don't mind if Mr Avery asks, Dave,' Diana responded. 'A friend of my mother's, who I actually called uncle, turned out to be my dad. And he sexually abused me.'

That was Diana in a nutshell - blunt and to the point.

'I'm sorry to hear that. No child deserves that,' I said. 'Actually, no person deserves that.'

'They've kept me in here because, if I'm released, I'll kill him,' she said matter-of-factly. 'Have you got any Carp?'

'Carp?' I said wondering what she was going on about and then looked down at the cards I was holding and it suddenly registered. 'Yes! Yes, I have.'

'So, how are Graham and Samantha?'

'Samantha was released from hospital soon after. She wasn't wounded too badly but she is finding it difficult regarding the death of her husband,' I answered. 'Graham is still in hospital. I went to see him recently and he almost died whilst I was visiting. The good news is that Tony, Gillian and Samantha went to visit him yesterday and he was awake and talking to them.'

'That is good news,' she smiled. 'And what about Gillian? Because Sue was married to Gillian, wasn't she?'

'She was,' I confirmed. 'It's hard to read Gillian at present. I know that she is suffering because the person she loved is dead, but it must be terrible to know that your partner is responsible for the murders of two of your dear friends.'

'Yes, it must be,' she agreed. 'Have you got any Perch?'

'Go fish.' Diana picked up a card. 'Have you got any Salmon?'

She handed me the card she had just taken from the pack. ' You were lucky,' she said. 'I was going to ask you for Salmon next.'

I put the card with my other three and placed set on the table between us.

'What do I go for now?' I pondered.

'I guess Sue was always going to turn out to be a bad egg,' Diana said out of the blue. 'I mean her brother was arrested for the murder of Graham Longmuir's sister and isn't her father in prison for killing his wife or someone?'

'He is in prison but he wasn't her father,' I said.

'I'm sorry, are you sure?' She said looking at me intently.

'Positive,' I replied. 'Her mum never registered her daughter's father. She had an affair with someone and Susan was the result.'

'Do you know who?'

'Richard Yeoman.' I watched as her eyes appeared to cloud over. She looked furious for a nanosecond. If I hadn't been looking at her then I would have missed it.

'But that can't be,' she almost whispered. 'I'm sure she would have told me.'

'You seem a little shocked.'

She glanced at the orderly who looked almost as shocked as Diana did. 'Richard Yeoman is my father,' she said.

Wow! What a story this could turn out to be. I had to play this very carefully. 'Now I think of it, you did look quite alike,' I said.

'Yes. Many people used to say that.' Diana was still speaking just above a whisper. 'Do you think she would have known he was her dad?'

'Well, if no one had told her, then I doubt that she would have,' I replied. 'I know that he had wanted to find her. He was heartbroken that she was hidden from him.'

'Was he?' She questioned. 'Or was he just upset that he was unable to abuse her as well?'

And then it clicked what she had mentioned a couple of minutes before. She had been the victim of a vicious sexual attack by that monster, Richard Yeoman. It now became evident that Michelle Duncan/Blackmore had done the right thing and had kept her daughter hidden.

'You have a point,' I conceded. 'I met a person recently, Tanya Sinclair, and she claimed that the politician had raped her. I don't think she thought anyone believed her. Many thought he was a womaniser but, obviously, he was worse than that. Much worse. This man needed to be punished.

'And I firmly believe that anyone who has done wrong will get their comeuppance in the end, don't you? Diana said.

'I certainly do, Diana.'

We continued our game which I managed to win. Diana was pleased about that. She thought I was a worthy opponent. Personally, I always thought that card games were just pure luck. The skill is not in the cards, after all you can only play with what you have been dealt. No the skill is making sure that your opponent cannot guess what you have got in your hand. Diana picked up all the cards and began to shuffle them. She was like one of the professionals you see in the movies. She split the deck in half and flicked the corners together so that the cards intermingled. She saw me watching her. 'When you're locked up 24 hours a day, 365 days a year, Mr Avery, you get a lot of time to practice.'

'I'm sure you do,' I smiled.

She dealt out the cards. 'I'm a little disappointed that you haven't mentioned anything about that email I sent you.'

'To be fair, Diana, I have had a lot to deal with recently,' I said.

'True. Very true,' she admitted. 'But I think you should at least listen to the attachment I sent with it. It will be very beneficial to you.'

'Uh-huh!' I said sorting out my cards.

'Now,' she ordered.

I glanced at her to see if she was joking. She didn't look as though she was. I took out my phone, carried out the fingerprint recognition and went into my deleted file for my messages. I soon found the one Diana had sent. I opened it and found the attachment. I downloaded it. It was a recording. I looked at Diana. She was sorting out her cards but I could see that she was smiling. I pressed play and was greeted by Chris Duncan's voice.

*"Well, sis. It wasn't quite the outcome I had in mind but I guess the result is just the same. It was always our little secret. And we're both going to get away with murder. I'm sorry that me killing Susan Adams sent you insane. I'm surprised that you didn't get in touch with me when you got released all those years ago. I'm hoping that it was to protect me. I don't need protecting now, sis. Tony has been arrested and will probably be charged fairly soon. So I've committed the perfect murder and gotten away with it but so have you. I mean you're not going to stand trial for the murder of Luigi Gustav and Tracey Gee. Graham Longmuir is fighting for his life. Samantha Adlington was wounded but is in a stable condition. You got away with it, Susan. You got away with it."*

I looked from my phone to Diana and back to my phone. I pressed play again

*"Well, sis. It wasn't quite the outcome I had in mind but I guess the result is just the same. It was always our little secret. And we're both going to get away with murder. I'm sorry that me killing Susan Adams sent you insane. I'm surprised that you didn't get in touch with me when you got released all those years ago. I'm hoping that it was to protect me. I don't need protecting now, sis. Tony has been arrested and will probably be charged fairly soon. So I've committed*

*the perfect murder and gotten away with it but so have you. I mean you're not going to stand trial for the murder of Luigi Gustav and Tracey Gee. Graham Longmuir is fighting for his life. Samantha Adlington was wounded but is in a stable condition. You got away with it, Susan. You got away with it."*

I looked at Diana again. She was smiling at me. 'This is dynamite,' I said.

'I thought you would like it,' Diana said.

'I've got to send this to the police.'

'I thought you would.'

'How? Why? No. How did you get this?' I asked.

'Is that important?' She answered. 'I mean, I don't have it anymore. You do.'

'Yes, but how did you come by it?' I persisted. 'The police will ask.'

'And we will inform them,' Dave the orderly interrupted.

I could sense that my visit was about to come to end. Diana and myself played the game we had just commenced. I let Diana win. She was ecstatic and couldn't stop laughing and smiling. Dave the orderly had stood indicating that my time was indeed over. But there was just one thing I needed to check. I picked up my phone again and selected the email I had received the other evening. 'Did you send this?' I asked.

'She was reading it. 'It doesn't look like one of mine,' she said convincingly.

'All messages are monitored before they are sent,' Dave interrupted. 'I'm sure, if you wanted, you can check if it had been sent from here.'

'I'm sure it hasn't,' I replied. 'It was just a stab in the dark. Thank you for our game of Go Fish, Miss King,'

'Oh, our battle is far from over,' Diana said.

I thought it was and odd choice of words. But she just smiled.

# 2018 PART TWO

The two girls were very excited. It was time to put their plan to the test. They were going to swap identities to see if anyone noticed. They had spent weeks learning all the different things about each other. They tested each other on favourite colours, singers, actors, where they started when cleaning their teeth, what subjects they liked, what subjects they hated and so on and so on. If they made a mistake, then they would start all over again. They then had to learn about each other's families. For example, what their fathers' and mothers' did for employment, previous addresses and schools. The list appeared to be endless but they taught each other everything. If they thought of anything new then they would question the other on it until the subject was exhausted and vice- verse.

Some of it was dead easy but some of it was tricky. Susan, like her brother Chris, could speak fluent French whereas Diana only had a very basic knowledge. So Susan had to give her a crash course in the language. Diana did question this because, as Susan never spoke anyway, how would anyone know she could speak French? Susan said that she was sure that her mum would have said something that would help the staff to try to get her to speak. She told Diana that some of the staff spoke to her in French just to see if she would respond.

The girls had to "suffer" an appraisal every two weeks. This basically meant being asked loads of questions over a twenty minute period. They had decided to swap roles at the next meeting. They both agreed that Diana, who would now be Susan, should remain silent so as not to draw to much attention to the switch.

Friday came and Diana was summoned. Amy Dunne accompanied her to the meeting room. Three senior members, two females and a male, which included psychiatrists and a doctor, were seated behind a longish table there was a jug of water on the table and three filled glasses in front of the professional people. A fourth glass was placed on the side of the table that Diana and Amy entered. A comfy chair was also placed that side for the "patient" to sit in. A further chair was at the side for Amy to relax in.

'Come and sit down, Susan,' the woman who was sat in the middle said.

Diana, as instructed by the real Susan, turned a looked worriedly at Amy.

The assistant, as always, smiled encouragingly at her. 'Go on, Susan. They won't bite.'

Diana did as she was instructed. After making herself comfortable, the questions began. To each one Diana remained silent. It was difficult for her because she wanted to answer a couple of them because of her own incarceration. Instead she bit her tongue, forcing her not to. Every now and again she would look at Amy for support who gave it in abundance.

After fifteen minutes of questioning, the panel obviously decided that there had been no change in the young lady. She had not spoken in six years. She must have witnessed something horrific to crawl back inside of herself and hide there.

Amy accompanied the pretend Susan back to her dormitory. She kept glancing at the teenager as if something was going on but she couldn't put her finger on it. When Amy left to fetch who she thought was the real Diana, Diana stayed in her room. A couple of members of staff popped in and spoke to her but she managed to keep up the pretence that she was Susan.

Susan, on the other hand, was answering the questions being

put to her by the panel; how was she? What did she think it would take for her to get out? Then they threw in a couple of curveballs. What was her favourite colour? What subject did she like? Who was her favourite author?

'Why are you in here, Diana?' The woman sitting in the middle of the three asked.

'Because I stabbed a man who I thought was my uncle but turned out to be my dad. And if I ever see him again I'll kill him,' Susan answered truthfully as Diana would have.

'But would you though?' The woman asked.

Susan thought for a moment. She wondered what Diana would say. She had no doubt that Diana probably wouldn't carry out that threat if she was released. And then she realised that they could have made their idea a lot simpler. But she now had to persevere with it.

'Yes. Yes, I would,' Susan replied.

The panel consulted amongst themselves. Susan could hardly hear what they were saying but "no change" was being mentioned occasionally. Susan smiled inwardly to herself. The plan was working.

'Thank you for your time, Diana,' The woman said. 'We will see you again in a couple of weeks.

Diana nodded to them. It was a gesture that was so easy to do but yet she felt Amy Dunne's gaze fall upon her. She stood up and waited for Amy to escort her out. When they entered the corridor and Amy closed the door they started walking back to the dormitory.

'I don't know what's going on,' Amy said. 'But you're not Diana.'

'Of course I'm Diana,' Susan snapped. 'If you think I'm Susan, then why am I talking?'

'I don't know,' admitted Amy. 'But something isn't right.'

They continued the walk back in silence. Amy didn't say anything to the eighteen year old when she left her in her room. She had to wait half an hour before Diana showed her face. Susan gestured for her to enter and to close the door.

'How did it go?' Diana asked.

'I believe we have fooled the panel,' Susan smiled.

'But?' Diana questioned. She could sense that her friend was about to add something.

'But we need to do something about Amy Dunne,' Susan answered matter-of-factly. 'I must admit that I thought she was stupid but she's a lot cleverer than I thought.'

Diana became anxious. 'Perhaps we should not go through with it,' she said.

'Don't be stupid, Diana,' Susan hissed. 'You want to get out of here, don't you?'

'Yes. But I don't want to go to prison for doing something illegal.'

'That's funny,' Susan smiled. 'I thought you were sent in here for doing something illegal.'

Diana stared at her and then they both burst out laughing. 'You're right once again, Susan.'

'Look, you leave Amy Dunne to me,' said Susan. 'The problem is that she is nearer to our age than any of the other staff and inmates.'

'Patients,' Diana corrected.

'Inmates - patients, it's the same thing in my book,' Susan sneered. 'All we need to do is find out Amy's shift pattern. And I'm going to need you to help me with that.'

A few days later, in the nighttime, Amy was doing her rounds. She was still concerned about what was going on with the two girls - well, young ladies now. She looked in on Diana who appeared to be asleep in bed. She then went and approached Susan's room. She unlocked the door and looked in. She couldn't see anyone in the bed. She stuck her head in a bit further. She felt the force of someone grabbing her head and pulling her inwards. Startled and caught unawares, she had no choice than to follow the momentum of her attacker. The door was pushed closed behind her. Susan had one hand gripping her throat and the other against her mouth to shut her up.

'If you scream or press your alarm, then you're dead. Do you understand?' Susan threatened. Amy slowly nodded. 'Now you see what happens when you do not follow the correct procedures? I'm sure the book states that you must not carry out your checks by yourself. I'm sure it states at least two people carrying out the rounds, doesn't it?' Again Amy slowly nodded. 'So you're breaking the rules, Amy. That's naughty. Very naughty. All I have to do is get the governor to have a look at the cctv. But it's your lucky night, Amy, did you know that?' This time Amy slowly shook her head. 'Well, it's your lucky night, Amy, because it's me that caught you and we're going to keep it our little secret, aren't we?'

Susan, tentatively, removed her hand that was covering the orderly's mouth but kept it within close distance in case she needed to replace it quickly. 'Which one are you? Diana or Susan this time?'

'Does it really matter?' Susan asked.

'Not really,' Amy said sounding really afraid. 'What do I have to do?'

'Just be like me,' smiled Susan, 'and don't say a word. Remember, if you dob us in, then a little bird will inform the governor of your little indiscretion about breaking the rules. And what you do to the "patients" when you're alone with them.'

Amy's eyes opened wide in terror as she got the gist of what Susan was implying.

'I…I…,' she stuttered but Susan shushed her.

'Do we have a deal?' Susan demanded.

Amy just wanted out of the room but she had no other option than to agree. 'Yes,' She squeaked.

'Good,' Susan smiled. 'Have a great rest of the night.' Susan let girl of the cowering orderly and opened the door for her. Just as Amy was leaving Susan continued, 'and remember, Amy, we're watching you.'

Amy left as fast as she could. She heard the door close behind her but she didn't bother to look back. She wanted to get away from this young psycho as quickly as possible.

The following day Susan visited Diana in her room. Diana looked expectantly at her friend. 'It's done,' Susan smiled.

'And she's going to help us?' Diana asked wide-eyed.

'Suffice to say that she was given no other option,' Susan smiled evilly.

# PRESENT - CHRIS DUNCAN'S REARREST

As soon as I got out of the institution, I eagerly reached for my phone and contacted Detective Inspector Martin.

'DI Martin.'

'Hello, DI Martin. It's Graham Avery here. And, boy, do I have some information for you,' I said. ' Can I have your email address so that I can send it to you?'

He gave it to me. 'Can you explain over the phone what it's about?' He asked.

I forwarded on the message that Diana had sent me. 'I think you need to hear it first,' I replied but I couldn't help smiling. I heard the recording of Chris's voice commence.

[1]

"Well, sis. It wasn't quite the outcome I had in mind but I guess the result is just the same. It was always our little secret. And we're both going to get away with murder. I'm sorry that me killing Susan Adams sent you insane. I'm surprised that you didn't get in touch with me when you got released all those years ago. I'm hoping that it was to protect me. I don't need protecting now, sis. Tony has been arrested and will probably be charged fairly soon. So I've committed *the perfect murder and gotten away with it but so have you. I mean you're not going to stand trial for the murder of Luigi Gustav and Tracey Gee. Graham Longmuir is fighting for his life. Samantha Adlington was wounded but is in a stable condition. You got away with it, Susan. You got away with it."*

It went silent for a few seconds and, for a moment, I thought that the call had been disconnected.

'Wow!' He suddenly exclaimed. 'That's a very powerful confession. I'm guessing that you want to be there when we rearrest him?'

'I'm in London so it will take me about four hours to get back,' I said. ' I really don't mind not being there. I'm just glad that Susan Adams will finally get justice.'

'Okay, Graham,' He said. 'I'll keep you updated.'

'Thanks,' I replied. 'I'd appreciate that.'

After hanging up I contacted Jude to find out where she was. It was no surprise to learn that she was in Samantha's Department Store. Apart from liking Samantha as a person and musician, Judith loved her clothing as well. I told her to buy a dress that she liked and I wouldn't question it. She hung up quite quickly after that, obviously eager to do what I had instructed her to do. I knew she would probably still be in there by the time I arrived. I made my way to the tube station.

Chris was just about to go out when the police arrived. Somehow the paparazzi had found out and it looked like a rugby scrum was taking place as they jostled to get the best position. Chris couldn't believe what was happening as a policeman read him his rights and he was escorted into one of the waiting police cars.

He called his solicitor from the station. She arrived just over an hour later and they were taken to an interview room. When DI Martin and DS Stevens entered and confirmed recordings were being made, his solicitor went right on the offensive.

'We had anticipated that my client was going to be released

and that Tony Gee would be charged with the murder of Susan Adams,' she fumed. 'As was witnessed by many people on the verbal confirmation that Susan Blackmore gave a few nights ago.'

DI Martin Just ignored her. 'Why did you you kill Susan Adams, Chris?'

Chris was about to reply but his solicitor cut him off. 'My Client has always denied that he murdered Susan Adams and continues to do so.'

'He was found guilty, by jury, in a court of law,' DS Stevens pointed out.

'A verdict which we will now get overturned in light of the recent new evidence,' the solicitor snidely responded.

'And we have some new evidence of our own,' DI Martin said. 'Please play the tape.'

'With pleasure, Sir,' DS Stevens smiled.

*"Well, sis. It wasn't quite the outcome I had in mind but I guess the result is just the same. It was always our little secret. And we're both going to get away with murder. I'm sorry that me killing Susan Adams sent you insane. I'm surprised that you didn't get in touch with me when you got released all those years ago. I'm hoping that it was to protect me. I don't need protecting now, sis. Tony has been arrested and will probably be charged fairly soon. So I've committed the perfect murder and gotten away with it but so have you. I mean you're not going to stand trial for the murder of Luigi Gustav and Tracey Gee. Graham Longmuir is fighting for his life. Samantha Adlington was wounded but is in a stable condition. You got away with it, Susan. You got away with it."*

'Do you recognise that voice, Chris?' DI Martin asked.

Chris looked at his solicitor. She shook her head. 'That could have been someone imitating my client,' she said.

'True,' DI Martin agreed. 'Would you care to play the video of the cctv footage, DS Stevens?'

'With pleasure again, Sir.'

The screen behind the two police officers sprang into life. A view of the Chapel Of Rest at the undertakers premises came into view. Chris is seen entering the room where his sister is in her coffin and, again, they get to hear everything of Chris's confession. The screen goes blank.

'May I have some time alone with my client, please?' The solicitor had certainly changed her tune.

'Of course,' Di Martin said as he and DS Stevens stood and left the room.

'I think it's time to confess, don't you?' Chris said.

'Looking at this new evidence, Chris, I really don't think you're going to have much of an option. I mean you could say that someone pressurised you into doing it.'

'Now that just doesn't seem plausible, does it, Malandra?' Chris responded. 'Can they use it as evidence? It was gained without my knowledge.'

'Unfortunately, Chris, the law changed in nineteen twenty-seven and evidence taken without the criminal's knowledge can be used in a court of law,' Malandra explained. 'Anyway, the cctv footage could be used as that was in the public domain.'

'In that case, Malandra, I suggest we come up with a statement.'

An hour later, DI Martin And DS Stevens reentered the room. They got the machines running and sat down, redoing the introductions.

'My client would like me to read a prepared statement,' The solicitor began. '"I, Christopher Duncan, confess to the murder of Susan Adams. We had arranged to meet in the wooded area as she said that she had something important to tell me. Whilst waiting for her I had whittled a branch of a tree to a sharp point. When Susan told me that she was pregnant, I grabbed her and shoved her against the branch, it acted like a spear and, with the force I was using, penetrated her back quite easily and went right through her body exiting through her stomach. She was probably killed instantly but I had to make sure so I stabbed her a few times. Was it premeditated? No. I didn't go there with the view of killing her but something had told me to take my knife so read into that what you may. What I didn't realise at the time was that my little sister, the late Susan Blackmore, had witnessed the whole event. I warned her to keep quiet - no, threatened her to not speak again, which, unfortunately, she took quite literally and never spoke for many years, I believe. I did convince her to say it was Tony she saw if she ever did decide to speak of it. But I have no idea why she decided to shoot those people at the party. I am sorry for the distress that I have caused; especially to Graham Adams, now known as Graham Longmuir, and his family. I am now fully prepared to to pay the penalty that will be bestowed on me.'"

'....Thanks for keeping me updated,' I was on the phone to DI Martin. Judith an myself were now driving home. 'I'm pleased that Chris has finally confessed. Although, I think we all knew it was him.'

'We did,' DI Martin agreed. 'But there was that element of doubt. And Susan Blackmore threw a spanner in the works when she said it was Tony. Obviously, we now know why. Drive carefully, Graham. I'm sure we'll catch up soon.'

The call was disconnected. I started whistling a happy tune. Jude started laughing.

'Well you're certainly in a good mood,' she said.

'I'll show you how good later,' I winked mischievously.

'Promises, promises.

My phone rang again. The caller display on my dashboard informed me that it was Parveen. I accepted the call as I continued to drive. 'Hi, Parveen,' I said. 'Some great news you'll be able to tell Graham. Chris Duncan has finally confessed to Susan's murder.' I suddenly heard that Parveen was crying. 'What is it, Parveen?'

'He died, Graham,' she said between sobs. 'About forty-five minutes ago.'

'What are you talking about, Parveen?' I asked although the knot in my stomach was getting tighter and tighter.

'Graham's dead,' she wailed.

# BOOK TWO

# THE AFTERMATH OF THE SHOCK NEWS.

We had to stop at the Taunton Deane service station. I must have driven there on autopilot. I don't know who was more in shock, Judith or myself. Jude had taken the news of Graham's death very badly. I was going to buy the coffees but Jude insisted that she needed the fresh air. And, besides that, Parveen had asked me to contact Samantha, Gillian and Tony as she just could not face it, Judith did not want to be in the car to listen.

After she had got out of the car, I conference called Samantha, Gillian and Tony. Fortunately or unfortunately, depending on which way you want to look at it, they all answered. They all sounded so cheerful as they greeted me. This devastating news was going to rip their hearts out.

'Great news about Chris Duncan's confession, isn't it?' Tony said. From the sound of his voice I could tell he was beaming.

'Terrific,' I said without much enthusiasm.

'What is it, Graham?' Samantha asked. 'You're sounding kind of sad.'

'I've just had a call from Parveen,' I said. 'There's no easy way to say this but Graham died about an hour ago.'

There was stunned silence emanating from my car speakerphone. 'That's sick, Graham,' Gillian said quietly. 'Why would you even say something like that.'

'Because it's true, Gillian,' I said equally as quietly.

'But he was talking to us yesterday,' said Tony.

'Parveen said that he suffered another haemorrhage,' I said and I felt the tears starting to flow. 'Unfortunately this one was fatal. We've lost him, guys. We've lost Graham.'

Again there was stunned silence. 'No! No! No! No!' Samantha screamed. I knew that she would take it the worst because they had been close and, obviously, were the songwriting pair.

'Look,' I said through the tears. 'Jude and me are travelling back at present. We've just had to stop at Taunton Deane services because of the sad news. We should be home in about an hour. Why don't you all come 'round and we'll grieve together?'

They all agreed to this. Judith came back to the car carrying the coffees. I pressed a button which opened the door for her. When she had got in I pressed the button again and the door closed. She handed me my drink. It was half full. Looking at her she must have been shaking with shock and had spilt much of the drink as she had walked back. I could tell that she had been crying.

'They're all going to be in for a shock when the news breaks,' she whispered, gesturing to the people milling around the services.

I watched as one couple took their Alsatian for a, relief, walk and met a woman who was walking her chihuahua. The little dog was trying to let the other know who was boss while the Alsatian was looking at it with much disdain. I got the impression it was thinking the chihuahuas was an insult breed in the canine world. 'Hmm,' I nodded. 'They say you remember where you were when your favourite celebrity died. My dad told me he was at his Granny and Granddad's home, playing cards, when a news flash came on the television informing the world that Elvis Presley had died. He could have only been about ten or eleven.'

'What did the others say?'

'As one would have expected. They didn't take the news

well. Samantha sounded like she was in hysterics. Gillian was in tears - I'm pretty sure that she blames herself again - and Tony sounded like he was in denial.'

'How are you feeling?' She tentatively asked.

'Numb,' I replied. 'I just can't believe it. I cannot believe that Graham is no longer with us. I think we're going to have to prepare for global mourning. I'm worried for Parveen and the guys.'

'Poor Mr and Mrs Adams,' Judith said tearfully. 'They'll be burying both their children within eight months of each other.'

'Oh, Jesus! This will break them'. The tears began to flow from both of us.

After a couple of minutes we had managed to compose ourselves. We sipped our drinks. They had cooled down quite a bit.

'How long before it's released to the press?' Judith pondered.

I knew it was a rhetorical question but I answered anyway. 'It wouldn't surprise me if we don't hear it on the next bulletin,' I shrugged. 'There's no way they're ever going to be able to keep this one quiet.'

We finished our drinks. I took Jude's empty cup, got out of the car and went and put them in the recycling bin. I got back in, buckled up and started the car.

'We'll have to ask Parveen if she wants us to help out with anything,' Jude said as I pulled away from the services.

'Of course,' I agreed. 'She's going to be grieving for quite a long time.'

'Thankfully she wasn't in the room to see Graham get shot.'

'She was, wasn't she?' I said, trying to wrack my brains to remember.

'She went to get drinks,' my wife pointed out.

'I thought she had returned with them just before Sue had entered.'

'No. I don't think she had.'

I drove on in silence. It's amazing how many details I couldn't remember from that evening a few days ago. I turned the radio on just in case they gave out a news flash about Graham's death. There was a report about Chris being sent back to prison.

It took us forty minutes to get home. We took the shopping in. Jude took it straight upstairs. She doesn't like things just being left in the hallway. I went to my study and did something I hadn't done for a long time. I took my old acoustic guitar out of its case and carried it with me through to the lounge. I sat down on the sofa. I started playing the introduction to "Teenage Dream".

'Wow!' I hadn't seen Judith standing in the doorway. 'You haven't played that thing in a long time.'

'It just felt right,' I said.

'I'll just go and make sure we've got enough drinks,' Judith said. At least she had stopped crying now.

While she was out of the room, my phone indicated that I had a message. I took it out and opened it to read. "CONGRATULATIONS. YOU'VE SOLVED ONE OF THEM ALBEIT WITH A LITTLE HELP. MAY CHRIS ROT IN PRISON. NOT MUCH TIME NOW TO SOLVE THE REST."

I read it and reread it. I decided to text back. "BECAUSE OF A RECENT DEATH, IM GOING TO NEED MORE TIME."

I waited for a few seconds before a response pinged up in my inbox. "AGREED. THE WORLD WILL BE IN SHOCK WHEN ITS ANNOUNCED THAT GRAHAM LONGMUIR IS DEAD. I'LL CONTACT YOU AGAIN SOON WITH A NEW DEADLINE."

I switched my phone off and picked up my guitar. I started playing "Its The Way You Make Me Feel". I started to sing along to my strumming. I do not profess to be a good singer but, I have been told, I can hold a pretty decent tune. I followed it up with a couple of Graham's tracks - "What If?" and "Only Time Will Tell". I then played "Tongue-tied."

When I had completed the song I heard some applause. I looked up and Samantha, Gillian and Tony were there.

'How long have you been stood there for,' I said, somewhat embarrassed.

'Since you started playing "It's The Way You Make Me Feel,' Gillian smiled.

I put the guitar down, stood up and we all embraced each

other in a group hug.

'I can't believe he's gone,' Samantha cried. I thought she was more grief stricken at the death of Graham than she was at Luigi's. But then I remembered that she had been wounded herself.

'I don't think any of us can,' said Tony.

'I wish I knew why Sue has done this,' Gillian sobbed. 'If only she had shot me.'

'She would never have done that, Gill,' said Tony. 'She loved you too much to hurt you in that way.'

We all sat down. Judith brought in the drinks; wine for Samantha, Gillian and herself, a rum and coke for me and a beer for Tony.

'It certainly put a dampener on what started to look like a pretty good day,' I said.

'You mean the news about Chris?' Tony questioned. I nodded. 'It certainly serves the bastard right. I hope he gets a longer sentence now.'

I had never heard Tony swear much and, judging by the look on the others' faces, neither had they.

'Has DI Martin been in touch to say that you are no longer being investigated?' Samantha asked.

'I am no longer a suspect in the the Susan Adams murder, for obvious reasons,' he said. 'But, because of the new information they received about the death of my first wife, they still have to investigate that. Although, as they are now aware that the source of the information may not have been telling the truth, then they are not setting it as a priority.'

I wondered if this was Tony's "secret." But dismissed it as now was not the appropriate time. We talked a while about Graham and about the past. Each one of them had a happy memory to share. Jude had turned the television on and it was playing in the background so that we could tune in if any announcement was made about Graham's death.

Sure enough, about forty five minutes later, Jude interrupted our conversation to say that a news flash logo had appeared on the screen. She commanded the volume on the television to increase (even I liked the voice recognition for these gadgets as it did away with all those pointless remote controls) and we waited for Newscaster, Monica Daniels, to start her report. A picture of Graham filled the screen behind her.

'Versatile performer, Graham Longmuir, has died. He was forty-nine. The hospital where Graham was being treated, after being shot at a party at his home on November the 24th, confirmed that he had died after complications from his wounds. His wife, Parveen, his children and his parents were with him when he passed away. Lorna McAndrew now looks back at the career of the superstar.'

I looked at the others, the tears were streaming down all our faces. They showed an early clip of the group.

'Do you remember the trouble we had getting him along to Danceworks in Newton, just after Ladies and Gentlemen were formed, so he could look professional in our dance routines on stage?' Samantha asked tearfully.

'Yeah,' Gillian sobbed, trying to laugh. 'He didn't know a cucaracha from a kookaburra. But Pauline and Rob were determined to succeed with him. Pauline obviously saw the potential in him where none of us could.'

'And then look at what he went on to do,' Jude interjected.

'Yeah. Who would have thought he would go on to become a world famous superstar?' Tony mused.

There was a few seconds hesitation before we all said simultaneously 'I did.'

'You do realise that the press are going to be trying their hardest to get hold of one of you,' Judith pointed out.

'My phones off,' Gillian said.

'So's mine,' Tony added.

'Mine too,' said Samantha.

'I guess it will be up to Parveen to make a statement,' I said.

'She's not going to be in any fit state to speak to the press for the foreseeable future,' Judith said. 'Perhaps one of you should contact her to offer help.'

'I think you should all go 'round and see her,' I added. 'I'm sure she would be grateful for the visit.'

'I'm leaving for Luigi's funeral tomorrow. You are all still coming, aren't you?' She asked anxiously.

We all confirmed that we would be attending.

'Tracey's funeral is a week on Monday,' said Tony. He looked down and I just knew he was trying to fight back the tears.

'When's Sue's funeral?' Jude asked Gillian.

'Oh, I'm not expecting any of you to attend that,' Gillian replied.

'When is it?' Jude repeated

'A week on Wednesday.'

'Graham and me will be there.'

I looked at her and she gave me one of those looks that only a female can give, that if I was going to say anything to dispute this, then she would win the argument that would bound to occur when we were by ourselves later.

'Are you sure?' Gillian asked.

'Of course we'll attend,' I confirmed.

'Thanks, guys. That means a lot to me.' I could see the tears in her eyes.

'I'll be there, as well, Gill,' said Tony.

'Oh, no, Tony. I couldn't expect that after what Sue has done,' said Gillian.

'I'll be there to support you, not Sue.'

After Tony said that the tears did start to roll down her cheeks. Whilst she was composing herself, I contacted Parveen. I thought her phone may be off but she answered it on the third ring.

'Hi, Graham,' She said. She sounded very tired.

'Jus wondered if you're up for some visitors tomorrow to help out with anything?' I asked. 'It will be Gillian, Tony, me and...' I looked at Jude who shook her head and mouthed "work". '...that will be it. Samantha has to fly over to Italy.'

I could tell that she was thinking about it. 'I am going to need some help, if that's okay. I don't really know what I'm meant to be doing.'

'I'm guessing the media are camped outside?' I asked.

'Security has informed me that a few arrived just after we got back,' she admitted. 'That could have been that they just followed me from the hospital. But since the news flash a few minutes ago, not only have the press congregated but the general public have been turning up with flowers. They're saying that there's quite a crowd outside now. It will probably be better if you use the secret entrance.'

'Okay,' I agreed. 'See you in the morning.'

We terminated the call. Jude had gone to get more drinks. When she returned we carried on talking; mainly about Graham. We chatted for a good two or three hours. I think it was Samantha who suggested that they do a benevolent concert in memory of Graham. At the time we thought it was a great idea. And then someone, it might have been Gillian, suggested that I play guitar. I think I may have replied along the lines of she had been drinking too much.

We decided to call it a night at about 01:30. Samantha had to leave for Heathrow at nine in the morning. Before I went up to bed, I sent the message I had received to Mark, asking him if he could investigate where it had originated. I wasn't looking forward to tomorrow/today. It was going to weird visiting Graham's home knowing that he will never be there again.

# ARRANGING A FUNERAL AND ATTENDING THREE OTHERS

I awoke to find that it was raining. Jude and I went downstairs to prepare breakfast for the others. We cooked a healthy fried breakfast; no tomatoes for me as I absolutely detest them. The smell must have wafted up the stairs as it wasn't long before Gillian, Samantha and Tony came jogging down.

'Something smells wonderful,' Gillian smiled.

'I haven't had a good fry up in ages,' Tony said smacking his lips.

'All vegan food for you, Samantha,' Jude said.

'And cooked in separate pans,' I pointed out.

'And guess who is doing the dishes,' Jude laughed.

'Who wants filtered coffee? And who wants tea?' I asked

Tony and Gillian went for filtered coffee whilst Samantha went for a black tea. I started to make the drinks when my phone started ringing. The caller ID notified me that it was Mark. I answered it.

'Morning, Mark.'

'I think someone is playing with us - well, you anyway.' There was no greeting or anything.

'What do you mean?' I asked. I felt all eyes staring at me.

'That message you forwarded to me was sent from Graham Longmuir's account.'

'But that's impossible,' I answered completely dumbfounded.

Judith nudging me brought me back to reality and I could see that I had overfilled one of the mugs. Jude was there ready with a cloth.

'I thought you would say that,' Mark was saying. 'I tell you this, the person who is doing this is very clever. It takes some extraordinary talent to hack someone's email account or computer these days.

I really didn't want to hear that. Now I was up against a talented criminal who every government, military or secret agency would try to employ. 'So, what do I do?' I stupidly asked. I knew that the others had not averted their gaze.

Mark informed me what I should do and we said our goodbyes. I finished pouring the drinks.

'Well?' Jude asked. 'What was that all about?'

'That last message I received was, apparently, sent from Graham Longmuir's account,' I explained.

'But that's...' Jude began

'Impossible. I know. But that is where Mark said it originated from.'

'How the hell is someone managing to hack into Mark's and Graham's account? Samantha asked putting a forkful of vegan sausage into her mouth and began to masticate it slowly.

'And whose is going to be next?' Tony asked.

'I don't know is the answer to both those questions,' I said, dishing out the drinks. I raised mine to my lips. Damn it was hot. 'But I'm an investigative journalist so I intend to find out.' I added it to my ever growing list of things that I needed an explanation for.

We finished our breakfasts and, then, went and got ready.

Samantha was heading straight to Heathrow. She had contacted the security company the group had been using since they had reformed. I had an instinct that the paparazzi were hanging at the bottom of my drive. Samantha also had the hindsight to order a car for Gillian and Tony as well. It was agreed that I would take my own car as a decoy and they would use the secret entrance.

The cars duly arrived. We said our goodbyes to Samantha, knowing that we would be seeing her again in a couple of days when we attended Luigi's funeral. Tony and Gillian got into the other car whilst I wished my wife a good day at work. I then got into my car and started it up. Electric cars were now the norm. They had become popular when the government at the time, I think it was in the mid to late 2010s, they announced that they wanted zero emissions by next year, 2050. Unfortunately, it does not look like they are going to achieve it. But, then, like most government and parliamentary statutes, they never seem to happen anyway. Hark at me! I'm starting to sound like Chris Duncan.

There were a few media people waiting for the electric gates to open - hey! I am a successful author, remember - and they now knew that I was quite close to the band. They shouted questions at me but I just carried on driving.

At Parveen's and Graham's, I had forgotten that the road was closed. I slowed up, though. The road and pavement, outside the entrance, was a blaze of colour from the flowers that had been laid there. I saw hundreds of people walking with more flowers and gifts. The hankies and tissues trying to wipe their eyes but the tears still coming from this shocking news.

Parveen greeted me when I arrived. She looked in a terrible state which was only to be expected. First thing first, we agreed that a statement should be released. I was also asked to go out and read it. The statement took about half an hour to write. Their were two, actually; one on behalf of the family and one on behalf of the group. Parveen contacted Stephen and Sally to read the statement to them. I think they must have started crying because Parveen began to break down. Victoria, their eldest daughter, took the phone from her mother and finished talking with her Granny and Grandad. Callum embraced his mother. Both Callum and Victoria had left home. Nathan was in his second year at Oxford university. Tanya had just started her last year at school - they leave at eighteen now. As long as her grades were acceptable, she was going to go to university after taking a gap year - Yep, they are still popular in 2049. Although still young, these children were showing a lot of maturity. It was what their mother needed.

When the time was ready, the security officer - the children had insisted on this as they didn't want the paparazzi or crazed fans trying to break in and steal something personal belonging to Graham - opened the door for me. I walked down the long, winding, driveway until I reached the mass throng of people. Cameras started clicking. Microphones were thrust into my face and a million questions were all being asked at once. I looked contemptuously at the reporters and the microphones were moved a little away. The television crews had trained their cameras on me.

'I am here to read two statements,' I began. 'The first is on behalf of the family and the second is on behalf of the surviving members of Ladies and Gentlemen.' This caught in my throat as the realisation hit me again that Ladies and Gentlemen would never perform as a quartet again. I looked down at the first sheet of paper and started reading it aloud. '"Yesterday, we lost a loving, son, husband and father. No words can express what we are feeling at the moment. No words can explain why Sue Bingham decided to do what she did. We ask that you kindly remember in prayers or thoughts, Samantha and Tony, who both lost their spouses, Luigi and Tracey, on that tragic evening on the 24th November 2049. Please also spare a thought for Gillian, who has also lost someone close to her.

We ask that you let us grieve in private. We appreciate that Graham was a public figure and you are shocked at his needless passing. But remember that Graham lived life to the full. He would not have wanted to see tears. He would want you to have happy memories. We will be releasing funeral arrangements in due course. We would like to thank the Intensive Care Unit where Graham was treated since the shooting. And to the staff who tried to save his life. We would also like to thank you, his fans. Graham would never call you fans. He always used to say you were his friends. How right he was there."' I let that sink in for a few moments before reading the next prepared statement.

'"Our hearts and minds cannot comprehend the death of our beloved colleague and "brother" Graham Longmuir. Our sincere and deepest sympathies go to his parents, Steve and Sally, and to Parveen, his wife, Callum, Victoria, Nathan and Tanya, his wonderful children. But our hearts also go out to you, his fans, who have been with him, and us, from the start. This reunion was meant to be new beginnings for us. Unfortunately, it is no longer to be. We will be announcing, in due course, what will happen to Ladies and Gentlemen. How we feel at present is that we will not continue. However, we will talk with our management team, Parveen and her family, Sally and Stephen, our own families as well as listen to your feedback. We believe that their should be a memorial concert. Graham would have wanted us to carry on but, without our charismatic leader, we do not know how. We miss you so much Graham."' Again, I let those words sink in. I then addressed the crowd. 'I will let not be answering any questions. I ask you to heed the family's request and let them grieve in private. Many gathered here today lost their favourite singer, actor, entertainer but please remember, although that is distressing, it is nothing compared to losing a son, a husband and a father.'

I turned and started to walk back up the pathway the way I had come down it. I could hear crying but then someone started applauding and, one by one, everyone started clapping. Journalists were shouting questions after me but I chose to ignore them. Instead I just carried on walking but, at least, I started to smile.

The door was opened for me before I even had to knock. I

went straight in. The others were still in the lounge. I joined them there. They all looked up expectantly at me.

'There's hell of a lot of people down there,' I said. 'The mourners certainly outnumber the media.'

Parveen's phone started ringing she answered it but left the room.

'How did they receive the statements?' Gillian asked. You could still sense that she blamed herself. It was like she should have known that Sue was Chris's sister even though there was no way she could have. Sue had played her - no, all of us - very well. We had no inkling as to who she was.

'They applauded,' I smiled. 'It was, as the statement said, remembering the happy memories they had of Graham. And, boy, there must have been quite a few.'

I thought I heard Parveen on her way back in but we all heard the ringtone from her phone.

'The flowers they are laying in memory of my father will be distributed to the hospital that treated dad and local charities,' said Victoria.

'I think there will be a few more days yet of people laying wreaths, bouquets and cuddly toys,' Tony said.

We all nodded our heads in agreement but took a few minutes for reflection. Parveen came back into the room. She had a look of disbelief on her face. We all turned and looked at her. 'That was the Very Reverend Michelle Taylor, the Dean Of Westminster Abbey on the phone,' she said. 'She was offering the Abbey for Graham's funeral.' And then she broke down in tears. Her children surrounded her and they embraced each other. They were all crying. I had to look away or else I would have joined them. I then saw that Gill and Tony were in tears themselves.

'That's a pretty good offer, Parveen,' Gillian finally said. 'But I thought you had to be at least had to be Knighted or a Dame to be offered that.

'Well, they're offering it as Graham was a "National Treasure". Their words not mine.'

'I think dad would want his funeral to be held in Devon,' said Callum.

'Yes. He was a Newton boy born and bred,' Victoria agreed. 'I mean, even when he was famous he never moved away.'

'You're right,' Parveen agreed. 'The funeral will be local.'

'Perhaps a memorial could be arranged for Westminster Abbey?' I suggested.

'Yes. That's a wonderful idea, Graham,' said Parveen. 'There is so much to arrange and we must start to do it.'

'The funeral is a private affair, Parveen,' said Gillian. 'It needs to be organised by you and the family. Listen to what the undertaker has to offer in the way of advice. But it is your choice. Maybe we can have some input on the memorial service.'

'Yes. That's a good idea, Gillian.' Parveen sounded very vague but I guess that wasn't very surprising given the circumstances.

'When we you be leaving for Italy?' Callum asked.

'Tomorrow,' replied Tony.

'You will give Samantha our best and apologise to her for us not attending,' Parveen said.

'I think it's safe to assume that Samantha will not be expecting you to attend,' I said.

'She was very close to Graham, you know,' Parveen said which struck me as slightly odd. But, again, I put it down to the present situation. 'It must have been very upsetting for her to lose Luigi and Graham.'

'I'm sure everyone in this room feels exactly the same,' I pointed out.

'Yes. Yes, of course,' Parveen replied. 'Please excuse me. I'm not thinking straight at the moment. I know he would want Samantha, Gillian and Tony to say a few words. But, for his eulogy, he would like you to say a few words Graham. He's known you since he was young.'

'Me?' I was flabbergasted. 'It would be an honour, Parveen. If that's what you want and what Graham would have wanted, then there's no way I can refuse.'

'Now! What about food?'

'Mum!' Victoria sighed.

'I meant for now. We can't have our guests going hungry, Vicky.' Parveen suddenly sat down. 'I can't believe he's dead.'

Again the children encircled her like a animal pack protecting their young or wounded. Parveen was definitely the matriarch but, in her current state, she was like a wounded, defenceless, animal. My heart went out to her.

'I can do something to eat if you would like,' Gillian offered.

'Thanks, Gillian. But I think I need to be keep myself busy. You can come and help, though,' Parveen answered. 'I'm sure everyone would like a tea or coffee; or perhaps something stronger?'

We all went for tea and coffees. Parveen and Gillian went to the kitchen. I didn't go in there but Gillian explained to me later that the place was spotless. Apparently she would not have realised the event that happened a week or so ago, it seemed a lot longer, if she had not been here to witness it.

We stayed for a couple of hours. The undertaker arrived just before Tony, Gillian an I decided to leave. We waited about ten to fifteen minutes to talk to the undertaker. Parveen was looking at us as though she was pleading that we stay. But this was the children's and Parveen's funeral to arrange. It was their dad/husband to be remembered. Anyway, we still had to get ready for flying out to Italy. Tony and Gillian sneaked out to their chauffeur driven car. I was about to walk down the steps to mine when Parveen called me back. She was carrying a large briefcase. She held it out for me to take.

'The children found these,' she said. 'I think Graham wanted Samantha to have them. There are songs inside.'

'I'll pass it on to her,' I promised.

I reached to take the case but she caught me off guard and pulled me towards her kissing me on the lips.

Luigi's funeral was a sombre occasion. It was held at the Duomo Di Milano, the largest catholic cathedral in Italy. It can hold approximately forty thousand people. Although I am not a religious person, agnostic I believe the description is, I do love studying the architecture of ancient buildings. Personally, though, my thoughts are that Jesus Christ, if he did exist, would not be too happy with the gold leaf and golden ornaments decorating this, in my view, wonderful building. I always thought Christ was a simple man who preferred the simple way of preaching. Wasn't he betrayed for thirty pieces of silver? But the building! Well, the building was simply stunning. I could have stayed for hours just admiring the columns and stained glass windows. I take some time to savour the history of the cathedral. No doubt I would have to do some research, but I'm pretty sure that the first cathedral was built around 388 AD. This one was circa 1386 with bits added over the next few centuries and restoration work which is still being carried out to this day. I spied the main statue that every tourist wants to see - the sculpture of Saint Bartholomew Flayed. It was riveting seeing the Saint using his flayed skin as a robe. Bartholomew was the apostle who was skinned alive for spreading his faith. You see what I mean about religion now? Two of my literary heroes, Mark Twain and Oscar Wilde, have visited the cathedral with differing opinions. Twain appeared to be in awe of it whereas Wilde was not complimentary. I stole a glance at Jude. I could tell she was astounded by its sheer beauty.

We had arrived yesterday and had to attend the wake. Like I said, I'm not religious so I don't know if it's a catholic thing or an Italian thing to do. To me it was a bit unnerving being in the same room as an open casket. To be fair, they had made Luigi look like he was asleep but it still gave me the creeps. Some traditions have not changed over the course of time. Funerals and weddings will always stand the test of time.

There were many tears. I couldn't follow some of the service as it was in Latin. I didn't know many of the hymns as they were in Italian. It was a very moving service. Samantha gave the eulogy. It was funny; it was heartbreaking; it was informative. I never knew that Luigi worked for his government. He collected data on whether Italy should leave or remain in the European

Union. Well, we all know what happened there, don't we? She cried but this only lead to many others in the congregation shedding a few tears - me and Jude included. If I looked to my left then I would have seen Gillian and even Tony with wet cheeks. Christopher, Luigi's stepson, looked sombre but I don't think it had hit him as hard as Davido, Stephanie and Charlotte. Rumour had it that he never really got on with Luigi but now was not the time to dwell on this.

After the mass and holy communion, family and close friends only, were shown to the graveside. There still must have been a hundred to a hundred and fifty people there. We watched as the coffin was lowered into the ground as the priest lead the service. I looked around to see various shades of black. It was depressing. But this was how Luigi's family wanted it. Samantha knew that he loved his family and this was his wish, so who was she to deny the man she loved what he wanted. Luigi's elderly mother broke down at the graveside and had to be supported by Davido and Stephanie. I think Samantha would have wanted Christopher to help out but he was having none of it. Not soon enough it was all over and we were flying back to England. It was time to get ready for Tracey's funeral.

This was a much more livelier affair even though it was held at the Torbay Crematorium. I had heard, over the years, that many people had complained that it was just like a conveyer belt mechanism. As soon as a group of mourners were ushered out the exit then the next lot were being greeted at the entrance. Well, folks, spoiler alert, since we have increased this countries population by millions over the last few decades, then what do you expect?

I think Tony was surprised to see the pathways lined with people and throwing alliums, Tracey's favourite flower, as the hearse went by. Screens had been erected for the public to watch the service. The council had been against this and if it hadn't have been for the colossal public backlash against them, then they may not have been put it in the first place. It's great to know that something's haven't changed over the years; and politicians being the scum of the earth is one of those things. The crowd were respectful and courteous. Although they did not really know Tracey, anyone connected to their favourite group felt like one of their own.

The funeral service did not take as long as Luigi's and we were allowed to sing three songs that Tracey loved. One of them was the song that had brought the group back together after splitting up for twenty five - "Close Your Eyes". Harrison and Leila, Tony's children from his first marriage, walked either side of Christian, holding his arms to support him. That poor little boy had gone through so much in his five short years. And I think it was the sight of that young child that definitely confirmed to Gillian, Samantha and Tony that the memorial concert should be staged to continue to raise money for the meningitis trust. He sat next to his daddy as good as gold. He probably didn't really have much of a clue as to what was going on. But he was so well behaved and that, I believe, helped his daddy.

Parveen did not attend but Victoria And Callum we're there as her representatives. I hadn't spoken to Parveen since Friday, although I had received a couple of messages asking to meet me. I knew I would have to go around as I was doing the eulogy. I didn't know why she had kissed me like she had. I was hoping it was just a friendly peck. But I had decided that I would take Jude with me.

The part I hate about any funeral is where you have to stand in line and give your respects to the devastated family. I mean, really, what do you say? They must be so fed up with hearing "sorry for your loss" so many times.

But it was Sue's funeral that caused the most talking points and most of them were not for good reasons.

# FUNERAL CAT FIGHT

Sue's funeral was for the Friday, two days after Tracey's. The morning had started off, weather wise, quite bad. It had been persistently raining since the early hours. It was now half past ten and it had been dry since quarter to ten. However, the tell tale puddles at the sides of the road indicated how bad it had been. In certain places you could see them stretching across the road like lovers trying to hold each other's hand. As Jude was driving us towards Ogwell, I could see a break in the clouds and it certainly appeared as though the sun was going to put in an appearance.

Jude and myself used to live in Ogwell when we first got married. It had changed so much over the years with new buildings being erected all over the place in order for the council to hit some government scheme. I always found it funny that the church was virtually opposite the Jolly Sailor pub. This had been revamped over the years and, although kept its historic facade, was completely modern inside. It even had one of those machines that when you selected your drink and paid for it by card, would pour it for you. It hadn't replaced the barperson completely - I think there would have been war if it had. The church itself almost closed its doors in the twenty-twenties because of a dwindling congregation. However, there was uproar in the village and the decision was revoked. And, because of how Britain was at that time, numbers increased and remain buoyant at present.

Jude knew the owner of the Manor House, which was situated right next to the church, and had been given permission to park in her driveway. There it was easy to get through her back gate and you were right in the church pathway. The road leading down to the village had to be cordoned off as the hearse and following cars would have been unable to drive down the road. Ogwell Green was packed with well wishers. They probably weren't there to give Sue a good send off but just to catch a glimpse of Samantha, Gillian and Tony.

We arrived in plenty of time. Deborah made us a drink and she and Jude had a good catch-up. I decided to step outside for some fresh air as the early December sun had managed to break through. I had noticed that a couple of paparazzi had managed to sneak into the field next to the church. I went and informed a security guard and watched as he made his way down to their hiding place. I decided to leave him to it.

Tony arrived not too long after us. Deborah made him a cup of coffee. Like us, he was dressed in colourful clothes. This had been Gillian's wish. She didn't want black at her wife's funeral. I was talking to him in the "Garden Room".

'Have you spoken to Gillian recently?' I asked.

'Yesterday,' he replied. 'She actually seemed in good spirits.'

'I doubt she will be in good spirits this morning,' I said.

'Have you heard from Parveen?'

'I've received a couple of texts,' I admitted. 'Jude and myself will be going over to see her later.'

'Is she coming today?'

'Doubtful,' I responded. 'She's got quite a bit to organise. I think she would like to be here to support Gillian. These last two or three weeks have been shattering, haven't they?'

'Yes, they have,' Tony agreed quietly.

All of sudden there was a loud wailing sound that seemed to be emanating from Tony. He pulled out his phone but the noise had brought Judith and Deborah running in.

'What the hell was that?' I asked.

'It's a new app,' Tony explained. 'It makes me aware that

someone is trying to hack into my account.'

'What does it do?' Judith asked.

'It responds to the hacker stating that they have been blocked and that a virus has now been planted in their software,' Tony answered.

'Wow! That's brilliant,' Deborah said.

'Does it actually do what it says?' I asked.

'I've no idea,' admitted Tony. 'But it would put the fear of God up me if I received that sort of message.

'I must download that app,' I said.

'Yes. You must,' said Jude.

We continued talking for a few minutes when Samantha popped her head around the door. Deborah asked her if she wanted a drink but she really only had time for a glass of water. Then it was time to leave. It only took us a minute to walk to the church from the Manor House via the back gate. It was starting to get really busy. It was weird to see Tony and Samantha at a gathering without their respective partners. I don't think I could even begin to imagine how they must be feeling at an event like this. For Tony it must be really hard after losing one wife to suicide and the other being murdered.

We went inside the church. Music was playing but not the standard piped music you usually associate with churches. Sue had apparently hated that kind of music, Gillian had told me. Sue had always liked Ladies and Gentlemen so it was their songs that were playing. I could make it that it was "Let You Go" coming through the speakers. I had an inkling that this would embarrass Samantha and Tony. I sneaked a peak at them as Jude and myself were sitting in the same pew and, sure enough, their gaze was looking downwards.

I picked up the service sheet. There was a lovely picture of Sue on it. She was smiling as though someone had said something funny but not funny enough to make her laugh. Underneath it had 2004 - 2049. She was only forty-five. She had many years left to give. Instead, she took her own life and three others with it. Such a waste.

It was Jude who noticed it first. She saw the concerned looks on the security personnels' faces. A couple left the church. Jude nudged me. 'Somethings going on,' she whispered.

I turned and looked but couldn't see anything. I stood up and walked out of the church. The gate was open. To my right was the back entrance to the Manor House that we had exited from a little while ago. In front of me was a tarmac lane that you could hardly drive a car up. It was here that a saw Gillian and her entourage blocking the way of Christopher Duncan and a few prison guards.

'You weren't invited,' I head Gillian crying.

'She was my sister,' Chris was arguing.

'You haven't seen her for - what? - forty years.'

'I didn't know where she was,' Chris said lamely. 'And she is still my sister.'

'I don't want you anywhere near her or this service. Or so help me God,' Gillian threatened vehemently.

'I'm allowed to pay my respects to my sister.'

'Can't he stay at the back of the church?' I offered as a compromise. 'I mean, I know he is a lying bastard but Sue was still his sister, Gillian.'

Gillian was looking daggers at the prisoner. 'Fine,' she relented. 'But he remains handcuffed.'

Judging by Chris's reaction, he realised that this was the best he was going to get.

'Perhaps he might get struck down by lightning before he enters the church,' I mused.

'If only,' Gillian muttered. 'I don't know why I had to go through with this. I mean, I'm not religious and Sue definitely wasn't.'

'I've told Judith to bury me in the garden,' I said.

'Well that will be a nice surprise for when the new owners move in and start digging up the garden,' Gillian smiled. 'Okay. Let's get this over and done with.'

Chris's appearance caused a bit of a commotion. I could hear people questioning why he had been let him. You see that's what

I don't get about regular church goers. I remember once, I think it may have been around 2019, there had been religious protests regarding "The Rocky Horror Picture Show" stage tour. I believe they were protesting about its homosexuality content. But I was thought that Jesus Christ said "he who is without sin may cast the first stone". And this was a guy who used to hang around with 12 males and a prostitute. My view, and the church has come on leaps and bounds in recent years, is that it matters not about the colour of our skin, our religious beliefs or our sexual preferences - we are all humans.

I must say that it was different, in a good sort of way, to see colour at a funeral. Black was always used as paying respect to the deceased. But now funerals are seen as a celebration to someone's life. It was strange celebrating the life of Sue after the way it ended. Not much was known about her young life. Gillian had pieced together a montage about things she had remembered from what Sue had told her. But there wasn't a lot of information there. Her love of dancing and choreography was well covered. The awards she had won were sitting proudly on the lectern near the coffin. There were quite a few of them. I remembered her putting those dancers through it on the Reunion tour. But, boy, could she move.

And then the service was over. The coffin was going to be taken to the crematorium later for a private gathering. We all stepped outside the church and stood in the surprising warm November sun.

I think we we all surprised to see Parveen staggering up the pathway to the church. I had a bad feeling about this. She stopped in front of Gillian and slapped her hard on the left side cheek.

'Your bitch of a wife killed my husband,' she shouted slurring her words.

'It was not Gillian's fault, Parveen,' Tony defended.

'She must have known she was Christopher Duncan's sister.'

'I didn't,' said Gillian.

A crowd was gathering. It couldn't really be helped as there was not much room outside the church. Parveen's shouting could probably be heard around Ogwell village. I just hoped that the paparazzi hadn't got a shot of these two.

'Take her home, Graham,' Judith whispered to me.

'Me?' I questioned. 'Surely it would be better if you went with her.'

'The eulogy you're doing for Graham would be the ideal reason to get her away.'

I knew she was right but something was telling me this was a bad idea. The shouting was still going on. I stepped between Parveen and Gillian. 'Now is not the time or the place, Parveen,' I said. 'And Gillian is certainly not to blame. Come on, I'll drop you back.'

I could see it in Parveen's eyes that she was about to argue but I placed an arm around her waist and gently pulled her away. She seemed to move into me. I was hoping it was because I was leading her but I remembered that kiss on the doorstep and just hoped that it wasn't anything else.

I was at the Drumbridges roundabout, on the road marked for the Liverton turn-off. Parveen hadn't said a word but I felt that something had to be said.

'You were in the wrong, you know,' I said.

I didn't think that she was going to respond. I just noticed that she had turned her head to look out of the window. 'I just miss him so much,' she said.

'I know you do,' I sympathised. 'But that doesn't give you the right to blame Gillian. She's going through as much grief as you are. Probably more as she knows that her wife killed Tracey, Luigi and Graham.'

Again it took her some time to reply. 'I know,' she finally said. 'I'll call her when I get in to apologise.'

'That's a good idea, Parveen,' I said. 'Knowing Gillian she'll forgive you immediately.'

'There's been a lot of forgiving recently,' Parveen's whisper was barely audible. It was certainly cryptic. I tried to clarify what she was saying.

'What do mean forgiving?'

Parveen suddenly seemed to come to her senses. 'Oh, it's just me wittering on. I've just got a lot on my mind at the moment.'

'Yes,' I agreed. 'You certainly have. How are the funeral arrangements going?'

'Mostly done,' Parveen replied. 'We're just planning the memorial service at the Abbey. I think we're going to have it early next year. Obviously it's going to have to be televised. Every channel I've heard of, and some that I haven't, have contacted me trying to get televised rights. But I think the public have the right to watch it on free per view, don't you?'

'I honestly think that the people who want to watch it will be in the capital itself on the day, to see it as it happens,' I replied. 'But you're right, Parveen. It's only fair that those who cannot make it can watch it free and not via the subscription channels.'

We drove on in silence. I turned in to the secret entrance. How Graham and Parveen designed this I had no idea. As she was in the car I decided to ask her.

'It was. Graham's idea,' she answered. 'I thought it made sense as there would always be fans blocking the main road. I probably won't have much use for it in the future.'

Her face broke and she started crying. She had already unbuckled her seatbelt so I unlocked mine and let the roller mechanism do it's work. I hesitated briefly before putting my arms around her to comfort her.

'It will take a long time, Parveen,' I said, not sure if I was consoling her or just making it worse.

'I know,' Parveen sobbed. 'Sometimes I feel fine but then it just hits me.'

'Like you hit Gillian?' I said trying to make light of it. I'm not very good at this comforting lark, am I?'

At least she laughed. 'No, nothing like that.'

'I think people call that grieving, Parveen.'

'Thanks, Graham. You very kind and good to me.' Her lips grazed my cheek and then she got out of the car. I followed suit and we went into the house.

She made me a tea but I declined something to eat. She phoned Gillian to apologise and, like I thought, Gillian immediately forgave her and they arranged to meet up for a drink. We discussed the eulogy in great detail. I was a bit confused that Parveen wanted Samantha named as his first real girlfriend and how they remained good friends throughout their respective successful careers. At the end I probably had enough material for five hours of solid speaking. And, knowing Graham's fans, they wouldn't have been bored if I did talk for that length of time.

'Can I get you another drink?' Parveen asked.

I looked at my watch. I certainly had time. 'Yes, please.'

I reread some of my notes, making amendments every now and again. I heard Parveen cough and sensed that she was back in the room. When I looked up I saw that she was completely naked.

# 2018 PART THREE

Susan was angry and Diana was sulking. They were stood at opposite ends of the room. Susan was staring out the window, clenching her fists. Diana was looking at the door.

'You're going to do it,' Susan fumed.

'I'm not,' Diana countered petulantly.

'But this is what we've been working towards,' argued Susan. 'We've spent months and years perfecting the routine.'

'I'm not ready,' Diana squawked.

Diana did not see Susan turn and walk quickly towards her. The next thing she felt was Susan's hands around her throat. Diana's head snapped back and hit the wall.

'I will not allow you to ruin the plan,' Susan threatened. 'Do you understand me?'

Diana opened her eyes in sheer terror. She knew that Susan had a short fuse but had always felt safe around her. But this had now changed that relationship. Unfortunately for Susan, when Diana is cornered she always comes back fighting and is very stubborn. She decided there and then that she would not go along with the scheme,

Amy Dunne put her head around the door. She surveyed the sight. It was so difficult theses days to tell the girls apart. The only way she could was by their personalities. It did not surprise her that Susan held the slightly older girl in a vice-like grip. Diana looked petrified. Amy could not blame her. She was scared of Susan herself. She made her presence known by giving a slight cough. Susan looked her way and loosened the hold on her friend.

'Who do they want first?' Susan asked.

'Diana,' Amy responded.

'Oh, Good. Let's get this show on the road,' said Susan as she marched out with Amy in tow.

Diana could not understand how her friend could be so threatening one minute and then so jovial and friendly the next. Perhaps Susan was a real psycho and did actually deserve to be in this place. But she was now resolute in her mind that she would not play along with Susan's game this time. She just wasn't ready.

Susan played her part as Diana sublimely. No, she didn't have any remorse for what she had done in two thousand and twelve. Yes, if she got out she would find her "father" and kill him. No, she didn't want to see her mother. She hadn't want to see her all these years so why would she want to see her?

Amy watched, fascinated by Susan's performance. To be honest it was getting more and more difficult for her to tell them apart. It was only every now and again that a little trait of their individual personality just reared it's head before disappearing again. She new that Susan, although the younger of the two, was the instigator and leader, Diana had a stubborn streak in her which could benefit her later on; or hinder her whichever way she decided to choose.

Soon it was Diana's turn, as Susan, to face the panel. Diana sat on the chair provided, as instructed. And then the interrogation began.

'So, Diana. It is Diana isn't it?' The female member said.

It was a trap. Diana was just about to reply when the name Diana hit her brain and reverberated around her skull. She shook her head.

'You're definitely Susan then?' asked the man sitting at the left of the table.

Diana nodded. She wasn't going to go along with Susan's plan anyway and she was glad that she wasn't. They would have tripped her up quite easily with the tactics they were using this time. She would have been waiting for a question about her and not focussing on Susan's background. Instead she just concentrated hard on nodding and shaking her head in the right places.

She didn't go back to Susan's room. Instead she just went to her own and stood at the window looking out at the fabulous garden. Diana must have been in a world of her own because she didn't hear Susan come in in and close the door. She didn't realise she was stood next to her until she felt the slight pressure of the other girl's hand on her left shoulder.

'I'm sorry,' Diana said quietly.

No, you're not,' the other girl replied. 'There was no way you were going to go along with that plan today, Diana. Well, guess what?'

'What?' Diana asked not taking her gaze from the garden.

'You passed the test,' Susan said happily.

This made Diana turn her head and look at the younger girl. 'Passed the test?'

'No one can make you do what you don't want to, Diana,' Susan explained. 'I had to make sure that no one could bully you in to doing things that you didn't want to do. When you get out, and it will be next time, you'll be pulled from pillar to post with people telling you to do one thing or another. I know and, more importantly, so do you that you'll be able to stand on your own two feet.'

Diana listened to what Susan was saying and, then, started nodding her head enthusiastically. 'You're right, Susan. You're right. Nothing will stand in my way.

'Except I will be controlling you,' Susan smiled to herself.

# BOOK THREE

# PRESENT DAY

I told Judith about Parveen; well not entirely true, I left out a couple of major details. Rightly she was not happy but she put it down to Parveen's distressed state of mind. I knew that she wouldn't go around and argue with Parveen. Jude's not like that. She tends to see the good in everyone. Anyway, I doubt if Parveen would have said anything. She was clearly as embarrassed as I was when I left.

I decided that it was high time I started work on my Danny Williams and the Virus Chasers book. I hadn't really worked on it since that dreadful November evening. I couldn't even put it down to writers block. I knew that one of the major characters was going to get killed off and that would leave the opening for book four which, I had now worked out, would be the final one. I knew how I was going to lead up to the killing. It was going to be a huge shock to my readership but, basically, I had taken this character as far as I could. Its significance would be similar to J K Rowling killing off Ron Weasley or Hermione Granger. Perhaps my readers would never forgive me but I'm pretty sure they would do when they read what was going to happen in book four.

I was typing away on my laptop. I must have written about a thousand words. It was flowing quite well. My phone made that noise that indicated I had a message. I looked and noted that it was Parveen. I opened it up to read.

"Hi, Graham. Just wanted to say how much I enjoyed earlier. I hope you did as well. Any chance we can have a repeat performance soon ������ Parv xxx."

I reread it again and smiled. It had, after all been a pretty good afternoon. I started to reply. "I enjoyed it very much, Parveen. Hopefully, we may be able to meet up again soon. We'll have to check diaries and arrange something xxx" I pressed the icon that indicated send. As soon as I did, I regretted it instantly. This poor woman was in no fit state. I had researched that some woman do have a brief personality change after the loss of a partner. Parveen was obviously in mourning. I should have just let things go. No, scrub that, I shouldn't have agreed to what happened earlier, even though I did enjoy it.

I didn't have much longer to ponder it, however, as my mobile pinged again. I expected it to be Parveen but actually noticed it was an email. I opened it.

"With Graham's funeral being next week, I'm going to postpone your mission until the new year. So you will commence on Monday 3rd Jan 2050. I'm going to allow you three months. That seems fair. The memorial concert for Graham Longmuir is a very good idea. If I were you I would get the others to arrange it quickly. Time is ticking xxx PS I now know your secret. Graham Longmuir will be turning in his grave...xxx"

I was shocked, stunned, gobsmacked and every other word that describes that feeling. I read it it and reread. Thoughts of my book were wiped from my memory. It had to be Parveen. She and I were the only two people who knew what happened earlier today. I forwarded the message to Mark telling him I needed to know who had sent it as a matter of urgency.

It had to be Parveen, I thought again. But how had she managed to find out secrets of the group members. Then I realised things may have been said when the alcohol was running freely back in the early days. But, then again, Graham met Parveen after the group had split up. This really wasn't making any sense. But it had to be her. It couldn't be anyone else.

I was mulling this over for about ten minutes when I heard that an email had arrived in my inbox. I saw it was a response from Mark. I quickly selected it and began to read.

"That was quite an easy one. It appears that your account has been hacked. I did warn you to get better protection."

I sent Mark a reply thanking him and that I would, indeed, but his recommendations for security in place. I actually downloaded the app that Tony had on his phone. It took me about five minutes to set up. It was probably a case of locking the stable door after the horse had bolted. I would get Jude to get it for her phone, too. Then a terrifying thought came into my head. The only other person who knew about Parveen and me, albeit an economical knowledge of the truth, was my beloved wife.

I had the alarming feeling that I was being watched. I looked up and saw Jude standing in the doorway. She had that look on her face that she had caught me up to something. I probably had the same look as a rabbit caught in car headlights.

'Are you coming to bed tonight?' She asked.

# GRAHAM LONGMUIR'S FUNERAL

Wednesday 18th December 2049 will go down as one of the most distressing days in English history. I don't mean that flippantly. I mean obviously the two world wars in the twentieth century clearly surpass that; actually, thinking about it, it probably wouldn't make the top twenty. But it was one of those days when everyone appeared to be shedding tears.

Parveen and her family had wanted Graham's funeral to be at the local church. But it soon became apparent that it had to be held somewhere much larger. Therefore it had to be moved to Exeter cathedral. The television companies, the funeral was being broadcast on virtually every network, had been setting everything up. It was/is unusual to see them working in tandem as they're usually vying for the best positions. However, I think that most senior executives had been devastated by the death of Graham Longmuir. He was their favourite actor/singer. He had starred in or appeared in many of their own shows. They had gotten to know him quite well and now they wanted to give something back. A day to remember and mourn Graham Longmuir.

The service was due to start at one o'clock but a large crowd had gathered around cathedral square two days prior to funeral.

I wouldn't even want to estimate how many people were there. To be fair, there wasn't much room between the boundary wall and the rear of the Main Street shops. But they must have been at least ten deep. Security barriers had been erected around the parameter, more to safeguard the cathedral green which always looked in pristine condition. I always wished that I could get my grass looking so good.

Exeter Cathedral has stood where it is now since about 1400AD. It did get hit in an air raid during the second World War. It has, I believe, the longest uninterrupted medieval vaulted ceiling in the world. Although I am overwhelmed when I see the beauty of its architecture, but I cannot help but think how wrong the church is when it comes to giving praise to God. It is a very rich and powerful commodity but like I have mentioned before, wasn't Jesus Christ betrayed for thirty pieces of silver? and didn't he drive out the tax men from the church? As I have said before, I don't think Christ would be happy with all the ornate ornaments it displays.

I don't think Exeter had seen anything like this in a long long time. Perhaps the VE Day celebrations would have brought the public out onto the streets, but today's service for the untimely death of Graham Longmuir would surpass that.

Guests started to arrive at midday. Seating arrangements inside the cathedral had had to be drawn up. Graham would have been tickled pink to think that Claire, Faye, Lisa, Lee and 'H' from Steps would attend his funeral. They had been touring with Ladies and Gentlemen before that unfortunate day and they had all become good friends. Graham had made it known many times that he did not want black at his funeral. He wanted it to be a celebration of his life.

Jude and I had been invited to join the cortège following the coffin into the cathedral so I only have the information that has been passed to me by witnesses. Richard Yeoman arrived at about twenty five past twelve. He acknowledged the crowd but most of them did not have a clue as to who he was. He arrived with a group of five other people. The descriptions of these varied; some were over sixty, There were three males and two females and one was black. I didn't know that Yeoman had been invited. It was probably more to do with Graham's mum and dad than Parveen.

Apparently, after he had taken his seat on one of the pews at the rear, he started to feel unwell. He started to sweat. People were concerned about him. When he collapsed on the floor all hell broke loose. The service was to supposed to start in twenty minutes. Thankfully a doctor was present but Yeoman's condition deteriorated. An ambulance was called.

My phone started ringing. It was an official from the cathedral informing me that there had been an incident and could we hold back the funeral procession until I got the all clear. I asked her what the "incident" was. She told me quickly about a guest collapsing and an ambulance being called.

The actual funeral cortège was about to commence on the agreed route which began at the Cathedral and Quay car park. The pallbearers were just about to take the coffin from the hearse. I quickly went over and stopped them.

'What's going on?' Parveen asked concerned.

'A guest has collapsed in the cathedral,' I explained. 'They've called for an ambulance and just want us to wait until the guest has been taken to hospital.'

'Have they said who it is?' Sally, Graham Longmuir's mum asked.

'No,' I replied honestly. 'I do know that it wasn't a family member as they were seated at the rear of the cathedral.'

Although they still looked concerned, I think this appeased them a bit. I looked at my watch and saw that it was ten to one. We heard the sirens in the background and assumed it was the ambulance on its way. The route it had to take would not bring it passed us but it would travel part of the designated procession. I could see why they didn't want the ambulance to get caught up behind us. If it was an emergency, and it certainly sounded quite bad, then it wouldn't take long for the patient to be lifted in to the ambulance and taken to hospital.

About five minutes later I got another call to say that it was all clear. I notified the undertaker. The pallbearers lifted the coffin out. I had a slight chuckle to myself as I thought that Graham would probably be laughing his head off at the events that had just unfolded.

Parveen and the children, her mum and dad, Graham's mum and dad started to follow the coffin. Gillian, Samantha and Tony fell into step behind them. Judith and myself joined the band members. It wouldn't have been the route I'd have chosen. I would have taken the subway at Coombe Street, turned left into South Street and then taken a right which would have lead straight to the cathedral. However, it was planned this way so that many people could pay their respects. Setting off from the car park, they would walk up Western Way. At the roundabout it would continue onto Magdalen Street before branching left onto Southernhay East and then onto Southernhay West. Entering Cathedral Close on the left would lead them behind the Cathedral. The final pathway would take the procession to the rear, around the side, to the main entrance.

When we left the the car park, I think everyone was surprised to see how many people had turned out to pay their respects to Graham Longmuir. We all knew that Graham was loved but there was an outpouring of heartfelt adoration and respect. I could tell that Parveen, the children and Graham's mum and dad were choked by the publics reaction. Flowers were being thrown towards the oak casket. Apart from crying, which I could hear, the only other sound was applause. I'm not a great lover of football but the minute applause instead of a minute silence of someone who had died connected to the sport was a welcomed introduction. I know that Graham appreciated this tribute more than the silence as, he felt, it was a way of celebrating their contribution. The crowd that had gathered were certainly showing their appreciation for their idol. It was very touching to see.

It took a good twenty minutes to walk a relatively short distance. But the pallbearers knew the pace they had to go at. The crowd must have numbered thousands, maybe even hundreds of thousands. There couldn't have been any space between them and they looked like sardines packed into a tin. The Christmas decorations were on. The council had discussed this with Parveen and she thought the Graham would have preferred them on. He loved Christmas. It was going to be so hard on Parveen and the children this year. It was only one week to go.

Thankfully the weather played its part. It was a sunny day but a bit on the cold side. There had been a slight frost in the morning but now the temperature had picked up, although it was probably still in single digits.

The Bishop Of Exeter met us at the main entrance. Obviously some sort of signal was given to the clergy inside as the organ began as Cat Perry's song "Over the Moon", an uptempo catchy tune, began playing. It was, according to Parveen, Graham's favourite song. Cat had been chosen to give one of the readings. I had spoken to her briefly, within the last few days, and she sounded very upset. She didn't know if she would be able to stand in front of the congregation and read the short passage. I didn't like to remind her of the millions who would be watching it on television.

The Exeter Cathedral Choir started singing "See Amid the Winters Snow" which was Graham's favourite Christmas Carol, and the procession, lead by the choir, commenced its interior journey. I could still hear the crying of all those that had gathered outside as I walked slowly into the historic building.

I must admit to being in a daze for most of the service. I looked at Gillian, wondering how on Earth she was feeling knowing that her partner, Sue, had been responsible for Graham's death. I heard Cat give her reading - He is Gone by David Harkins

He is Gone (She is Gone)

You can shed tears that he is gone
Or you can smile because he has lived

You can close your eyes and pray that he will come back
Or you can open your eyes and see all that he has left
Your heart can be empty because you can't see him
Or you can be full of the love that you shared
You can turn your back on tomorrow and live yesterday
Or you can be happy for tomorrow because of yesterday
You can remember him and only that he is gone
Or you can cherish his memory and let it live on
You can cry and close your mind, be empty and turn your back
Or you can do what he would want: smile, open your eyes, love and go on.

To her credit, Cat managed to hold it together whilst she spoke but, on returning to her seat, she broke down. I hope that the camera had the decency to move off her. There was another hymn which was "Guide Me O Thy Great Redeemer" which was supportive of Graham's love of Welsh Rugby.

And then it was my turn. A silence descended the cathedral as I made my way to the lectern. This made me even more nervous. I turned and faced the congregation. I noticed all the television cameras directed at me and felt the billions of eyes worldwide staring at me.

'I could start by telling you of the time that Graham helped fill the salt cellar by using one of large refillable containers. He did not sense Parveen watching him until he heard her laughing and told him that he needed to place his finger over the hole to stop the salt from piling into the sink. And there he saw the contents of the entire refillable container in a perfect salt pyramid.' This brought the laughs I had hoped it would bring. 'Or when he wanted to push Victoria in her buggy, for a walk in the park, only to discover that after completing the first lap he was, in fact, pushing and empty buggy.' More laughter. 'Yes, Graham Longmuir was a world famous icon but he was also human. A loving husband to Parveen; a wonderful dad to Victoria, Callum, Nathan And Tanya. A loyal son to Peter and Helen.

'Or I could tell you that Graham Longmuir was one of the

most successful artiste that this country has ever produced. He was one quarter of one of the most famous male/female pop groups of all times - Ladies and Gentlemen. When they split up in two thousand and twenty four, he founded Kids Stuff with his cousins Chris and Andy. After three number one albums and singles, tragedy struck when a close member of the group was killed in a crash involving the tour bus. In his memory, they decided not to continue. Graham Longmuir went on to have nine solo singles peak at number one and eleven albums.

He was also considered to be one of Britain's best actors. He won three Oscars - "The Night Chicago Died...' (here I imitated his most famous line in the film) ..."Like the American City but with a R", "The Magpie" and "Friends". But it was the role that he had always wanted but couldn't accept that he kept on mentioning. He even told it on the comeback interview in March. And that role was - if I may conduct this - Ted Moseby in...'

And all the congregation joined in...'How I Met Your Mother,' which brought quite a few laughs.

I waited for quiet before continuing. 'Or I could tell you of the Graham Longmuir...Graham Adams...that I remember. I was fortunate to be taken on by Peter Adams and was introduced to his children, Graham and Susan, they were ten and twelve respectively. I was given the immediate impression that Graham was going to achieve success. He could play the guitar, keyboards and the drums. I would hear him sing along to songs and his voice was just amazing. He wasn't your "usual" teenager during those dark days when everyone seemed to belong to a rival gang. Knife crime was at an all time high. No! Graham deplored violence of any kind. Samantha and Graham even wrote "Revolution Of Fun" which was against all kinds of hatred. The only "gang" he ever got involved with was his good friends at the music and drama society. And, although Graham could never fathom this, he was well loved. Not just by his family and friends. No, the entire world loved Graham Longmuir. You just have to say his name and everyone smiles. The response to his untimely death just shows how much he was loved by the world. So, many, many, many millions of people loved Graham Longmuir. And Graham Longmuir loved all of his fans. However, only a few, close, people could say that they were loved by Graham Adams. His wife, Parveen and their four wonderful children. His mum and dad, Sally and Stephen - you know it's wrong that a parent should have to bury their two children within a matter of months of each other. He also loved Samantha, Gillian and Tony. Or, as we all know them, Ladies and Gentlemen. A group that the world welcomed into their hearts thirty years ago and, also, a few months ago. Those three colleagues of Graham are now going to sing for you. A song which was written by all the members of Ladies and Gentlemen and, which is believed to be, the last piece of music written by the man we are saying goodbye to today. I give you Ladies and Gentlemen with "Never Said Goodbye".

In hindsight, the guys probably would not have agreed to sing a song at the funeral. However, at the time when it was discussed, everyone thought it was a good idea. But as I went back to my pew and sat beside Jude, the gang started the song. The tears started almost immediately. I looked around the church and saw everyone, even the clergy, with tears in their eyes. The crying could clearly be heard from the crowd outside. It was at that precise moment that everyone realised that they would never get to hear Graham Longmuir singing live with Samantha, Gillian and Tony ever again.

It was Samantha who started the vocals;

*You closed your eyes*
*Then you were gone*
*But you'll always be remembered*
*In your songs*
*When I hear your voice*
*It's very clear*
*It's like you're just standing here*
*But you're not*
*And I ask why*

THE REUNION 2

*I never got to say goodbye*

*You may be gone*
*But you're not forgotten*
*And I thank you*
*For letting me share it with you*
*But the memories make me cry*
*Cos I never got to say goodbye.*

*(Gillian)*
*You were embarrassed*
*By your fame*
*You always thought*
*It was just a game*
*Your voice so tender*
*And that's no lie*
*But I never got to say goodbye*

*You may be gone*
*But you're not forgotten*
*And I thank you*
*For letting me share it with you*
*But the memories make me cry*
*Cos I never got to say goodbye*

*(Tony)*
*We were friends*
*Since first day of school*
*You were clever*
*But acted the fool*
*But now is see*
*Tears in eyes*
*Because we never got to say goodbye*


*You may be gone*

119

*But you're not forgotten
And I thank you
For letting me share it with you
But the memories make me cry
Cos I never got to say goodbye*

*(Samantha, Gillian and Tony)*

*You may be gone
But you're not forgotten
And I thank you
For letting me share it with you
But the memories make me cry
Cos we never got to say goodbye.*

After the song, remarkably, I could hear cheering and clapping from all those outside who had, moments before, been sobbing their hearts out. Then a cacophony of;

*You may be gone
But you're not forgotten
And I thank you
For letting me share it with you
But the memories make me cry
Cos we never got to say goodbye.*

It was, honestly, the most moving thing I had every heard and experienced. If anyone was having second thoughts on how popular Graham Longmuir was then this reaction certainly laid them to rest. But the group had not finished. Gillian waited for a bit of silence.

'After discussions with Graham's immediate family, we would like to announce a memorial concert for our beloved friend. Newton Abbot Racecourse has kindly agreed to host the event. It will be held on Saturday 26th March 2050. It will start at five o'clock and finish at approximately eleven thirty. It will be shown live on television via a subscription channel and all proceeds will be divided between The Meningitis Trust and Cancer Trust charities. Not only will we remember Graham but also Samantha's husband, Luigi and Tony's wife, Tracey. There will be surprise guest stars. Graham gave the world so much. It's only right that we do this for him. Thank you.'

Again the applause was deafening. Graham deserved this tribute. Whilst the group had told me they were planning this, I had no idea that it had all been confirmed. And the the funeral service was over. The procession followed the casket out of the cathedral to a montage of Graham Longmuir songs commencing with "Teenage Dream".

# THE AFFAIR?

Christmas was a bit subdued. Not surprising really after the events over the last couple of months. The only thing I noticed, well Judith did really, was that Gillian and Tony seemed to be growing closer together. We had invited them to spend Christmas with us but they decided to spend it with each other. Samantha spent it with Luigi's family. So it was just a small, family Christmas for us.

We did spend New Year's Eve with the band although no one really felt like celebrating and, more surprisingly, no one drank very much. The guys were soon into rehearsals when 2050 began. They wanted me to write a book covering the concert. It goes without saying that I waived my rights to royalties.

There were arguments. There was bound to be. To be fair to Chris and Andy, Graham's cousins and "Kids Stuff" members, it was always going to be difficult for them to reform without Graham and Steve. But they agreed to do a couple of their hits if the right guest artists could be found.

I also found the time to spend with Parveen. I told Jude where I was going but, obviously kept certain things secret. However, one evening, Jude and I were settled down in bed; she was watching the news and I was writing my "Danny Williams" novel, when my phone went off. I looked at it but didn't recognise the number. Usually I would not answer a number I didn't know but something made me answer this call.

'Graham Avery,' I said.

'Mr, Avery! This is David Carmichael.' The name meant nothing to me. He must have sensed this. 'I look after Diana King.'

'Oh. Good evening,' I replied. 'It's a little late, isn't it? Is Diana okay?' I could sense Judith taking an interest in my call.

'Unfortunately, that is the reason for my call,' David Carmichael explained. 'Diana found out about the death of Richard Yeoman. We have had to sedate her.'

'Just because of Yeoman's death?' I asked incredulously.

'I knew that sounded wrong as soon as it left my lips,' David laughed. 'No, she became agitated because she has learned that the committee is recommending releasing her.'

'Releasing her? Why?'

'Well, the reason they kept on detaining Diana was because she always vowed to kill her father. Now that he is dead, she can no longer seek her revenge.'

'Okay. I get that,' I said. 'But what's it got to do with me?'

'Diana says that she is not going to cooperate with anyone until she has had a word with you,' said David.

'I'm kinda busy at the moment,' I replied.

'Diana is now on suicide watch,' David continued. 'She just needs to talk to you. I promise you that you will not have to play "Go Fish".'

I looked at Jude. Her reaction was encouraging me to go. 'Okay,' I relented. 'I'll be there tomorrow. I'll try to get there for about midday.'

'Thank you, Mr Avery. That's very kind of you.'

'No problem. See you tomorrow.' I hung up.

'Sounds serious,' Jude said.

'Hmmm. It does,' I agreed.

'But?' Jude quizzed. She knows me so well and soon figured out that something was bothering me.

'It just doesn't sound like something that Diana King would do?'

'I must admit that I was thinking exactly the same thing,' Jude nodded. 'Sounds to me like she is just seeking attention like she has always done.'

'Well, no doubt I'll find out more tomorrow,' I said.

I decided to take the train. Not only did I not like driving but it would give me about three hours working on the new book supporting Graham Longmuir's memorial concert in March. I purposely left my phone at home. It would only distract me on my journey to the Stratford Mental Institution and I had been informed that, because of new security measures, it would be taken from me on entering anyway.

I, actually, got quite a lot of work done. I only touched lightly on the dreadful November, Wednesday, evening. I went into more detail on the funeral. Graham would have been proud to see the reaction he got that day. And I don't mind admitting that a few tears leaked as I remembered that day.

Before I knew it, the train was pulling into Paddington station. I stashed all my things in my case and alighted the train. I took the steps down to the underground. I chuckled to myself as I watched the public, like little ants, scurrying to their respective platforms to catch their tube trains. As I sauntered towards the underground line that I needed my mind, for some strange reason, was cast back to March 2020 when the Coronavirus hit the world. There had been outrage at pictures of idiots cramming onto tube trains after ignoring all the warnings to stay at home and to just let the key workers get to their jobs. Those cretins cost hundreds of lives as well as having a negative impact on the economy.

It took many years to recover from that disease. In fact some people claim that we are still feeling the effects 30 years later. Although online shopping was the final nail in the coffin for the high street but the Coronavirus certainly had a devastating effect.

It took me about forty minutes to get to the Stratford Institution and another twenty minutes to get passed the security measures. After that, David met with me and showed me to the same room where I always met Diana.

Ten minutes later Diana was shown into the same room and

sat in the chair she always sat in. She did not look particularly well. No. Correction. She looked formidable.

'They're trying to release me,' she said suddenly.

'I know,' I replied.

'But why?' She demanded.

'Well,' I responded. 'You were being kept here because you kept on threatening to kill your father if you were released. He is now dead so you are no longer a risk.'

'I'll spit on his grave,' she said vehemently. 'Worse I'll pi...'

'I get the picture,' I interrupted. 'I remember talking about Richard Yeoman, with you, the last time I was here.'

'Did we?' She seemed to backtrack.

'Yes. I vaguely recollect that you were quite shaken with the news that you and Susan shared the same father.'

'It's not something we spoke about,' Diana replied.

'That's funny,' I said. 'I would have thought that you two would have found it interesting that you shared something.'

'Obviously not,' she replied.

'So why don't you want to be released?' I asked.

'I've been incarcerated so long, I wouldn't know how to live in the real world,' she answered honestly. 'Since I was a young girl and my mum, Melanie, took me to Ullacombe House, this is all I've ever known. I'm comfortable with this living. I've got no family on the outside. David is my only friend. My only friend on the outside went and killed herself. I would have no where to go. I wouldn't have a clue what to do.'

'I can see why you would be frightened,' I agreed. 'But from what I've seen about you, Diana, you're a very strong minded person. Yes, it will be strange for you at first but you will rise above it. I'm sure you'll be successful at whatever you choose to do.'

'I've always loved dance,' she said. I'm sure she had already told me this before but I kept quiet. 'Sue and me used to come up with all these routines. We always enjoyed doing that.'

'There you go,' I encouraged. 'Look, I may be able to help you get into choreography if that's what you desire. I do have contacts in that field.'

Her eyes widened in surprise. 'You would do that? For me?'

'Of course,' I smiled. 'I may even play a few games of "Go Fish" with you.'

'Now you're just messing with me, Mr Avery,' she laughed. 'But I may take you up on that.' We went quiet for a few seconds. 'I've been rereading your Danny Williams trilogy. I can't wait for the fourth instalment. Can you give me any spoilers?'

'Well, one of the characters turns out to be not who they claim to be,' I replied. I stopped and stared at her. I searched through the conversation I had just had with Diana. And then it hit me. 'You said your mum's name was Melanie. That was Sue's mother's name.'

'I-I must have made a mistake,' she stammered.

'You don't make a mistake like that, Diana. Or should I call you Sue?' I said. 'You're sisters and you probably looked quite similar. You two swapped identities. Oh, my, God. You're Chris Duncan's half sister. You're Susan Blackmore.'

Sue actually smiled. 'It was all my idea,' she admitted. 'I was the stronger sibling even though I was younger. At first it was just a game to us - to see if we could get a way with it. I was quiet when I was first institutionalised by my mother. I didn't speak for the first six months after I had witnessed my brother murdering Susan Adams. But Diana probably had more call to be silent. That bastard, Yeoman, had abused her for most of her life. No wonder why she wanted to kill him. I would have tortured that slimeball for what he did to her.'

'But Diana was released what? Twenty years ago?' I said. 'Why did she never attack Richard Yeoman?'

'Unfortunately, Diana was a very weak person,' Diana explained. 'Although she threatened, she never had the strength to carry it out. Although, something must have triggered her to react in the way she did on that November evening last year.'

'I remember that she took a phone call from someone when Judith and myself arrived,' I replied.

'I have no idea who that would have been,' Diana sighed. 'The initial plan was to get her out so that she could seek revenge on Yeoman. I'm not sure who - or why - someone would have instructed her to do what she did that night.'

'I guess that was my fault,' I said. 'She must have thought I was getting to the truth. Although I had her as Susan Blackmore. I don't ever think I would have made the connection that she was, in fact, Diana King. I'm surprised that the institution's committee didn't see through your plan.'

'Like many of those panels, they couldn't see beyond the end of their noses,, Sue said bitterly. 'I don't think that Diana or myself needed to even look alike. If someone had told them that it was Diana in front of them, then they would have taken it as gospel.'

'Hmmm,' I said thoughtfully. 'Why would she name Tony as Sue Adams's killer? Surely she would have known that it was your brother?'

I thought, for one moment, that I saw hesitancy in her eyes. 'My guess would be that as she felt the net closing in around her, then she probably made mistakes.' I conceded that could have been the point. 'Or she may have mixed up two murders.'

I stared at her. 'Are you insinuating that Tony killed his first wife?'

'I'm not insinuating anything,' Sue retorted. 'I've been in castigated for most of my life. What on earth would I know? Except...'

'Except what?'

'I knew she was doing a lot of research into Ladies and Gentlemen,' Susan continued. 'They were her favourite group. Actually, we both loved them. We got to watch them on television whenever we could. Obviously I knew them but Graham was always my favourite. I couldn't believe it when I heard that Diana had killed him. But Gillian was Diana's favourite. She always said that she would end up marrying her.'

She carried on but my interest had been piqued. Diana had been doing a lot of research? Had she discovered that Tony had killed his first wife? Is that the secret that Tony had been hiding?

'...I always thought that Diana would have made a pretty good investigative journalist,' Sue was saying. 'She would have given you a run for your money.'

'You're probably right there,' I laughed.

We sat in silence for a few minutes. Both mulling over the conversations we had just had. I certainly had a few notes that I wanted to investigate but Susan could have been thinking about anything.

'I've decided to go through with it,' she said suddenly. 'You argued it very well, as I knew you would.'

'You'll do well on the outside, Sue,' I said. 'You could always stay at Chris's place while you get settled.'

'I want nothing to do with that murderer,' she said quite forcefully. 'I can still see vividly what he did to Susan. I had nightmares about it - I still do.'

'And yet you never came forward to the police?'

'I didn't speak to anyone for twelve months,' Susan tried to justify. 'My mother was right sticking me in a mental home. I definitely had mental issues. But wouldn't you have if you had witnessed what I had?'

'True,' I conceded. 'No one should have witnessed what you did at any age. You'll have to let me know when you are released and we'll arrange to meet up.'

'Sounds like a plan,' she smiled.

I thought about the meeting on my return journey. It had knocked me for six that Diana King and Susan Blackmore had changed identities. They would have made terrific actresses because they, obviously, had gotten away with it for many years. But something was bothering me. Something that I just couldn't put my finger on

I was glad to get home, though. I used the voice recognition to open the front door. I dropped my case in my study and then walked through into the kitchen. I was surprised to see Parveen sitting on one of the stools by the island.

'Hello, Parveen,' I said kissing her cheek. I walked around the other side and went to kiss Jude but she only offered her cheek, which I duly pecked. Something was wrong. I sat down on another of the stools.

Jude threw my phone onto the island. 'Are you two having an affair?'

# ANOTHER INVESTIGATION BEGINS.

I looked from Jude to Parveen and then at the phone. I read what Parveen must have sent earlier - "Fancy coming around later and finishing where we left off��" to which a reply that my wife must have written "Why don't you come here instead? ����."

I looked at Parveen again. She turned her attention to Jude. 'I wish we were, Jude,' she began which made Jude and myself gape at her. 'Unfortunately, the real reason behind those messages is that Graham has been helping me get back into singing and writing songs. I'm hoping to perform at the memorial concert. We've been working on a couple of songs but I'm not sure if they're good enough.'

'Oh, really,' Jude said sceptically.

'Can you get your guitar?' Parveen asked me.

'Do you think you're ready?'

'One way to find out.'

I went and fetched my guitar. When I got back I perched on the stool I had been sitting on. Jude and Parveen hadn't moved a muscle. 'I'll just tune it,' I said, more to break the silence than anything else. 'Shall we start with "You"?' Parveen nodded.

I gently counted her in and started playing the tune we had written.

*If everyday*
*Was like the day before*
*Would that*
*Make me love you any more?*
*You know*
*I think that it would*
*When I'm with you*
*Everything seems brighter*
*Could you hold me*
*Just a little tighter?*
*I know*
*That you could.*

*When you smile*
*I get a little warm*
*All my emotions*
*Caught up in a storm*
*When you laugh*
*I feel so dreamy*
*I just want you*
*Near me*

'...and that's how far we've got on that one,' Parveen finished.

We both looked at Jude. 'Well, if you want to keep borrowing my husband to come up with music like that, then feel free,' she smiled. 'That was good. Very good. Why on earth did you ever give up singing, Parveen?'

'Oh, children, etc etc,' Parveen said. 'However, I always secretly wanted to get back to singing but my confidence was very low. Why would people want to listen to me?'

'I did explain to you, in a round about way, what Parveen did when I was in the room?' I said.

'You told her?' Parveen said sounding completely embarrassed.

'You obviously wasn't in the right frame of mind,' Jude comforted.

'I m still not,' Parveen said tearfully. 'I'm missing him so much.'

Jude went to Parveen and embraced her. I put the kettle on using the voice command. Why is it that a cup of tea or coffee always helps in times like this?

'My mind is all over the place,' Parveen continued, her voice quivering. 'That day, when I stripped off, I didn't see your Graham sat there. I saw mine. I see him all the time. It's so hard.'

'I can only dream that my Graham was Graham Longmuir,' Jude smiled.

'Well, thanks a bunch,' I replied.

This made Parveen laugh. 'It's hard putting on a brave face for the children,' she said. 'In some ways I feel like they are dealing with Graham's death better than me. I get his fans saying all nice things about him. And that makes it even worse. I wish they would just stop and let me have some time to grieve.

'I can understand that, Parveen,' my wife soothed. 'But they have also lost someone close to them. Your children are probably putting on a brave face for you. You should talk to each other. But what I really want to know is are you going to be dragging my husband up on stage?'

Parveen laughed again. Jude was certainly performing her role very well. 'The other guys don't know yet so we may not get the chance.'

'No. I'm sorry,' said Judith. 'But this really is too good a chance for you and Elvis the Pelvis here. From what I can remember, Graham always wished that you hadn't given up your career. Didn't he always say that you were his most favourite singer?'

'He did,' Parveen confirmed. 'But he was just saying that.'

'No, he wasn't,' I smiled. 'He meant every word. Wait there and I'll prove it to you.' I went quickly to my study and opened up the cabinet marked audio. It only took me a few seconds to locate the tape I required. I picked up my dictaphone and loaded the tape - still old school, I'm afraid. I went back to kitchen and pressed play on the machine. My voice was heard first.

"So what first attracted you to Parveen?" And, then, eerily, Graham responded. "I heard this beautiful singing voice a long time before I saw the precious person it belonged to. It was like a breath on the wind. I was mesmerised. This voice should not belong to someone on backing vocals. This should be a lead singer. And, then, I saw the most beautiful woman I had ever seen, standing next to the microphone, in the recording booth. For me, it was love at first sound and sight. I just stood there, watching a listening. My only regret is that I wish I had been a better husband to her."

I turned the tape off. I don't think I had ever heard it so quiet in our house before. It must have only lasted seconds but it seemed like an eternity. I could see the tears falling on Parveen's face. When I looked at Jude, she was crying, too. Even my eyes were moist.

'But he was a great husband,' Parveen sniffed. 'I couldn't have asked for anyone better.'

I finally managed to make the drinks. Parveen had a black, decaf, coffee whilst Jude and me had a cup of tea. We talked about the upcoming memorial concert. Parveen was being asked for her input. I had a few meetings to attend over the following week, regarding the concert and suggested that Parveen should accompany me. I, jokingly, added that perhaps Jude should also join us in case she thought we were up to something. Jude punched me, theatrically, in the arm.

Later that night, when Jude and myself were in bed; she was drinking a hot chocolate whilst I just had my standard cup of tea, Jude was going through some paperwork whilst I was mapping out a new idea for a novel.

'I'm sorry that I accused you and Parveen of having an affair,' she said suddenly. 'But when I saw those texts...well, I just jumped to conclusions.'

'I should have told you,' I admitted. 'I mean, I told you the worst part when I saw Parveen stark naked and you didn't jump to conclusions then. I could have just added what we had been doing.'

Jude nodded. 'I did notice that you were reluctant to discuss how your day went.'

I took a sip of my drink. 'Diana King is actually Susan Blackmore.'

'What? How?' My wife splurged out.

'They were half sisters,' I explained. 'They shared the same father, Richard Yeoman. Apparently, they did look quite alike. I think there was only six months between them. Yeoman used to abuse Diana - sexually and mentally - until she retaliated. But she wanted Yeoman dead. So the girls hatched a plan that would break Diana out of the institution. They switched identities.'

'But wouldn't it have been easier for Diana just to say she didn't want to kill Yeoman?'

'Of course it would,' I replied and took another sip at the now perfect temperature tea. 'But you need to think like young girls who had both been traumatised by what they had witnessed. To them it was the only way out.'

'And once embroiled in the lie they would have found it difficult to come clean,' Jude pondered. 'But why did Susan - sorry - Diana single out Tony as the murderer? Surely Susan would have told her that she saw her brother, Chris, murder Graham's sister?'

'This was the only thing I didn't understand out of the conversation I had with Susan,' I said. 'Susan said that Diana must have been confusing it with a different murder. But when I quizzed her, Susan couldn't explain why. I may have to ask Gillian if I can go through Diana's belongings.'

'This is going to hurt Gillian a great deal,' Jude pointed out. 'She's been married to a complete stranger.'

'I hadn't thought of that,' I said. 'This will hit her hard. I may need your help when I go over. You're much better at comforting people.'

'All depends when you're going over,' Jude replied. 'I'm going to be pretty busy at work. Perhaps it may be better, on this occasion, if you go by yourself.'

I mused this over. I wanted to do this sooner rather than later. But I had to appreciate that Jude was busy at work. They had, recently, won a very large contract and were negotiating for another large one. This would mean her going to America some time soon. She had asked me to accompany her and I was thinking about going. I needed to do some research anyway. And, perhaps this news was better coming solely from me.

'You're right,' I said finally. 'I'll give her a call in the morning and see if I can pop over.'

# SUSAN BLACKMORE/ DIANA KING POSSESSIONS

I called Gillian as soon as I got downstairs in the morning. Thankfully she had nothing much on and would be glad of my company. I was thinking that she won't be so glad when she hears what I have to say.

I got to her house at about ten o'clock. She lived in a lovely historic building on the outskirts of Newton Abbot. It was a very secluded spot. Gillian had also purchased quite a lot of the land surrounding the property to stop developers building on it. Newton had, unfortunately, been ruined by over ten thousand new builds since the start of the new millennium. It had destroyed the character of the town and the quality and look of these deployments was an eye sore. However, we were all responsible for this. Thanks to the baby boom that happened in 2020/1, thank you Coronavirus, that smashed the death tally by 3-1, people were clamouring for houses and, to be fair, developers were already having a nightmare trying to keep up with demand. Gillian was offered large amounts of money, and I mean LARGE amounts of money, but she never succumbed. Her name was dragged through the press but she also had her fair share of supporters. I mean why would we want Londoners buying second homes down in Devon as our youngsters couldn't afford the new properties?

Gillian made me a cup of tea. With the news I had to tell her, I would have preferred something stronger. I thought it best if I came right out and said it.

'I saw Diana King yesterday,' I said.

'How is she?' asked Gillian.

'She's not Diana King,' I said rather too bluntly.

Gillian gaped at me. 'Then who is she?'

'She is, in fact - this is lovely tea.'

'Graham! Just tell me.'

'She is, in fact, Susan Blackmore - Chris's sister.'

It went deathly quiet. 'You know I thought you were going to say that,' said Gillian. 'I'm going to need to sit down before I fall down.' We went through to the lounge. Gillian slumped onto the sofa. I took the armchair nearest to the door. 'So the person I married and thought I loved was a complete stranger.' I reluctantly nodded. 'So tell me what you know so that I can get my head around it.'

So I told her everything I had learnt the previous day. About how the two young girls had come up with this plan to switch identities. How ludicrous it sounded to us but to those young girls, it was what kept them going whilst they were being incarcerated. Gillian did not interrupt me. She nodded at certain parts and was almost in tears as I described how Yeoman molested Diana. After I had finished we both stared at nothing - lost in our own thoughts for a while.

'In hindsight, does Susan regret doing what they did?' Gillian asked.

'No,' I replied. 'She thought that she was helping her best friend - her only friend. I know that she thinks that even now.'

'So I was married to Diana King,' Gillian said in what sounded like a dreamy voice. 'I really thought she was not from around these parts. I remember, once, I said something about school, I think it was smoking behind the history huts, and she replied that they were no longer there. I wondered how she knew what

I was talking about. Susan must have told her everything. She certainly played the part of Susan Bingham well. She had me fooled all those years.'

'One thing that Susan did tell me was that she and Diana King were great fans of Ladies and Gentlemen,' I said. 'And Diana always told her that she would end up marrying you.'

I saw Gillian's eyes mist over. 'What a shame I didn't know the real Diana King, wasn't it?'

'Would you have any idea who she was on the phone to, when we arrived that evening?' I asked.

'No,' Gillian confirmed. 'The police did take it for evidence but were unable to trace the number of that last call. Usually, the experts can trace a call even if it has been wiped. However, according to DI Martin, no calls, at all, were found on that phone. Apparently there wasn't anything left on her phone.'

'What? Nothing?'

'No apps, no internet browsing, no messages - not even to me.'

'That's strange,' I said. 'She definitely took a call just after we arrived.'

'It makes no sense,' Gillian agreed.

'I'm just confused as to why she named Tony as Susan Adams's killer,' I said.

'You said that Sue thought that Diana may have mixed up two murders?' Gillian questioned. 'Do you think she was referring to Tony's first wife?'

'That's what I initially thought,' I said. 'But Tony has a cast-iron alibi for that. 'He was at a cafe enjoying a toasted sandwich and a coffee. His phone puts him there.'

'So, what was she accusing him of?'

'I've no idea,' I replied. 'Her mind may have just snapped which could explain why she did what she did and said what she said. Would you mind if we went through her possessions? Just to see if we can find out if she was on to something?'

'Be my guest,' Gillian said. 'I must admit that I haven't touched them since - well, since that night. Come on, I'll show you where they are.'

I followed her out of the lounge into the large hallway. The staircase, which resembled the one on the Titanic, was in the middle but at the platform split both left and right. We took the left hand side. She walked by the first oak panelled door but stopped at the second. She turned the round knob handle and pushed the door open.

I was surprised to see that there wasn't that many items. 'I thought there would have been a lot more of her stuff.'

'Oh, this is just the first room. There's another five to go yet,' Gillian replied. 'And they're crammed to the rafters.'

'Five?' I almost shrieked. 'Better get started.'

'What exactly are we looking for?' Gillian asks.

I didn't really have a clue. 'Anything that reveals her true identity or what she was up to, I guess.'

We started searching. Although there wasn't much in the room, the boxes had stacks of paper concealed inside them. Most of them were sketches of dance moves with written descriptions. Some look very complicated indeed but Diana or Susan or both must have performed them and this was the way the detail was recorded.

We must have been looking for a good half an hour when I suddenly became aware of Gillian crying. I looked over and, sure enough, she was. She was clutching a small, cute, teddy bear to her chest. I went over, knelt down and put my arm around her.

'It was my proposal teddy to her,' she wept. She held the teddy so I could see the writing on the front. "WILL YOU MARRY ME" was emblazoned across it. 'I thought she would have thrown it away. She never appeared to be the sentimental type.'

'Perhaps Susan Blackmore isn't,' I replied. 'But Diana King may have been.'

'I don't think I can do this,' Gillian said. 'It's too soon. You carry on. The room next door is full. I'll go and make a drink.'

The next couple of boxes had clothes in. Actually, everything else in this room was of little interest. She was right about the next room, though. It was crammed but I could tell instantly that most of it would not help me on my quest. I managed to manoeuvre the boxes so that I could get into the room.

I noticed a pile of boxes marked "PRIVATE." I went straight to these and opened them. I was surprised to discover that she was actually writing a novel. It was meticulously planned out. She made copious notes that were easy to follow. I sat down and started to read. It was about a guy who was killed but his "ghost" started to investigate people he knew who had secrets. One of them was the murderer.

'I told you the place was full.' Gillian was stood in the doorway holding two mugs. 'Have you found something?'

'Probably a red herring,' I said. 'Did you know she was writing a book?'

'She always said that she was going to,' Gillian smiled. 'She never told me she had written one, though.'

'Do you mind if I borrow it?'

'Feel free,' Gillian said hand me one of the mugs. 'It's not like Diana's going to be doing anything with it, is it?'

The next couple of rooms were fruitless. However, Gillian was getting to grips with it now and I realised that she was now deciding what was staying and what she was finally going to throw away. The last but one room was not as cluttered as the others. I could move more freely in this one. Gillian followed me in. She went straight to one box, opened it and pulled out a photo album.

'A photo album?' I exclaimed. 'I thought everyone had kept them on SD cards or uploaded them for at, at least, forty years.'

'That's where she was different,' Gillian replied. 'She loved printing out photos and arranging them in these albums.' She opened the one she held in in hands. 'Wow! This one was about all her tours she did.'

I peered over her shoulder. 'Holidays, you mean?'

'No. Tours,' she confirmed. 'Her choreography took her all over the world. This one was of her in Washington. She planned the routine for the dance troop on "THE MEMBERS" tour.'

'That was the venue for Ladies and Gentlemen last gig the

first time round, wasn't it? I asked.

'Yes, it was.'

'Did they stay in the same hotel you did?'

'I only think the group did. I think she said that most of the crew stayed in a slightly cheaper hotel,' said Gillian. She stopped on one photograph. 'Sometimes she took pictures of the outlandish things. I mean, would you take a photo of yourself at a car rental place?'

'I could think of better landmarks to photo,' I replied. 'Especially in Washington. Do you mind if I borrow those, too?'

'You think it could throw up something?'

'It might. Probably won't.

'Sure you can borrow them.'

We carried on looking. Gillian got more and more surprised at the sentimental things that Diana had kept. At the back of the room there was another box labelled "DO NOT OPEN ON FEAR OF DEATH." I glanced at Gillian who nodded. I carefully opened the box. It was full of her diaries.

'Take them,' Gillian offered. 'I don't think I'm up to reading them just yet.'

And that was the last thing I found of use within Diana's possessions. So I had the book and the photographs. Didn't seem like much and I suddenly got the feeling that I was clutching at straws. Maybe Diana was still having mental issues. Maybe those pictures of Tony and Chris, that were shown on the reunion interview, had just confused her and, perhaps, she thought she was standing in front Chris that fateful evening. I soon dismissed that as she had actually named Tony.

Later that night, when Judith and myself had taken our drinks to bed, I showed her the photo album. She laughed at a few of them but she stopped at the car rental place.

'Nobody takes a photo of car rental office and puts it in an album,' she said.

'It looks like one of those joke pictures,' I said.

'No, Graham, listen to me Jude said. 'Nobody takes a photo of a car rental office and puts it in an album.'

'So why would she do something like that?'

'I've no idea but she must have had some reason,' Jude replied. 'Oh, by the way, we'll be going to the States three weeks today. You still interested?'

'Yes, I am,' I smiled. 'It will give me a chance to do some research on a couple of things.' I closed the photo album.

# REHEARSALS AND AMERICA

I kept on thinking about the car rental lot in America. But the puzzle was certainly missing a piece. However, something was happening that made me forget about it every now and again. The memorial concert for Graham was now well underway and rehearsals were happening regularly. It was now the end of January so there were about five or six weeks to go. The group had decided that they would rehearse daily with two weeks to go. The guest line up had been kept to a bare minimum. The guys were going to perform their hit songs, with a surprise element, and the "guests" were going to sing some of Graham's solo songs. Possibly the biggest surprise of the concert was that the two surviving members of Kids Stuff were going to reunite to perform their biggest hit "If The Kids Are Alright".

When Kids Stuff played the memorial concert for Steve, who was killed in a crash while the band were on tour, they had a hologram of the lead guitarist projected on the stage and it did look like all four members performing together. It was eerie as well as mesmerising. Perhaps the group were going down these lines.

Kelvin and Olivia had been hired to do the set design again. Samantha, Gillian and Tony wanted to keep it simple. The designers had come up with this brilliant montage that showed

Graham's life. The show was to last about three hours and the video would run on loop until the very end. There were tears in everyone's eyes as we watched all the images of Graham. It truly would be in memory of him.

Parveen had now told the others about our little song and they were gobsmacked when we played it for them. They definitely wanted Parveen to be a part of the show and even asked us to compose a second one. And so we knuckled down to writing another track. Just before Jude and myself flew off to America, Parveen and me had come up with these lyrics so far.

*Is that your face at the window?*
*Or am I seeing things again?*
*Your ghostly image*
*Or a picture made by the rain*
*Do you know how much I miss you?*
*Can you sense what I say is true?*
*I see you all the time*
*And know that you're still mine*

*I'll never say goodbye*
*You're always here*
*You're looking over me*
*I can feel you near*
*I want you back*
*Because I love you dear*

I certainly could not become a composer full time. This was really draining me. We'd write some lyrics and try to fit it to a melody. Some words just would not fit so we had to change them and, then, the new lyrics did not gel with the other words so we changed the tune. And, you've guessed it that made the rest of the music seem odd. Composers will probably be laughing at me right now or just telling me to get on with it. Graham Longmuir would probably be in hysterics. To be fair to Parveen, she did agree with me on most things - or was it the other way round.

I had always liked America. The people are friendly and funny. We flew into JFK Airport. A car was waiting for us to drive us down to Washington. It would take about four hours to get us to the hotel we had been booked in to.

I had read part of Diana's book on the plane. It was a very good plot if you let your imagination run wild a little bit. But, so far it had not garnered any clues. The text message I received stated that someone had all the clues. There was a bit about some twins who used to switch identities to get things they wanted. That bit was easy to work out. I was sure that I was on to something but just hadn't found it yet.

I don't read or write on car journeys, mainly because I'm driving, that's just a little joke. Apparently, if I do it makes Jude feel ill. She's not a good traveller in the back of a car, even in the smooth modern cars. I'm not good on cars. As long as it has four wheels and a steering wheel then that is generally fine with me. This one seemed quite luxurious but that's about as much as I could tell you; oh, except it had a black exterior and dark tinted windows.

I dozed on and off on the trip down to Washington. Jude will not snooze in the car. She likes to watch the scenery. To be honest, it hasn't changed that much over the years. Okay, the skyscrapers have gotten slightly bigger, if that's possible in America. And some of the green landscape that I remembered had been built on. But, overall, there were many landmarks I could recall.

We got to the hotel about four thirty in the afternoon. We were staying at the Jefferson Hotel, which was just under a mile from the White House, in one of the Grand Premier Rooms. We had the evening to ourselves. We had a fantastic meal and a couple of drinks. We were actually asleep by half past nine.

It was good job that Jude set the alarm for half past seven in the morning because I probably would have slept the entire day. We went down for breakfast at eight. We decided just to have the continental. I think we were both still recovering from the journey yesterday. I was still pretty full from the wonderful meal last night.

Jude had to be at her meeting for ten o'clock. I was going to do some research. I definitely wanted to find this car rental place. I also wanted to take a look at the venue where Ladies and Gentlemen last played in America. A car was waiting to take Jude to her destination while I had asked reception to order me a taxi that would pick me up roughly the same sort of time. We gave each other a brief kiss as we alighted our separate transport.

I could have walked to the formerly named Capital One Arena. But, hey, I was still pleading tiredness. It hadn't changed, much, since that fateful Ladies and Gentlemen concert. The roof had been sloped a little more. The inside had been updated with all the new technologies - lighting and sound systems and all that jazz. I think when the group played here, the stage was situated at the 7th Street entrance end. I know that Samantha, Gillian, Tony and Graham desperately wanted to play here again. Unfortunately, that would now never happen.

Whilst I was walking the parameter, I noticed I was being followed. A couple of young teenage girls. They were carrying a hessian bag. I decided to see if they were genuinely following me. I crossed over 6th Street and walked down F Street. Judiciary Square was on my right and the National Building Museum on my left. I stopped to look at Federal Bureau of Investigations offices before turning right to walk down 4th Street. The U.S Attorney's Office was across the road on my left. But I quickly turned right and stopped. The two girls came running around the corner and almost knocked me down.

'Hello, girls,' I said in my best American accent. 'Now, how can I help you both?'

'We know who you are,' one of them said excitedly.

The other one pulled two books out of the bag. I was surprised to see they were both mine - The Reunion Book and the first Danny and the Virus Chasers novel. 'You're Graham Avery. We're big fans.'

'Thank you,' I said. I was flattered. I don't get recognised often. 'How long have you been following me?'

'Not long,' the first girl admitted. 'We saw you get out of the taxi. We were on our way to our book club at the Warner's Theatre. We just couldn't believe our luck when we saw you. Would you sign these for us?'

'My pleasure,' I said. 'What are your names?'

'Paloma and Adele,' Paloma replied.

'I can't believe Graham Longmuir is dead,' said Adele. 'It must have been difficult for you?'

'It was. There you go,' I said passing back the books.

'Will there be another Danny Williams book?' Paloma asked.

I smiled. 'I'll tell you a secret. There's going to be another two.'

The girls squealed with delight. 'Oh, please don't kill off Del Sol,' Adele cried.

'These lips are sealed,' I smiled.

'Thank you for signing our books,' Paloma said.

'No problem,' I replied. 'Just out of curiosity, where is the best place to hire a car around here?'

'Take your pick. There's loads of them,' Adele responded. They asked for a selfie with me which I duly obliged and then they waved goodbye.

Great! That's all I needed. An army of car rental places was all I needed. I did have an itinerary that I wanted to follow. One was to find the car rental place that was in Diana's photo. I wanted to visit the hotel the guys had stayed in when they were last here - The Watergate Hotel. I wanted to find out a bit about Wayne, the waiter behind the incident involving Gillian and Tony. But, now, I just decided to do some site-seeing before heading back to the hotel.

When I got back, I went straight to the room and put the television on. It was just after two in the afternoon. The temperature was similar to Devon at this time of year but, in the room, with the heating on, it was quite toasty. I had no idea what time Jude would be back so I started to flick through the channels.

I stopped when I saw one of them rerunning the the reunion interview. It had only just started. I became engrossed and then I got to bit which interested me a great deal.

*Chris - Were there any other times you played together? As a threesome?*
*Gillian - You make it sound dirty. (Laughter). Samantha, Graham and myself played at my wedding to Robert. But I think that was it.*
*Samantha - Yep. That was it. I don't think we even talked about getting back together again until last year, did we?*
*Tony - 'No. I think we just sent birthday and Christmas cards.*
*Gillian - I sent more to you than you did to me.*
*Tony - There was a good reason for that.*
*Gillian - You hated my guts.*
*Tony - That may have had something to do with it.*
*Chris - And are you two getting along better now? Or is their still a friction there?*
*Tony - I think the friction has definitely gone. As we mentioned earlier, we're writing together and our families are meeting up.*
*Gillian - And, everyone, if it wasn't for Tony magnanimously accepting my apology, then we wouldn't be sitting here now.*
*Tony - Correction, if Gillian hadn't had the guts to apologise then we wouldn't be sitting here now.*
*Chris - I wanted to ask you, Tony...*
*Tony - My twin as we were called at school.*
*Chris - Yes, we were. It was uncanny how much alike we looked. Most people thought we were brothers, didn't they? If only we could get photographs up of us in our school days...it appears that we are going to show a photograph.*
*Graham - I'd forgotten how much you two did look alike. What went wrong?'*
*Tony - I aged much better.*
*Chris - And I went on to interview politicians. But as I was saying, Tony, What reaction did you receive after the fake news had been reported?*
*Tony - It wasn't very pleasant. When it broke back in two thousand*

*and twenty four, I thought we were living in a modern environment where people were accepted of gender, race, religion etc. However, I had graffiti on my house - suffice to say that homosexuality was not accepted. Friends, or people I thought as friends, shunned me. The thing that hurt me the most was that people I thought knew me, believed Gillian. They didn't question it. Except for Graham and Samantha, who I had sworn to secrecy, it seemed that everyone thought I was capable of what Gill had said. And that hurt. The snide comments dwindled over the years but every now and again people would say something thinking I had never heard it before. What these people, at the time, didn't realise was that it was affecting those closest to me. My first wife took her own life because she couldn't stand the hurt and ferocity the comments were said with. They targeted her, sent her things which were not very nice. Although the verdict was suicide, I blame those people who hounded her. They murdered my wife and the mother of my first two children.*

*Chris - I'm sorry to hear that, Tony. It obviously must have been a horrible time for you. I would have thought that you would have wanted your version of the story told? To finally clear you?*

*Graham - I think as far as Tony was concerned, was that it was still down to Gillian to admit that she had lied. When we heard the tragic news that Tony has just revealed, Samantha and I offered to go to the press and give the truth about what happened.*

*Tony - But I turned them down. As far as I was concerned, it was my word against Gillian's. Graham and Samantha were not there so the press would have just laughed at their statements. The only person who could put it right was Gill.*

*Chris - Well, there was one other. I'm surprised the male involved didn't come forward. He would have made quite a bit of money giving his story.*

*Gillian - I'm ashamed to say he was well paid to keep quiet. Unfortunately he was also killed in a car crash a few months later.*

*Chris - How did you learn about that?*

*Gillian - The hotel informed us.*

I paused the telly. 'She never looked him in the eye when she said it,' I thought. There was definitely no eye contact which could imply that Gillian was telling lies. I went and found Diana's book. I read. There was a character called Jillian Lucas. I flipped through the pages for mentions about her. There were a few but the one that made interest was near to the end. She hired a car and ran over the primary character. Was this too much of a coincidence?

I looked at my watch. It was just after half past three which meant it would be just after half past eight at home. I dialled my contacts number and waited. Within five minutes my phone rang and then went quiet. It rang again straight after. I snatched it up.

'You're not in this country,' she observed.

'I'm in Washington,' I replied. 'My wife is negotiating a large contract.'

'And you're there because?'

'Site-seeing and research,' I replied.

'Of course,' she said. 'But less of the small talk. What do you want?'

'I need you to find something out for me.'

'Obviously. Or you wouldn't be on the phone.'

'You know I love your sarcastic tones. We really must meet up,' I said.

'Ain't gonna happen.'

'I need you to find out if Gillian Tindall was ever investigated for the murder of a hotel worker in two thousand twenty four or five,' I said.

'Wow! Interesting,' said my contact. 'I'll get back to you soon.'

The line went dead. I wondered how long it would be before she got back to me. An half hour later Jude walked in. She kicked off her shoes and collapsed on the bed. She didn't move.

'Tiring day?' I asked. Jude pretended to snore. 'Are you pretending? Only you do actually snore when you're asleep.'

'If I hadn't have taken my shoes off I would have thrown them at you for that remark,' she laughed.

'Tough day then?'

'Americans are known to be tough negotiators,' Jude replied. 'However, we know what we want, if they don't come close, then our competitors can have it.'

'So you're not a million miles away from each other, then?' I asked rhetorically.

'The opening offer was within five per cent of our best outcome,' she squealed, standing up, running over to me and throwing her arms around my neck and kissed me. 'How was your day?'

'Well, I don't want to put a total dampener on your day,' I began, 'but I believe Gillian was connected with the death of the waiter twenty five years ago.'

She kept her arms around my neck. 'Wow! That's quite a serious accusation, Graham. What makes you think that?'

'During the reunion interview she never looked Chris in the eye when she mentioned that he had been killed,' I replied. 'I have no evidence. At the moment it's purely gut instinct. I'm going to check out the hotel they stayed in and try to find that damn car rental office. But that sounds like it's going to be a needle in a haystack. Apparently their are hundreds of them in Washington.'

'And that one in the photo may not have even been in Washington,' Jude said.

'Yep. That went through my mind as well,' I replied. 'But I'm hoping that when I show the photo to the Washington office then they might recognise which one it was.'

'Unless, of course, it's an independent rental showroom with only one office.'

'Yes. I had thought of that, too, but decided to put it to the back of my mind,' I said. 'And here's another thing, there's a person in Diana's book called Jillian Lucas who does a hit and run on the main character.'

'Sounds like, at best, circumstantial,' Jude responded. 'Albeit very strong circumstantial. I don't think Gillian is, or was, capable of murder. But, if Diana was giving clues, surely she would have given the character an alias that you would have recognised. I mean, I know Gillian went by her birth name, Tindall, but her mother's maiden name was French and her adopted name was Young. Why pluck Lucas out of fresh air?'

'There's got to be a connection somewhere,' I said. We pulled apart from the embrace. 'I've asked my contact to look into the investigation over her. Anyway, back to your good news. Doesn't sound like the negotiations will last all week. In fact it looks like it will be a done deal tomorrow.'

'Whoa there. I'm not counting any chickens until the t's are crossed and I's are dotted. Now help me out of this dress.'

'Now you're talking,' I smiled.

'I'm not going to stop you,' she said looking back over her shoulder seductively.

# THE AMERICAN INVESTIGATION CONTINUES

We got down to the dining area at half past eight. Jude needed to straighten her hair. And we both needed to let the deep flush in our faces to subside a little. After a fantastic meal and a few drinks, we were back in bed by ten thirty and, boy, it was great.

At three o' clock the following morning we were woken by my phone ringing before it stopped after four rings. Then it rang again before cutting off. Then it went for a third time. I picked it up knowing it was my contact.

'You know it's three o'clock in the morning here?' I said sleepily.

'Yes,' she said. 'Gillian Tindall was interviewed by the police about Wayne Degradio. Now listen closely to this, according to records, Gillian Tindall did not leave the country at that time.'

'Damn!' I said. 'Are you sure?'

'Definitely,' she replied. 'It was fully investigated at the time and GILLIAN TINDALL did not leave the country.'

'But she could have gone under an alias?' I said more to myself.

'Good. Finally listening. Perhaps I should phone you at three o'clock in the morning more often.'

'Can you find out if Gillian can be connected to the surname Lucas?' I asked knowing the answer already.

'Consider it done.' And the line went dead.

'Sounds like a lead,' Jude mumbled.

'It certainly does,' I replied. 'If she can just connect the name Lucas to Gillian, then I'm afraid it's not looking good for her.'

'What will you do if it was Gill?'

'I really don't know,' I admitted. 'I just hope that I'm completely wrong about this.'

I snuggled down with my wife and started kissing her neck.

'Wow! Three times in a few hours?' She said. 'I can't remember the last time you managed that.'

Jude had already left by the time I managed to drag myself out of bed. I think that I had managed to mumble "goodbye." And I could have sworn that she said that she wanted a repeat performance later. I had managed to miss breakfast so was at reception by about ten thirtyish.

I sat and waited in one of the many plush armchairs until the front desk was clear of customers. I took Diana's photo out of my pocket and walked over.

'Good Morning,' I said cheerfully.

'Good morning, Sir,' she replied smiling. 'How may I help you?'

'I wondered if you recognised this car rental office?' I handed her the photograph.

She seemed to study it quite closely. 'I'm afraid I do not, Sir. However, I'll show it to a couple of colleagues if that's okay with you?'

'Fine,' I acceded.

She was not gone too long. 'Unfortunately, no one recognises it, Sir,' she apologised. 'I can only suggest you try some of the local rentals. They may be able to assist you.'

'Thank you,' I replied. I had already worked that out.

'Is there anything else I can help you with?' I shook my head. 'Then have a nice day, Sir.'

'You, too,' I smiled, turned and left the hotel.

Although it was chilly, it was dry so I decided to walk to the Watergate Hotel. I'm guessing it would normally have taken ten to twenty minutes, depending on pace. However, I stopped off at a a couple of the car rental places en-route. I showed the picture but all I drew were blanks. This was going to take time. I got to the Watergate in forty minutes. I was always intrigued by the political history that governed this area. It brought down a President. As an author I have to chuckle, I don't think anyone could have come with a fictional plot like that. However, the fifteen floor Watergate Hotel looked fantastic and I wondered if room 214 was currently occupied. When I entered the front reception, I could tell why Ladies and Gentlemen loved staying here when they were at their height twenty odd years ago. Although it had been refurbished about eight years ago, it still made you go "wow" when you walked in. It still had its modern, curvy, decor look which seemed to calm you when you entered. The swirling front desk filled the rear wall and I knew the view from the reception waiting area was of the meandering Potomac River. Yes, they certainly knew how to make hotels in America.

I walked over to the concierge who was dressed in her dapper, grey, Watergate uniform. She smiled as I approached. ' Good morning, Sir,' she greeted.

'Good morning,' I replied. 'I'm Graham Avery. I'm an...'

'Not the author?' she gushed before becoming professional again. Her identity badge informed me that her name was Maria Swartz. 'Sorry about that, Sir, it's just that my parents had all your books in our library. And I have read "Danny Williams" to my children.'

Okay, now that made me feel a bit old but I just smiled. 'I'm doing some research for a new book.' It wasn't a total lie. An idea was forming about a famous celebrity being found dead in a swank hotel. 'I just wondered if I could arrange a meeting with someone who worked in the early to mid twenties?'

'We have four people who have been employed since the

twenty twenties. If you could just wait here...' she replied.

'Sure,' I said. I spent a long time just gazing around the foyer. If the lighting blended in well with the decoration. They weren't quite chandeliers but were lavish and large. People were starting to mingle in the reception area. However, I could count the number on both hands. It was getting close to checking out time - this was usually now about midday - so it would only get a bit busier.

The concierge returned. 'Emma Erickson, the Watergate's House Keeping Manager, as agreed to see you tomorrow at four o'clock pm, if that's convenient?'

'That's very kind of her, thank you very much,' I smiled as she keyed it into the electronic diary. I pulled out the photograph. 'Just out of curiosity, do you recognise the car rental showroom in this photo?'

She took the picture from me a looked at it. 'No, sorry, it doesn't look like any from around here,' she said, handing the photograph back to me.

'Please, don't apologise,' I said. 'It really was just a stab in the dark. Thank you for your time. See you tomorrow, Maria.'

I left the Watergate and decided to go back to the Capital One arena. I stopped to have a good look at the White House. I must have stayed there, just gazing, for a good quarter of an hour. I was imagining Nixon and what he must have been thinking in those final hours. I had read that he thought he may be able to see it through. Did he really think that he would be able to stay in office? I guess no one knows how they would react in desperate times.

I walked on towards the Capital One arena. There were a couple of car rental showrooms on the way there so I called in but no one could identify the office from the picture. It was now looking more likely that it was not taken in Washington which meant that it really would be looking for a needle in a haystack. Just as I approached the arena my phone buzzed four times before ringing off. It went again. The third sequence I answered my contact.

'Hi,' I greeted.

'Gillian's adoptive mother's maiden name was Lucas,' she said.

'Really?' I asked.

'No. I'm pulling your leg,' she said sarcastically. 'Of course really.'

'That's a great help. Thanks,' I said.

'Anytime,' she replied and hung up.

Now that was a turn up for the book. Diana had based her character Jillian Lucas on her wife. This made me more determined to prove that Gillian did murder Wayne the waiter.

Knowing that it was a very slim chance, I entered the car rental business located within the arena complex. One of the sales personnel approached me.

'Good afternoon, Sir...' he began and then a look of recognition swept across his face. '...I'm sorry, but are you the author Graham Avery?'

'Guilty,' I said.

'Wow! This is an honour. The Chicago trilogy - "like the American city but with an R" - is the best fiction I've ever read,' he said excited and pumped my hand in a firm handshake.

'I think they're a favourite of mine, as well,' I commented. I was also thinking that I barely get noticed back home but in just over twenty four hours I had been recognised three times. I quite like America. I pulled out the photograph. 'I'm doing some research for a new book and wondered if you knew where this place was?'

He studied the picture but shook his head. 'It's not one of our offices,' he said. 'Tiffany! Jake! Annalouisa! Frampton! Come over here and see if you recognise this place.'

The four members of staff walked over to us. They took in turns to look at the photo. Tiffany, Annalouisa and Jake could not be of help. Frampton stared at it long and hard. 'It looks like a plot I remember in Philadelphia,' he finally said. 'I can't swear to it but it certainly looks the same. I'll write down the street name for you.

'Thanks,' I said as I took the photograph back and he went to jot down the address. 'It's the best lead I've had since I started looking.'

Jake handed me the address on the car rental personalised notepaper. 'Like I said, don't build your hopes up. It only looks similar. Please don't blame me if it's not the place.'

'I promise,' I smiled.

After posing for a group selfie and shaking their hands, I left and walked back to The Jefferson. On the way back I searched for how long it would take to get from Washington to the address I was just given. By car it would take me about two and a half to three hours to get there, depending on traffic. That meant if I left at six in the morning, I could be there by nine o'clock. Even if I spent two hours searching for the car lot I would still be back in Washington to make my four o'clock appointment at the Watergate.

When I got back to The Jefferson, I went over to the reception. Marco, that's what his badge label said, was on duty. I booked a taxi for six o'clock and a wake up call for five-fifteen. Jude was already back in the room. She popped a bottle of champagne as I entered and poured it into two empty champagne flutes. She put the half full bottle on the drinks cabinet, picked up the two glasses and walked over to me. She handed one to me.

'I take it the day was successful for you,' I smiled.

'The best,' she replied. 'We got the agreement four percent over our best case scenario. This is the biggest contract the company has ever won. They're taking us out for a meal tomorrow evening. They're all big fans of yours and want to meet you.'

'That's nice,' I replied. 'Fancy coming to Pennsylvania tomorrow?'

'That would be great.'

'Good. We're leaving at six.'

My wife had just taken a large sip of champagne. The look on her face indicated that she didn't know whether to spit it back in the glass or gulp it down. She chose the latter and started coughing, like she was choking.

'Six?' She said after recovering.

'Yes. I need to be back at the Watergate Hotel for an appointment at four,' I explained. 'By the way, Gillian's adoptive mum's maiden name was...'

'Lucas,' Jude finished for me. 'So Diana was trying to tell you something. Your hunch was right.'

'Yyyesss,' I said hesitantly. Jude looked at me, expecting me to say more. 'At the moment all the evidence is pointing towards Gillian. Even I said that before. But it was something you said when I suggested it. You didn't think Gillian was capable of murder and, deep down, I don't think I am either.'

'But?'

'But there's something I can't put my finger on yet,' I replied. 'I think the car rental place is key. If Gillian did rent a car at the time of the murder, then it's not looking good for her. I'm really hoping I don't find it.'

'Then why look?' Jude ask. 'No. Scrap that question. It was stupid. Since we've got an early start, I suggest that we get ready for our evening meal and then get to bed.'

'Repeat performance?'

'You bet.'

I was already awake before the early morning alarm call. I let Jude take a shower first and I went in whilst she was drying her hair. We had a continental breakfast pack-lunch waiting for us at reception. The taxi was waiting for us.

It took two and three quarter hours to get the address. We walked up and down the road. We asked a couple of people and they pointed further down the road than where we had walked. It felt like we had walked Route 66. When we found the car rental place I was disappointed. It looked similar but it was not the one I was looking for. To be honest, I was not having high expectations for this trip but I had to follow every lead I was given. The message hacker had given me until the memorial concert which was in about three weeks. So far I had two - Diana King really being Susan Blackmore and Parveen wanting to get back to singing - there were still four to go; Tony, Gillian, Samantha and Graham's still to go.

We got back to Washington at two o'clock and Jude treated me to a very light lunch. We did a little sightseeing, for her benefit mainly. She then went back to The Jefferson while I made my way over to The Watergate. I stopped at a bookstore en-route and purchased the two "Danny Williams" books. I got a long look from sales person. It was like they recognised me but did not know from where. I stepped outside the shop, took my pen from my inside jacket pocket, took the books from the paper bag and signed them. I had checked to make sure that Maria Swartz was on duty.

She smiled as I entered the lobby at ten to four. 'May I offer you a beverage before your meeting?'

'A latte will be gratefully accepted, Maria.' I smiled. She obviously put the request through via the computer. I put the books on her desk. 'I know you've already got these but I've signed them for you as a small thank you for arranging the meeting.'

She gasped in excitement before regaining her professional standards. 'Thank you, Mr Avery. I will treasure these copies.'

Maria showed me to a meeting room just off of the reception area. This one was pretty lavish so I could only imagine what the larger ones would look like. I sat down, Maria made sure that I was comfortable and left when my latte arrived. I took a sip and, yes, it was scalding hot. Why do we do it?

Emma Erickson arrived about five minutes later. She was a stylish woman whose face gave away that she liked a bit of fun. Her hair was the same colour and style as Marilyn Monroe. Her Watergate Hotel uniform was in pristine condition and her gold name badge told me that she was the House Keeping Manager. She had long fingered with perfectly manicured nails which indicated that she rarely did the dirty work in the rooms these days. I assumed that she must have been in her late forties although she could have easily passed for mid-thirties. She looked kind of excited to meet me.

'This is an honour, Mr Avery,' she enthused pumping my hand vigorously.

'Please, call me Graham,' I replied.

'Emma,' she introduced herself as she wanted to be called.

'Thank you for agreeing to meet with me, Emma,' I said.

'Maria informed me that you were doing some research for a new book. How can I be of help?' Emma said getting straight down to business. I liked that.

I took a sip of latte. It was now at the perfect temperature. 'I am,' I said. 'I'm looking at celebrities accused of murdering people in famous hotels. I bet you've had many, many, celebrities staying here.'

'Quite a few,' Emma smiled. 'The first ones I remember were Ladies and Gentlemen. I hadn't been working here that long so it must have been twenty twenty four. It was the evening they split up, regrettably. What with the Watergate scandal and the break up of the worlds best group, this hotel has certainly got itself a reputation.'

'What were they like? Were they typical pop stars?' I asked.

'They were fantastic,' responded Emma. 'I idolised Graham Longmuir. And he was absolutely fantastic. I was pleasantly surprised by Samantha. She was ever so lovely. She took time to have a conversation. My colleagues had more involvement with Gillian and Tony. They also said that the two were fantastic. It was a shock when we heard the news the following day that there was an acrimonious split.'

'Did you see any of the group the day the news broke?' I asked.

'No,' she replied. 'They were ushered out, separately, by their security.'

'Did any of them return within a few months?'

'Graham did. I think he was over here to film Grease. Gillian also came back. I believe she was promoting her solo album,' Emma answered.

I thought it best if I explained a bit my the book I was planning albeit very loosely. 'There are elements of my story that are based on actual events,' I began. 'Although I have twisted it for plot reasons. A well known celebrity is stalked by an employee of a swanky hotel. This leads to their death but who actually killed them?'

'Sounds like an excellent premise for a novel,' Emma smiled.

I was now getting to the crux of the interview. 'Did you watch The Reunion Interview special last year?' Emma nodded. 'Gillian announced that the waiter, who Tony caught her in bed with, died a few months after.'

'Died?' Emma said scathingly. 'Rumour has it that he was killed by a hit and run driver.'

'Did you know him?'

'Not really,' she admitted. 'We rarely bumped into each other on the days we worked. Obviously I would hear all the gossip. But no one deserves what happened to Wayne.'

I noticed that she had used his name for the first time. 'Gillian admitted that Wayne was being paid a lot of money for his silence. Would he have been the sort of person to try and extort more money? Like my stalker character?'

'From the stories I remember at the time, Wayne didn't want any money in the first place. He always felt responsible for Ladies and Gentlemen splitting up.'

'Would you say that he was suicidal?' I asked.

'Ohhh! That's a good question,' Emma said. 'Is that a twist for your character?'

'The character is developing during this conversation,' I smiled. 'I'll have to mention you in the acknowledgements page. So, was Wayne suicidal?'

'I didn't hear that he was,' she said. I could tell that she was scanning her memory. 'But he must have been depressed if he thought he was the cause of the greatest pop group of all time.'

'I guess he must have been.' This had been an angle I hadn't considered. Perhaps Wayne had wanted to end his life and had jumped in front of that car.'

'But he was definitely killed,' Emma was adamant. 'Witnesses saw the car steer towards him.'

Bang went that theory then. I pulled the photograph from my left inside jacket pocket. I handed it to Emma. 'Do you recognise this car rental place?'

She studied the picture long and hard. 'No,' she said. 'Sorry. Don't recognise the place at all. I don't think it's anywhere local. I know that woman, though?'

'You do?' I asked.

'Yeah. She booked in roughly the same time as Gillian did, when she came to promote her solo album.'

My interest was piqued. 'Oh, really?'

'You talk about one of your characters being a stalker,' Emma said. 'She was following Gillian quite closely.'

'Was she now?' I said. 'I don't suppose you remember her name?'

'Funny thing was that she was called Jillian, too,' Emma smiled. 'But with a J.' I could guess what was coming next. 'Yes. Jillian Lucas.'

'And you're definitely sure that's her?' I asked.

'Positive,' she forcefully replied. 'Why do you ask?'

'Do you know what happened to her?'

'No,' Emma said shaking her head. 'I'm guessing she didn't sink back into obscurity.'

'Far from it,' I replied. 'She is actually better known as Susan Blackmore.' I saw Emma's face drop. She obviously knew who that was. 'However, recently I discovered that she was really called Diana King. She was married to Gillian. She was responsible for the murders of my friends Luigi Gustavo and Tracey Gee - and Graham Longmuir. So your hunch about her following Gillian quite closely was spot on.'

'Oh my God,' she said. 'Do you think she murdered Wayne?'

I was starting to wonder that myself. Perhaps Luigi, Tracey and Graham were not the first people she had killed. I mean, after all, she was institutionalised for threatening to murder her biological father. However, 'there is no evidence to suggest that, at the moment,' I said.

'But you're going to find the link,' Emma encouraged.

'I believe the clue is in that photo,' I said. 'If I can find that car rental place then, I believe, some answers will be forthcoming.'

'Good luck with that,' she said.

I proffered my hand. 'Thank you for meeting with me Emma.

You've been a great help.'

Emma shook my hand. 'Wait a minute,' she said. 'The research you're doing for your book has had me wondering. Do you think Gillian from Ladies and Gentlemen killed Wayne?'

'Initially the evidence pointed that way,' I said. 'But, now, I'm not so sure.'

'Do you think Gillian is capable of murder?'

'No,' I replied. 'But, then again, I didn't think the person posing as Susan Blackmore was either.'

# THE FINAL TWO DAYS IN AMERICA

I recounted my meeting with Emma to Jude as we got ready for our evening meal with her new colleagues.

'So you think this is a wild goose chase?' She asked.

'I missing something,' I admitted. It definitely felt that my instincts were letting me down. I was guessing that this had something to do with getting older. 'I can see why the evidence points towards Gillian. I mean she was paying Wayne to keep quiet about that night. But why would Diana follow her out here and use a name associated with our friend?'

'You'll figure it out,' Jude replied. 'You've still got those box of diaries to go through. Can you just put this neckless on for me, please?'

'I don't think it will suit me,' I quipped.

'Very droll,' said Jude. 'Now shut up and do it up.'

She had put the two ends of the chain around each side of her neck. I took them from her and fastened the clasp. 'There you go.'

'Thank you,' she smiled. 'So what are you going to do? I mean, that car rental place could be anywhere and we only have one full day left.'

'I've no idea,' I grimaced. 'That rental yard is the quay. It holds all the answers. Anyway, that's my problem. Come on. Let's go.

We don't want to be late for the meal.'

We dined at The Plush Restaurant near Capitol Hill. It had been around since the late twenties. It was actually started by a chef from Devon just after the Coronavirus pandemic in twenty-twenty one. It catered for the social distancing crowd and developed over time. By the year two thousand and thirty, he had a restaurant in many countries. Apparently the presidents enjoyed eating there as it wasn't too far from the White House.

Judith introduced me to Davis Rembrandt the third. His wife, Mary Ellen. Michael Buchanan was the co-partner in the firm, and his wife Hazel. I instantly liked the group. Being respectful and praising of Judith will always put me in good spirits.

The quality of the food was breathtaking. The scallops, that I had, just melted in the mouth. We had drinks while we waited for the main course. I'm glad Jude had warned me that her knew colleagues admired my work because they bombarded me with questions.

'How on earth do you come up with all you plots and subplots?' Mary Ellen asked.

'Could be anything,' I replied. 'Something may be said around this table tonight that will spark an ember of a story. I actually got the idea for "The Magpie" sitting on a train, listening to a family of four, who were heading back home after their holiday.'

'Do you write a book as we read it?' Davis asked. 'From start to finish.'

'I, personally, write a book like it's a journey,' I answered. 'I know where I'm starting from and I know where I want to go. The exciting part, like any journey, is what happens with getting to your destination. So many obstacles can occur on the route so you may have to do a detour. I don't think any of my books were completely as I initially envisaged - except for the start and the end.'

'And how do you construct your characters?' Hazel asked.

'You really don't want to ask him that,' Jude laughed.

'I people watch,' I explained.

'So, basically, anyone sat around this table could be included in his next novel,' Jude said.

'Excluding you, honey,' I smiled. 'I would never be able to create a character as perfect as you.'

This brought a huge laugh from around the table. I took a sip from my rum and coke.

'Give me an example of people watching?' Hazel asked. 'What are you thinking at the time?'

'Okay. The couple at table one, over in the corner there,' I began and my evening meal friends turned their heads to look at the couple. The woman had long auburn hair and was wearing a plain green skirt and a frilly white blouse. He was wearing a casual blue shirt and plain blue trousers. Both were looking at their phones. 'They had a massive argument before they came out. He wasn't going to come so she must have caused the issue.'

'She's having an affair?' Mary Ellen was really getting into this.

'Could be,' I said hesitantly. 'But they're here so I'm guessing it's more to do with her job. She's dressed plainly so, obviously, did not have time to dress as he wanted her to. This was meant to be a special occasion.'

'Anniversary?' Mary Ellen said.

'Perhaps,' I shrugged. 'However, look at the way they are gripping their phones. Look at their faces. There is concern etched on them. This may have been an anniversary but there has been some bad news. But what is that news? And that builds up your characters. Has he had some bad news about his health? How will he cope with it? How will she cope with it? What made her late for this meal? There you go. Ten seconds and I've asked four questions and, trust me, it could have been a lot more. As an author it is my job to to answer those questions in a way that is acceptable to the reader. I can't suddenly say he's an astronaut and he's just been called in to replace someone on an important mission, if I haven't mentioned it anywhere else before.'

'You get all that information from just looking at someone?' Michael asked. 'I just see a couple out having a meal.'

'Not looking, watching,' I amended.

'Drives me barmy,' Jude laughed. 'It can take us four or five hours to eat a meal at a restaurant back home.'

We all laughed. 'Is there anything you won't write about?'

'Yes,' I replied my face clouding over. 'I will never write about that terrible November evening.

'Are you working on anything at the moment, Graham?' Mary Ellen asked.

'I'm working on three projects at the moment,' I answered.

'Three?' Hazel said. 'Do you ever mix them up?'

'No, he doesn't,' Jude answered on my behalf as I took another sip of my drink. 'He makes copious notes. He can tell you the ancestry of all his characters - major and minor ones - and what they've had for breakfast.'

'I keep them all very separate,, I continued. 'If an idea comes to me, I will know instinctively which story it will fit.'

'So, are you allowed to say what you're working on at the moment?' Michael asked.

'I'm working on the next Danny Williams novel,' I began. 'The second is about a cul-de-sac and the people living behind the doors of the property. The third is about a death of a person and a well known celebrity is the suspect. I'm currently doing some research on it while over here. In fact I've been trying to track down this car rental place.'

I took the photo from out of my jacket pocket and put it on the table. Mary Ellen picked it up, looked at it and passed it to Davis. He shook his head and passed it on to Hazel. She looked hard and long at it.

'That looks like Frank's place,' she said holding the picture for Michael to see.

'Looks the spitting image,' Michael finally agreed.

'Frank is my brother-in-law,' Hazel explained. 'His parents started the car leasing business near the Washington Airport. I think the first one was opened thirty years ago and now operates about ten nationwide. I believe this one is in New York - near the JFK.'

'When would that have been opened?' I asked. I was excited but knew that this could be my final chance to get answers.'

'It opened in two thousand and twenty two, just after the Coronavirus pandemic,' Hazel said. 'Although my brother-in-law runs the business now, his mother and father still like to be involved.'

'Would it be possible to arrange a meeting with your brother-in-law and his parents for the day we travel back to England?' I asked.

'Consider it done,' said Hazel. She took out her phone.

'Oh, you don't have to arrange...' I said hastily but Jude stopped me.

'Hi, Frank,' she said. 'You're not going to believe who I'm sat here with...No, not the President...Who's your favourite author? Yes, that's right? Graham Avery.' She took the phone away from her ear and held it out to me. 'He wants to speak to you.'

I took the phone. 'Hello, Frank.'

'Are you really Graham Avery?' He asked. 'Or is my wonderful sister-in-law pulling my leg as always.'

'Well, I'm definitely Graham Avery,' I replied. 'Although I realise that it's difficult to prove over the phone. I'm here with my wife, Judith, who is on a business trip. We're currently having a lovely meal with Hazel and Michael - and with Mary Ellen and Davis Rembrandt.'

'It's good to talk to you, Graham Avery,' Frank said.

I passed the phone back to Hazel. She stood up and exited the restaurant as we were getting looks from the other diners which were totally justified. Jude will tell you that one of my pet hates is people talking on their phones whilst I'm eating. She came back in just as our main course was being served. One thing about America that has never appeared to have changed over the years is the size of the portions.

'All arranged,' she smiled as she sat down.

The rest of the meal seemed to fly by even though we must have been there for a further hour and a half after that phone call. I was convinced that these four people would become very close friends of ours.

We spent our last full day in Washington sightseeing. Jude wanted to visit the FBI headquarters. We went in to both the Smithsonian museums. Jude is fascinated by history, particularly ancient American history. We then had to do many of the memorials; Jefferson, Martin Luther King, the Lincoln Memorial Reflecting Pool. We went and had a look at the White House. Personally, I think, she preferred Buckingham Palace. We saw Lyndon B Johnson memorial, Theodore Roosevelt island before heading over to Arlington National Cemetery. We went and stood at John F Kennedy's and Jaqueline Bouvier Kennedy Onassis gravesite. We saw the eternal flame. This sparked an idea in my head for yet another Danny Williams novel.

Jude snuggled in closer to me. 'Do you think he would have been a successful President if he hadn't been assassinated?'

'I think Kennedy would have been successful in anything he wanted to do,' I replied.

'Such a great pity that his life was tragically cut short,' Jude said.

'I couldn't agree more.'

The following day we left for New York for our meeting with Frank and his parents before flying home. The driver dropped us right outside the car rental lot. He was going to wait so that he could take us to the airport.

I took the photograph from my inside left jacket pocket. I held it up and looked from it to the showroom. I walked about twenty five metres to my right and, when it was safe, went to the other side of the road. I checked the photo against the actual place again. Jude followed me. She looked at the picture.

'It definitely looks like the right one,' she said.

Frank was very enthusiastic at meeting me. He was pumping my hand so vigorously I thought it might come out of his socket. Jasmine, Hazel's sister, was also there. Unlike her sister, Jasmine was quite shy. It took her a little while to pluck up the courage to ask me to sign some of the books they had brought in specially for the occasion. As the meeting progressed she came more and more out of her shell and I got the feeling that she would become a life long friend.

Mrs Malone was a striking woman. Although well into her seventies now, she could easily have passed as someone in their forties. I always thought Jude looked great for her age but Veronica was immaculate. She did, however, blush a little when I complimented her on her appearance. Frank Senior did look his age but his wit and charisma made my sides ache with laughter.

After all the introductions and humorous banter, I handed them the photograph. They studied it.

'Well, it's definitely this place,' Frank senior confirmed. 'All we do, externally, is give it a fresh coat of paint. It keeps in with our branding. We've changed the interior many many times.'

'Do you keep ledgers of everyone who's rented a car?' I asked.

'From about twenty five years ago,' Jude completed for me.

'We have to keep all the details for legal reasons,' Veronica confirmed. 'Apparently it can help when the law enforcement officers have to solve a crime that could have happened twenty, thirty or more years ago.'

'At least technology has developed at a significant pace since we started,' said Frank Senior.

'So what period are you looking for?' Frank junior asked.

'I'm looking for two thousand and twenty four to twenty five,' I answered.

'Any names would be a great help,' Veronica said.

'Try Gillian Tindall,' I suggested.

'You surely don't mean the Gillian Tindall, do you?' Jasmine asked.

'The very same,' I replied.

'Am I missing something?' Frank Senior asked. 'But who is Gillian Tindall?'

'Oh, Frank,' Jasmine said incredulously. 'Have you not been watching the news these last few months? Gillian is in the best pop group in the world - Ladies and Gentlemen - it was her wife that murdered Graham Longmuir in November.'

'Consider myself informed,' Frank Senior smiled.

Veronica typed in the name. It didn't take too long to get a response. 'Well,' she began. 'Gillian Tindall has hired cars from us.' Not what I really wanted to hear. 'But not in between the years you stated.'

'What about Diana King?' Jude asked.

Veronica tapped in the name. Seconds later, 'nothing.'

I think I may have sighed loudly in relief when Gillian's came back negative. 'What about Jillian Lucas? Jillian is spelt with a J,' I asked.

'That's the woman in the photograph,' said Frank Junior. All heads turned to look at him.

'Jillian Lucas hired a car here in April twenty twenty five,' Veronica confirmed.

'How did you know that the woman in the picture went by the name Jillian Lucas?' I asked.

'Normally I wouldn't have taken any notice,' he explained. 'However, Gillian Tindall was always my favourite in Ladies and Gentlemen. So when this woman said she was hiring a car on Gillian's behalf, obviously my interest was piqued. She even gave me a signed photo of the star.' I suspected that this was probably a fake. Or one that Diana had requested from Gillian. 'It's those types of memories that you tend never to forget.'

'Was she with anyone?' Jude asked.

Frank seemed to give this some thought. He looked at the photograph again. 'I don't recall anyone else with her but someone must have taken this picture, mustn't they?'
I looked at Judith and she looked at me. How the hell had I missed that? I was definitely losing my touch. 'I can tell you who it wasn't, though,' Frank continued. 'It wasn't Gillian Tindall. I was such a fan that I would have recognised her through any disguise.'

'If Frank can think of anything else, is there some way we can contact you?' Jasmine asked.

I exchanged telephone numbers with Jasmine, Veronica and Frank Junior. Frank Senior did not bother as, in his words,

"Pointless, because I won't be around for much longer."

Veronica made us a drink and we talked, mainly about my books. They tried to pry some more details out of me regarding the new Danny Williams book, but I wasn't giving anything away. Soon we were on are way to the airport terminal. Just as we were about to arrive, my phone vibrated. I looked at it and saw that it was an email. I pressed on my inbox and saw that it was from Dominica Robertson. I read it.

*Dear Graham Avery*

*As discussed at our last meeting, I have attached my book for you to critique. I appreciate that a lot has happened since we met and the pressure that you must be under so have waited until now to send it to you. I'm not expecting an immediate response as, I expect, you're probably pretty busy at the moment. But I look forward to hearing from you soon.*

*Kind Regards*

*Domy*

There were two attachments with the message. One was titled synopsis and the other was called The Heroine in a Man's World. At least it would give me something to read on the journey home.

# TONY'S FIRST MARRIAGE

I actually got totally engrossed in Domy's book. Basically it was about a woman during the First World War whose husband goes missing. She then dresses like a man and enlists in order to try and find her husband. She discovers that one member of the squadron is a German spy. There were a few factual inconsistencies that I pointed out in my response. For example, the Bren machine gun was introduced in nineteen thirty-eight so she could not include it in the First World War. I told her that she could use the Browning which the British used in the period she was writing about. I offered to meet up with her to advise on next steps. Although I was considering keeping the story for my own use. I know they call it plagiarism but I had done it once before. I had received the manuscript for "The Magpie" from a person. I had written back rejecting the book. But I kept the story with me so when Heather wanted to co-write a novel, I outlined the thesis of the book I had received and declined.

I went in to my study. Jude had gone to work, probably to celebrate the deal she had negotiated with her colleagues. Initially I was going to work on the Danny Williams book. I was close to completing. However, for some reason I took out my phone. I looked at it and pulled up the message I had received anonymously regarding the secrets of the members of Ladies and Gentlemen. I started writing.

*'You think that Gillian killed the waiter that Tony found her in bed with.'*

I only had to wait seconds before a reply.

*'I don't think. I know.'*
*'Well, I think you're wrong,'* I texted. *'And I'll get the evidence to prove it.'*

Again, the response came immediately. *'Can't wait. You've still got Tony, Graham and Samantha's secret to figure out and the concert is only two weeks away. Good luck. I think you're going to need it.'*

Well, whoever I was communicating with here, they were certainly correct in stating that I needed some luck. I know that I had yet to read Diana King's diaries. Instead of going on the Danny Williams file on my laptop, I searched for "The Reunion Interview." I thought there may be a clue in there. At least something that could help pinpoint a date in the diaries. When I had found it I pressed play. I got to this part of the interview.

Samantha - And that is how we got back together,
Chris - How is Christian now?
Tony - As well as can be expected,
Chris - And you are a dark horse, aren't you? Nobody knew you were married and no one knew you had three children with Tracey.
Tony - Well, Harrison and Leia are from my first marriage.
Chris - So you were married before?
Tony - Yes. My first wife died and that's all I'm going to say about that

I immediately pressed pause, rewound to the section I needed to see again and pressed play.

Samantha - And that is how we got back together.

Chris - How is Christian now?

Tony - As well as can be expected,

Chris - And you are a dark horse, aren't you? Nobody knew you were married and no one knew you had three children with Tracey.

Tony - Well, Harrison and Leia are from my first marriage.

Chris - So you were married before?

Tony -Yes. My first wife died and that's all I'm going to say about that.

I pressed pause again before listening to it once more. It came as a bit of a surprise to everyone that Tracey was Tony's second spouse. Then I remembered that after Tony had been released on bail and came here, he had asked me to investigate this very thing. And it had been mentioned a few times since then. Boy, I was definitely losing touch. There was quite a bit of a difference in age between Leia and Christian. Leia was now sixteen and Christian was five. Apart from that, I had no knowledge of her name or when they got married. However, this was my bread and butter. It would be quite easy. I knew both Harrison and Leia's birthdays. It didn't take me long to pull up their birth certificates online. Deidre Gee was registered as being the mother. After a few more minutes I had managed to trace Tony and Deidre's marriage certificate. Her maiden name was Robertson. I couldn't find a death certificate. This puzzled me as Tony definitely said in the interview that she had died.

I went and made myself another hot drink. I returned to my study with it and hadn't taken a sip to see how hot it was. I guess there is a first time for everything. I clicked on the clip once more.

Samantha - And that is how we got back together.

Chris - How is Christian now?

Tony - As well as can be expected,

Chris - And you are a dark horse, aren't you? Nobody knew you were married and no one knew you had three children with Tracey.

Tony - Well, Harrison and Leia are from my first marriage.

Chris - So you were married before?

Tony - Yes. My first wife died and that's all I'm going to say about that.

Yep, he definitely confirms that his first wife died. But there was no death certificate which could only mean one thing, her body had never been found. The cogs were ticking in my brain. As far as I could see there could only be three reasons for this;

1. Deidre may have fallen into the sea and her body was swept away.
2. Tony killed Deidre and hid the body.
3. Deidre was still alive.

I didn't go much on option two but it had to be considered. I picked up my phone and dialled my contacts number. After the coded reply, I picked up.

'Wow! So soon? People will start to think we're having an affair,' she said.

'I'm starting to wish that we were,' I laughed. 'It would be simpler.'

She must have sensed the tenseness in my voice. 'How can I help?'

'I need everything you've got on Deidre Gee, maiden name is Robertson,' I said.

'Gee?' She queried. 'With your circle of friends, I'm taking that this is related to Tony?'

'It's his first wife,' I said.

'I'll get back to you as soon as I can.' And the line went dead.

I tried to research Deidre Robertson/Gee. There wasn't really much to go on. She was reported missing in 2037. I was surprised to see that there wasn't much about her on the online press. But, then again, Tony did very well in hiding her from the general public. There was limited information about the woman. Apart from the marriage licence, I could not find anything linking her to Tony. Mind you, the press had already had Tony labelled as a homosexual so would not have associated Deidre with him.

My phone interrupted my thoughts. I grabbed it up and saw a message from Sam. "Are you coming to rehearsals?" It read. I looked at the time on my phone. It was eleven twenty-two. I remember agreeing to meet with them at ten thirty. "Apologies. I'm on my way. Will be about twenty minutes."

I quickly closed my laptop, unplugged it and stuffed it in its case. I grabbed my pad and a couple of pens and put them in the case, too. As I left the house, I voice activated the alarm. Judith would be impressed as I usually forget to do that.

I was getting out of my car, at the warehouse, eighteen minutes later. Ashamedly, I didn't keep to the speed limit. Normally I've very conscious about that. A friend of ours youngest child was knocked down by someone speeding. Fortunately she survived but is in a wheelchair for life.

I walked into the warehouse, the same one as the guys had rehearsed in for the reunion tour, with a smile on my face. It was soon wiped off, however, when I saw Graham Longmuir performing "Teenage Dream" on the stage.

It took me a few moments to regain my composure. It was, obviously, a very good, realistic, hologram. Technology had made giant steps forward, in this field, in recent years. It was like the person was actually performing.

'Wow!' However, was all I could say.

I could see that Samantha, Gillian and Tony had all been crying. Samantha was sat on the sofa, strumming her guitar. Her mind, clearly, elsewhere. Tony and Gillian were sat at the table. They were a few pieces of paper so they must have been in the middle of composing a song.

'Finally,' Tony said without looking up.

'What do you think?' Gillian asked.

'It's lifelike,' I said. 'It's like he is really up there performing.'

'We're not sure whether to use it,' Samantha said quietly. 'It's quite eerie. We're finding it difficult to perform with him.'

'It's like he knew something was going to happen so he got Kelvin and Olivia to film him performing over various concerts,' Tony said.

'We're supposed to interact with the hologram,' explained Gillian.

'And you can't because?' I queried.

'It's like he really is here,' said Samantha. 'He even laughs and jokes with us.'

'We're just wondering if the general public is ready for that,' said Tony.

'Do you want my input?' I asked. They all nodded. 'The fans are never going to be able to see Graham Longmuir perform live ever again. I honestly think they would accept seeing Graham as a hologram because it would mean seeing him. Sure, there are bound to be tears. From the stains on your faces, it appears that there already has been. I think that if you mention the holographic image first, then it won't freak people out. What does Parveen think about it?'

'She's all for it,' said Gillian. 'I'm guessing that she's trying to hold onto the memory of her husband forever.'

'And who can blame her?' Samantha agreed.

'Well, if it's alright for Parveen,' I pointed out. 'Then it's good enough for me.'

'Did you know she was thinking about selling the house in Cardiff?' Samantha asked.

'She did say something,' I admitted. 'She has always preferred the home here in Devon.'

'It will be a shame, though,' Gillian mused. 'I mean, that was the house where we all played together for the first time in twenty five years.'

Kelvin and Olivia came in from the other room. They smiled

politely when they saw me.

'Hello, Graham,' said Olivia.

'Olivia. Kelvin,' I acknowledged them.

'What did you think of the projection?' Olivia asked.

'Very realistic,' I said. 'It was almost as though the real Graham Longmuir was performing up there.'

'That's what we were hoping for,' Kelvin admitted.

'Mind you,' said Olivia, 'it was very difficult bringing him back to life. Not in the way of projecting him but from a mourning experience. We very nearly didn't suggest it. But Graham had some reason for wanting us to film him at concerts. I'm hoping that we can portray him tastefully enough.'

'If anyone can, then it's you two,' I replied.

I watched as they started rehearsals. I actually had tears in my eyes as I watched them perform. It took me back to the night of June 4th last year, at Newton Abbot racecourse. It was the first concert on the Ladies and Gentlemen Reunion Tour. It was so realistic. The guys were having conversations with each other. Olivia and Kelvin had scripted it. Yes, there were a few mistakes, but this was what rehearsals were for. They still had two weeks to perfect the routine. And perfect it they would

They took a break at one o'clock. We sat around the table drinking teas and coffee. Kelvin and Olivia were in the next room working on, what they thought, a hitch with the projection. I don't think any of us noticed it.

'How was America?' Gillian asked.

'Exciting,' I replied. I wondered if I should say what I discovered. 'You remember how we all received those weird texts a couple of months ago.' They all confirmed they did. 'Well, so far I have discovered the secrets of Chris, Parveen, Diana King and - yours, Gillian. Although I do not agree with it.'

'What did they think it was?' She asked. She looked very concerned.

'Would you prefer to do this in private?' I offered.

'I have no secrets from these guys,' she said.

'Well, whoever sent those messages believes that you killed Wayne the waiter,' I answered. 'The person Tony caught you in bed with all those years ago.'

'There's no way Gillian killed that guy,' fumed Tony.

'Very kind of you to say that, Tony,' Gillian smiled. 'And you're right. I didn't kill him. I felt sorry for him. He was a young kid. He was happy with the money I was sending him...'

'To keep him quiet,' I interjected.

'Yes, to keep him quiet,' Gillian admitted. 'He didn't deserve any of what happened to him. He was a - sweet - kid.' She went quiet for a few minutes. All you could hear was the sound of us breathing. 'I was in America the day he died, you know.' We all looked at her. Although this was not news to me, it certainly appeared that Samantha and Tony had never heard it before. 'I was promoting my first solo album. It only took me three months to write and record. And it shows.'

'I, personally, thought it was the best thing you did,' said Tony.

'Thank you,' said Gillian. 'You always were good at saying the right thing at the right time, Tony. I was questioned by the Washington police. But it was soon proved that I was not in the area where Wayne died. There was an eye witness who gave the model and colour of car. It was completely different than the one my management team hired. Mind you, if I had been at the wheel, then there probably would have been a trail of bodies.' It was a feeble attempt to lighten the mood and the rest of us did have a little chuckle. 'But, perhaps it was in my imagination, I had a strange feeling that I was being followed. Now it just sounds like an excuse.'

'You were being followed,' I said. Now all the attention was on me. 'I've discovered that Diana King followed you to America. She hired a car under the pseudonym Jillian Lucas. That's probably a name you're familiar with, Gillian.

Gillian gazed intently at me. 'It's a name I used - no, still use - regularly to cover my true identity. I use it in honour of my stepmum. So Diana or Susan was following me back then?'

'It would appear so,' I replied. 'Unfortunately, at present, I have been unable to discover any evidence of her being involved with the death of Wayne. It could be that his death was just an accident.'

'But you don't think so?' Sam asked.

'I think it too much of a coincidence that Diana was in the States, the same time as Gillian, when Wayne died,' I replied. 'I've tracked down where she rented the car from - it was just outside J F K airport. One of them remembers Diana being there as she gave them a signed photo of you, Gillian. He was a big fan of yours.'

'Well, that's two I had,' Gillian joked.

We all had to laugh at this. 'I believe someone else was with her.'

'Who?'

'Unfortunately, I don't know yet,' I admitted. 'I'm hoping my contact at the car rental place will come good. But, anyhow, it still leaves me with a problem.'

'What's that?' Tony asked.

'I've got two weeks to discover the secrets whoever it is knows about Samantha, Graham and you, Tony,' I said. 'Any suggestions?'

'I can't think of any that haven't already been reported,' Samantha replied.

'The only one I can think of would have been the Gillian and Wayne incident,' said Tony. 'But that's now been laid to rest thanks to Gillian.'

'You did mention in the reunion show about your first wife,' I prompted.

'I think I also said that I wouldn't discuss it any further,' Tony said.

'You said she died,' I persisted. 'But she has never been certified as dead.'

'I really don't want to discuss it, Graham,' warned Tony.

'I'm afraid you may have to, Tony,' I said. My voice slightly rising. 'If this person does know anything about it, then you can bet in a little over two weeks the whole word is going to know about it.'

'And what if all this is a con?' Tony said. His voice also rising. 'What if someone is just making you out to a mug?'

'Tony...' Gillian put a hand on Tony's arm.

'No. He's right,' I conceded. 'But are you prepared to take that risk, Tony? If you are, then, I promise, I'll back off.' I was a bit surprised by Tony's outburst. After all, hadn't he wanted me to investigate her death when he came over to our place when he was released on bail? Perhaps it was because the others were here.

It went quiet again, for a few minutes, before Tony began speaking. 'I had taken a couple of weeks off. We hadn't gone very far, just local. We were on a day out to Babbacombe. We had left Leia and Harrison with my parents. I think Dee wanted some time alone. She had been suffering from post natal depression after Leia was born. But that was three years prior to this. I had never seen her like it. But she appeared to be her old self when we visited Babbacombe. She was laughing and joking. There's a railway that takes you down to Odicombe beach.'

'I think we know it, Tony,' said Samantha.

Tony smiled, apologetically. 'Dee wanted to go down to the beach. I wasn't interested. Obviously, I wish I had gone with her now. But I chose to stay in the cafe at the top of the cliffs. No one else was in the train as it descended. I watched as it started its journey. Deidre was waving to me. That was the last time I saw her. I've now always thought that she was waving goodbye. They found some of her clothes on the rocks.'

Tony went quiet. 'But they never found her body,' I virtually whispered.

'No,' Tony admitted.

'So the evidence the person may have is that you're a bigamist,' I said. All eyes were on me. 'You never reported her dead, Tony. Even when the seven years elapsed without a body, you still need to apply for a declaration of presumed death. You married Tracey without that.'

'Yes,' he replied.

My phone rang and then stopped. It went again and stopped. 'I'll need to take this,' I said as it rang for the third time. I stood up and walked towards the exit.

'Hello,' I said.

'You probably know all this already but Deirdre Gee went missing in March 2037,' my police contact said. 'She suffered from mental depression caused by post natal depression. Tony was interviewed about her disappearance but his phone and a witness place him in a cafe. Deidre Gee's clothes were found on rocks at Odicombe beach. It is thought that her body was washed out to sea.'

'Does your report indicate if she threatened suicide before?' I asked.

She was obviously reading the report as she took a few seconds to respond. 'There's nothing to say that she threatened suicide before. She did have regular therapy sessions.'

'How regular?'

'Every other week. From when Leia was born through to her death.'

'That's pretty regular,' I said.

'She must have meant something to Tony,' my contact said. 'He was paying for her sessions.'

'So whoever knows all the secrets of the group, must think that Tony is a bigamist,' I said, more to myself than to my contact.

'Bigamy? What on earth are you on about?' I could hear her tapping keys on her keyboard. She must have been looking something up.

'Tony never applied for a declaration of presumed death.' I was a bit surprised that my contact was being slow on the uptake here. 'In the eyes of the law he was still married to Deidre when he married Tracey.'

There was a slight pause. 'I thought you were supposed to know everything about the members of Ladies and Gentlemen.'

'Of course I do,' I said irritably.

'So you know, then, that Tony and Tracey never got married.'

'Never got...' Her words struck me like a thunderbolt. 'He...She...Are you sure?'

'Thought you were an investigative journalist?' She said. 'It's easy to look it up. So, whatever it is this person thinks they know, it's definitely not bigamy.'

# ANOTHER SECRET SOLVED?

Judith and I were laying in bed later that night. We had Diana King's diaries strewn across the bed with us. I had been searching for anything from around twenty thirty-seven. There were four volumes covering that period.

'Are you sure Tony and Tracey never got married?' Jude asked.

'I've looked at all the websites and can't find a thing,' I replied. 'There's no reason to doubt my source.'

'What did Tony say?'

'I didn't actually mention anything to Tony,' I admitted. 'There's obviously something he doesn't want to tell me.'

'So if his secret isn't bigamy, then what is it?'

'I've no idea,' I said. 'I mean it still could be bigamy if the person hasn't done their research properly - very much like me.'

'But you don't think so?'

'It's unlikely,' I answered honestly. 'Whoever has all these secrets has been given actual information. How they got it I cannot say. Perhaps Diana followed them and fed back the information. But I'm really clutching at straws.'

'This is all such a mess,' Jude said sounding as frustrated as I felt. 'Why would someone want to wreck the lives of Gillian, Samantha, Tony, Graham, Parveen and all their families?'

'If I knew the answer to that, then I could do something about it,' I replied. 'I take it that you haven't found anything in that diary.'

'Nothing worth mentioning,' she answered. 'I take it that it's the same for you?'

I nodded. 'Diana does tend to use the letter D quite a lot,' I pointed out. 'She must be referring to someone because, listen - "D was not impressed when I updated her."'

'I've had quite a few of them as well,' Jude said. 'But I just took it that she was referring to Diana.'

'But it's Diana writing it. Why would she be referring something to herself?'

'I read it like she was Susan at the time and Susan was Diana.'

I hadn't read it like that. 'That makes a lot of sense,' I smiled and leant over and kissed her on the cheek. 'That's why I married you. Do you fancy another drink?'

'I'd fancy something else,' she said and gave me a lecherous wink.

'Unfortunately, darling, we've still got a couple of diaries to go through. It's going to be a late night. So, drink?'

'Better than nothing,' she said, reaching for her cup and passing it to me.

'Be careful or ill make you ordinary coffee instead of a decaf.'

I got out of bed and went downstairs. I voice activated the kitchen lights. It's all fine when the internet is running properly but, as I've already mentioned, I'm not technically minded. I'm more of a technophobe. When we first moved in to this house, I got up one night to go down and make a drink. I thought I was being clever using the voice activation sensor. I couldn't figure out why it was dark when I got down to the kitchen. I commanded the unit to put on the lights again. They came on but ten seconds later they went off. Unbeknown to me, Judith was awake and was deactivating them. I could have switched the kettle on from the bedroom. However, since I was the last one to use it before we went up, I knew damn well that I wouldn't have refilled it. I took the kettle off its stand, walked over to sink, took the lid off the kettle, turned the tap on, stuck the kettle underneath and filled it so that there was enough for two mugs of tea. After putting the lid back on, I went and placed the kettle back on its stand. I pressed the button for it to start boiling the water. I was stood next to it so it was quicker than asking the voice command unit to do it for me. One thing I do like about this modern technology is that the kettle boils the water within seconds. In fact you don't get much time to put the coffee and tea-bag in the cups. When the kettle switched itself off, I poured the water in the cups. Just as I got the milk out of the fridge and added the quantity I required to make the tea the consistency I liked I heard Jude shout.

'Oh my God! Graham, get up here now.'

I quickly put the milk away, picked up the two mugs and walked quickly upstairs. I was quite pleased not to spill any. I did notice the tea-bag bobbing up and down in my drink. Oh, well, too late now.

When I returned to the bedroom, Jude was holding out the diary, she had been reading, to me. I passed her her coffee, placed mine on the bedside table and took the book from her. She indicated that I should start reading from the entry dated Tuesday March 17th 2037.

*"I had followed them to Babbacombe. They went to the Model Village. I hadn't visited this attraction since I was a little girl. Mum and that traitor bastard, Yeoman, took me when I was six. It had grown a lot bigger and I particularly enjoyed the Jurassic World exhibition. They must have stayed there about three hours. I was getting a little bit bored. I thought they would have gone back to their car but Tony and his wife walked to their next destination. I mean I'm a dancer but this seemed like miles. To be fair, it probably wasn't that far.*

*They stopped at a cafe which had a cable car kind of ride which took you down to the beach. Their was a bit of a heated discussion. I thought Tony was going to hit his wife. In the end he stormed into the cafe and she took the ride down to the beach. I thought that was going to be it but about an hour an a half later I noticed Tony slipping out the back entrance. He virtually ran down the steps next to the cable* car track. I didn't think that I would be able to catch him up but there could have only been one place he could have been heading.

The wife was standing on the rocks. It was a windy day so I doubt if his wife heard Tony approach. I saw him grab her by the throat. He strangled her and then pushed her into the sea. He looked around to see if anyone was watching but I captured everything on the video on my phone from my vantage point. D now has it for safekeeping."

I read it all again but a bit more slower. 'Bloody hell,' I said.
'Tony wouldn't hurt a fly,' Jude said resolutely.
'We know that,' I agreed. 'But what if there is a video? I mean, his reaction today was out of character. It was almost as though he did have something to hide.'
'Hang on a minute, Graham,' Jude said. 'The person who sends all the texts thinks that Gillian killed that waiter bloke. You think that Diana may have killed him herself. Couldn't she have done exactly the same thing in this scenario.'
I gave it a lot of thought. 'Look, we both do not think Gillian and Tony are capable of murdering anyone. However, this person - this crazy person - could have evidence to the contrary. All I have been tasked with is finding out what those secrets are.'
'You will investigate this first, though, before you respond to this bloody lunatic, won't you?' I could clearly hear the pleading in my wife's voice.
'Of course I will, Jude,' I replied. 'If I'm wrong about this, then I don't particularly want to give them any more information.' I got back in to bed and felt my wife looking at me. I glanced her way. 'What? I asked.
'Aren't you going to phone your contact?'
'Jude, it's quarter past midnight. My contact does have to sleep, too, you know,' I replied. 'I'll call her first thing in the morning.'
'Promise?'
'I promise. Now how about we drink our tea and coffee and then get down to something you were suggesting before I went down there make them?'

'Sorry, darling, but I'm not in the mood for that now,' Judith said.

It was still dark when I got woken up so it must have been before six-thirty. It felt like I was elbowed in the ribs. I turned over.

'Oh, you're awake, are you? Jude said. She was sat up, her v-pillow propping her head up.

'What's the time?' I asked sleepily.

'Nearly half past six.'

'You're awake early,' I was still quite groggy.

'Couldn't sleep.'

'Did you dig me in the ribs?'

'Now why would I do that?' I thought it looked as though she was smiling but, to give her the benefit of the doubt, it could have just been my tired eyes. 'You were probably having a bad dream. You were twisting and turning most of the night.'

I couldn't recall the dream but Judith could have been right. I mean, the news I went to sleep on was not entirely brilliant, was it?

'Are you going into work today?' I asked.

'No,' she replied. 'Thought I would hang about with you. Are you going to call your contact?'

'It's six-thirty, Jude,' I responded. 'Let's go down and have some breakfast first. If I contact her this early, then she'll probably quit being my contact and that will not help us.'

Jude, begrudgingly, conceded this point. So we went downstairs and had breakfast. She just had dry toast as she, really, was not in the mood for anything. I had tropical granola. After eating and tidying up and after looking at our emails and messages, I could tell that Jude was getting a bit impatient. It was now eight o'clock so I reached for my phone. Jude sat to attention on a bar stool. I dialled, hung up and waited. It didn't take long before the coded return came through.

'May I suggest that you move in with me,' she said sarcastically. 'I think you've spoken to me more times than you wife recently.'

'After being rudely woken up by my wife this morning, I make take you up on that suggestion,' I laughed.

'How can I help?' I could hear the hint of joviality in her response.

'I'm back on the Tony and his wife, Deidre, thing again. Was there any cause for the police to think that her disappearance was suspicious?'

'Every investigation they treat as suspicious,' she replied. 'Tony was questioned but his phone and a witness places him in the cafe for well over an hour. Probably longer. Another witness puts Deidre on those rocks by herself.'

'Could someone have climbed down from the top to the bottom, killed her and then walked back up again?'

'It's always possible. It is known that Deidre went down on that train thingy by herself. Other people, apart from Tony, witnessed that. She was in a very depressed state. Some of her clothes were found on the rocks which forensics say indicate that she undressed herself. It looks as though it points towards suicide but...'

'But without the body it cannot be confirmed,' I finished the sentence for her.

'Correct.'

'So you don't think it's plausible for someone to have sneaked out the back exit and gone and murdered her and snuck back?'

'It's just a question of the timing,' my contact pointed out. 'It's not a five minute walk from the top to reach Odicombe beach. The witness places Tony in the cafe for a quite a while.'

'Okay. Got ya,' I confirmed. 'Thanks for all your help.'

'You're welcome. Can't wait until your next call.'

I lowered the phone. 'Well?' Jude asked.

'An eye witness and Tony's phone place him in a cafe for quite a long time,' I replied. 'Someone saw Deidre alone on the rocks. Forensics say that the evidence suggests that she removed her own clothes.'

'So Tony couldn't have done it.'

'As we thought all along.'

I could feel Jude's stare. I looked at her. 'But?' She asked.

'We need to go and have a look at scene,' I replied. 'Something's not right about this. I just can't put my finger on it.'

Two hours later, I was parking the car near to where the former Babbacombe Theatre stood. Unfortunately, this was one of the many venues that failed to recover after the second wave of Covid19. However, a consortium was looking at modernising it and running it as a working theatre. They had purchased it a few years ago and had turned it into a museum. Likewise, many of the former hotels that stretched virtually the entire length of the road, had been developed into luxury apartments. Jude and myself viewed one about five years ago. The views were amazing. We saw it on a clear day and could see all of Torbay. However, Jude found the rooms on the small size, so it was a no go. As I got out of the car, I looked up at the apartment we had viewed. It was starting to look a little tired. But when I turned around and saw that view, it was something I would never get tired of. Fortunately, it was a clear day for March and I could see for miles. I know that they say you can see the Dorset coast on a very clear day. I couldn't quite make it as there was a little sea mist in that direction. An impatient sigh roused me from my daydream.

'Oh, you are with me, then!' Judith exclaimed sarcastically as she started walking towards where the Babbacombe Cliff Railway was situated. I took one more look at the scenery before joining up with her.

Going at Jude's pace it, we did not take long to cover the distance from the car to the railway. The cafe was situated right next door. It was extended in two thousand and twenty-four, the year Ladies and Gentlemen split up. It was, and still is, a family run business which was very popular with the tourists in the summer and the locals in winter.

I had phoned beforehand to make sure that it was okay to meet with Sebastian and April Marchland. They had been running the cafe since it was extended. I was not expecting any miracles about them remembering anything from thirteen years ago. Although a celebrity involved in a missing persons case is pretty memorable.

It was April who greeted us when we entered the cafe and showed us to a table near to the window. The view was breathtaking. We purchased a coffee and a tea to drink. We finally decided on a cheese scone for a snack. It was a lovely cheese scone. Jude thought it delicious.

We made small talk with April whilst Sebastian served a couple of other customers. He made sure that they were happy with their order before joining them.

'You said on the phone that you wanted to talk about Tony Gee and his missing wife,' said Sebastian. Blunt and to the point, I liked that.

'Yes. I just wondered if you remember the incident?' I asked.

'Remember? That sort of incident is something you never forget,' Sebastian said.

'It's not everyday that we get a world famous celebrity in your cafe,' April almost shrieked. 'And within hours his wife goes missing.'

'Can you talk us through that day, please?' Jude asked.

'I first saw them outside the cafe,' April remembered. 'It must have been about lunchtime. 'Tony was gesturing with his hands so I assumed they were having some kind of heated discussion. Anyway, his wife took the train down to the beach and Tony came in here. He ordered a a bacon and Brie jacket potato.'

'You remember what he ordered?' I asked.

'Like I said before, you never forget when a famous celebrity comes into your cafe,, April replied. 'He also had a coffee.'

'He sat by the window, back there, didn't he?' Sebastian said.

'Yes, he did,' April concurred. 'He was gazing out of it quite a lot. I guess he was seeing if he could see his wife.'

I looked out. I couldn't see the rocks where Dee's clothes had been found. I could see the beach. Although it was a lovely sunny day, there was quite a breeze and I could see the white horse trying to gallop to their freedom. To my left I could see where some red, sandstone, cliffs had collapsed onto the beach and rocks below. The sea was definitely trying to reclaim the land.

'Did he stay here the whole time?' I asked.

'Yes, he did,' April smiled.

'Well, he did go to the toilet,' Sebastian pointed out.

'Oh, yes he did,' said April.

My interest was piqued. 'How long was he away from the table?'

April and Sebastian looked at each other.

'Ten...' said Sebastian.

'Fifteen minutes,' said April.

'Was it ten or fifteen?' Jude asked.

Again they looked at each other. 'Ten,' Sebastian confirmed. ' I know what you're thinking but the police checked his phone and he didn't exit the cafe.'

Some more customers entered so Sebastian went to serve them.

'How long does it take for the train to descend to the beach?' I asked.

'About two minutes,' April replied.

I took some time to calculate this in my head. It just didn't add up. If he was only gone for ten minutes then there wouldn't have been enough time for him to ride down to the beach, find Dee, kill her, undress her and fold her clothes neatly, throw her body into the sea and catch the train back up. 'How long does it take to walk down?'

'About ten minutes,' April replied.

That also ruled out the likelihood of him going down that route. We finished our drinks and scones. As we were leaving we promised that we would return. We took the train down to the beach and it did take just over a couple of minutes. We walked hand in hand to the rocks where Deidre's clothes had been discovered. Fortunately the tide was out. I looked back towards the cliffs but, from this angle, could not see the cafe. I could not see any way in which Tony could have got down here in the time restraint that was stated. This actually made me feel relieved but confused. This person who appeared to know everyone's secrets must have some startling evidence.

'Where's my phone?' I heard Jude saying in a panicked voice.

I looked at my phone and smiled. 'It says that you're still in the cafe.' As soon as those words left my lips we both stopped and just stared at each other.

'Oh, shit,' Jude said which normally would have surprised me as she rarely swore, but those words were exactly what I was thinking.

'If April and Sebastian were wrong with their timings...' I began.

'And Tony left his phone, on purpose, in the cafe...' Jude interrupted.

'Then Tony would have had a small window of opportunity to murder Deirdre,' I concluded.

'Shit! Shit! Shit!' Jude exclaimed.

'My sentiments exactly,' I said. 'I think we need to go back up to the cafe and ask April and Sebastian a couple of more questions.'

We walked up. It took us about 15 minutes but we were ambling. When we entered the cafe, April smiled and handed Jude her phone. 'Tony did exactly the same,' she laughed. So that answered one of the questions.

We ordered another tea and coffee. When April brought them over we both took a sip - will we never learn. Sebastian also came and joined us.

'Did the police make anything about him leaving his phone?' I asked.

'Not really,' Sebastian said. 'I mean we told them that he only went to the toilet and was gone like ten minutes.'

'I know it was a long time ago - virtually 13 years to the day - But can you remember if you were busy that day?' I asked.

I looked around the cafe. It wasn't particularly busy. Only three tables were being used, four, if you included ours. 'Not overly busy if I recall correctly.'

'We did have a delivery though,' Sebastian butted in.

'How long does that take you to do?'

'About 30 to 45 minutes depending on the size of delivery,' Sebastian replied.

I looked at Jude and she stared right back at me.

'I can see what you're thinking,' I heard April saying, 'but we're sure that Tony was sat here in the cafe whilst we were doing the delivery.'

'That's what we told the police and I can see no reason to change the story for you guys,' Sebastian said. 'It's the truth.'

'I'm glad it is,' I said. 'Tony is a very good friend of ours. We certainly can't see him harming anyone but someone else has certainly got it in for him.' Then something else came to me. 'Did you notice anyone else hanging around?'

April and Sebastian looked at each other. 'Nothing out of the ordinary,' April finally said. 'Although I did notice a couple of females who walked past the cafe a couple of times. I mentioned it to the police.'

'And what did they say?' Jude asked.

'I believe that they tried to find them but no one came forward.'

'Can you describe what they looked like?' I asked.

'The older one was black,' said April. 'The younger one was wearing a pink coat.'

It wasn't much to go on. 'I'll tell you this, though,' Sebastian said. 'The one wearing the pink coat looked like a younger version of that woman who murdered Graham Longmuir.'

Well, that confirmed Diana's version of events. She must have been here but who on earth was this Black female?

# THE FINAL SECRETS

I texted the number which all those messages stating that they thought Tony had something to do with the disappearance of his first wife. I waited a couple of minutes and, as expected, I got a reply.

*"Like my reply to Gillian's secret, I don't think - I know. I am impressed, though. Getting that one only leaves you with Samantha's and Graham's left to guess. But you only get to the day of the concert. And that's a week on Saturday."*

There really was no need to tell me that. This person was certainly messing with my head. I had quizzed Samantha a couple of times but got nowhere. I did have a feeling that she was hiding something but, whatever it was, I just could not pry it out of her. It goes without saying that there was no way I could ask Graham what his secret could be. I did broach it with Parveen a couple of times but nothing came to light.

Parveen and I rehearsed our segment with the group. They were all excited for us. I, on the other hand, was getting as nervous as hell. I kept on cursing myself for agreeing to do this. Jude and my two, wonderful, children found it highly amusing. Parveen, however, was having a wail of a time. You could tell how keeping her secret all these years had melted away when she started singing. Her only regret, she informed me whilst we were rehearsing, was that she hadn't plucked up the courage to perform live again when Graham was alive. He had tried his best to persuade her to get back into singing. He had written her solo songs. He had even composed quite a few duets. But she was not having it. I don't know why, Graham was right, she had a terrific voice - a cross between Karen Carpenter and Aretha Franklin with, perhaps, a hint of Annie Lennox.

I worked constantly, for the next few days, on the Danny Williams novel and the book to accompany the concert. Danny Williams was nearly finished. Like I had already mentioned, I did kill off one of the main characters. It was critical to the plot. I was sure that the legions of followers would be dismayed but, hopefully, they would read volume four, which was about half-way through, that would give a thorough explanation.

It was a couple of days until the concert and we were at the racecourse to carry out a technical run. They were going to pack so much in that it was going to start at five o'clock and finish about elevenish. The television company that were covering the event had cleared their schedule. There were to be some ad breaks. When it was announced, businesses were clamouring to show their products to the world. The TV company and Ladies and Gentlemen reached an agreement where a certain percentage of the advertisement revenue would be donated to the Meningitis Trust.

There was a slight hitch with Graham's hologram but Olivia and Kelvin managed to sort it out. There were going to be a few surprises during the evening. I knew that Cat Perry was going to do a couple of songs from Grease. Steps were accompanying Ladies and Gentlemen "The Way You Make Me Feel" and "One For Sorrow." The guys had asked Parveen to sing "Close As I've Ever Been" which was one of the new songs that Graham had written. But Parveen politely declined. She just wasn't ready to sing a song which, she thought, was about their loving relationship. If she knew at that precise time what that song was really about, well, the concert probably would not have gone ahead.

Parveen and me rehearsed our section without any issues at all. Parveen was singing two songs - the two that we had written. Parveen seemed to be in her element. I did notice that she kept looking up at the sky. Soon it was time for us to make way for the next section.

'That went well I thought,' Parveen said as we made our way to the wings.

'Not too bad,' I agreed. 'I saw you looking up quite a few times, at the sky.'

'I was just wondering if Graham was looking down and laughing his head off,' Parveen smiled wistfully.

'Well, he probably was looking down but I doubt very much that he was laughing,' I said. 'He is probably so proud of you. You know that all he ever wanted was for you to get out there and sing again.'

I noticed that her eyes started to water but she managed to regain composure. 'So are you ready to have billions of eyes watching you?' And that was the worst thing she could have said to me. I didn't get a wink of sleep that night.

The following day there was a full rehearsal. I never get bored of watching all this. Although this was a memorial for an icon, the camaraderie on stage was fantastic. It was full on and how there were no accidents I'll never know. The technicians were working like a well oiled machine and did not get in anyone's way. The dance troupe were slick and were on and off the stage for costume changes well within their allotted times.

The hardest parts for me to watch was the opening segment, the solo segment and the ending. Parveen, Gillian, Samantha and Tony, along with Kelvin and Olivia had planned something for the finale. I don't mind admitting that I was very unsure about it but it was not my call. More about that later.

At eight o'clock that evening, we finally managed to meet up at the hotel the band were staying at for a bite to eat. Samantha was there with two of her children. Christopher was running a bit late. Gillian and Tony were seated next to each other with Harrison, Leia and Christian were with them. Tony and Gillian were spending a lot of time together, recently, and seemed to be getting on very well. Christian was enjoying his food. The little guy was now nearly six. And the questions he was asking about the gig would put any journalist to shame. Parveen was on the table next to them with Callum, Victoria, Nathan and Tanya. I was quite touched when Tony asked for a minutes silence for all the lost love ones. I thought I heard Parveen scowl and look towards Gillian. Thankfully, Gillian was oblivious to this as she had her head bowed in prayer.

Jude, again, was talking to everyone very excitedly. I don't think she could get over the fact that she could count the members of one of the worlds most famous pop groups as her friends. I had to smile. She reminded me of a teenager.

I was just tucking in to my prawn salad when Christopher finally walked in. He went straight over to his mother and kissed her on the cheek. He also embraced his half-siblings. I noticed Jude do a double take.

'What is it?' I asked, being rude by speaking with my mouth full.

'If I hadn't have known better, I could have sworn Chris looks like a young Graham Longmuir,' she whispered to me so that no one else could not hear.

I looked long and hard at Samantha's eldest son and, sure enough, he did look like Graham. Then I looked at Davido. He definitely looked like his late father, Luigi. The girls, Stephanie and Charlotte, however, despite looking a lot like their mother, I could still see certain features that belonged to Graham. The eyes, for one, were Graham's. I couldn't believe what I was seeing.

'Oh, my, god!' I exclaimed.

'What?' Jude asked.

'That's the final secret,' I said.

'What is?' Jude said. She wasn't quite with me yet.

'Graham is the father of Christopher, Stephanie and Charlotte,' I whispered.

Judith looked taking in what I had just told her. I saw when the realisation dawned on her.

'Bloody hell! You're right,' she said. 'Their eyes are exactly the same as Christopher's. And his are exactly like Graham's. Christ! Graham is the father of Christopher, Stephanie and Charlotte.'

I lost my appetite and pushed the plate away from me. I took a sip of my tea but decided that I needed something stronger. I stood up and walked over to the bar. It didn't take too long for the barman to ask what I wanted. I went for a double rum and coke and a double gin and tonic for Jude. When I put the drink in front of her, she downed it in one and held her empty glass out for me to get a refill.

'I take it we're getting a taxi, then?' I asked.

'I need another drink, Graham, to settle my nerves for the shock of I've just had,' Jude replied.

I put my drink down and went and got Jude her top up. She drank this one a lot more slowly when I placed it in front of her. I sat down and took a sip of mine. Like Jude, my head was reeling. I took another sip and, then, another thought entered my head - I had no proof. But how would I get proof? I could just ask Samantha. But seeing that she hadn't said anything in twenty odd years, I doubt very much that she would come out and admit it. The person who appeared to know all the secrets, however, obviously thought they had some sort of evidence. But I needed to know if this was, in fact, the final secret. I took out my phone and opened the message from the stranger. I started typing.

"Final secret. *Graham Longmuir is the father to three of Samantha's children?*"

I had to wait a few minutes before a reply popped onto my screen.

"*Wow! That is exciting news. One to add to the collection*�� ."

I nearly threw my phone across the room. I managed to refrain myself as that would have drawn attention and I would have to explain why. Instead I showed it to Jude. She opened her eyes in surprise as she read it.

'So what the bloody hell is it?' Jude hissed.

I had no idea. I thought when Jude said that Christopher looked like Graham, that was it. That was the last secret. Now I didn't have a clue. And the secret, whatever it was, would be released to the world on Sunday. My phone indicated that I had another message.

*"Fooled you. That was the secret really. You have bingo. Now all you have to decide is what are you going to do with all the information I have given you."*

I showed it to Judith as I gave it some thought. What actual information had this person given me? Nothing. Only Parveen had admitted that her secret was that she wanted to perform again. I had seen no evidence regarding Tony's, Gillian's, Samantha's and Graham's secrets. Although Graham's and Samantha's was kind of staring me in the face. But, having just said that, I still had no proof. I started typing a reply.

*"What information? You haven't given me anything. I have seen no evidence to suggest that the secrets I've texted you are, in fact, actual secrets. For all I know, you could just be making the whole thing up.'*

I knew that this response would probably antagonise whoever it was but, at this point, I didn't really care. I heard my phone make a noise but I stuffed it back in my pocket. I wasn't in the mood to play mind games with this idiot. I finished the rest of my drink in one gulp and went up to buy anther one. I brought Jude another one. Definitely would be taxi now.

We left at about eleven thirty. Parveen and me had been booked in for a sound check at midday. Jude used her voice to let us in the front door at five to midnight. She went a made a drink. I asked for a coffee. I'm not usually a coffee drinker but I was in the mood for one, that's for sure. We took the drinks right upstairs. Although we prefer a bath, we both decided to have a shower that night. Jude went first. It was then I remembered that I still had to read that reply.

I was a little surprised to see that I actually had an email and not a message. I really will get used to the different tones one day - on second thoughts, strike that, I'll never get the difference between the two.

The email was from Hazel Buchanan, who we had met in America. I opened it.

*"Hello, Graham*

*How's the books coming along?*
*Frank found a picture he took at the time Gillian Lucas hired a car. As he mentioned, he was infatuated with Gillian Tindall. So anything that had a connection to her, he took a photo. As the person in the photo gave him a signed picture of Gillian, naturally he had to take this as a memento.*

*However, less of the waffle, I think you'll be more interested in the other person. Frank says that he cannot remember her but thinks, can't be sure, that Gillian Lucas knew this person.*

*Love*
*Jasmine*

I scrolled down and the picture came into view. I could clearly see Sue/Diana but it was the person standing just behind her and to the left in the picture who grabbed my attention. She was black and was looking at Susan as though she was waiting for her to instruct her to do something. I instantly recognised her as I had met her only a few months ago. I was looking at a younger Amy Dunne.

I immediately recalled our little meeting. I had her age at sixty five, but she must have been nearer to my age of fifty six if she was, in fact eighteen when she entered the caring profession in two thousand and twelve. She told me that she had been doing her job for forty seven years which must have been a blatant lie, unless she was older in two twelve than she said.

But why lie about something like that? If that was a lie, then I'm guessing that her saying the working with children was a "specialised" area could also have been fabricated. But, again, why? Amy had nothing to gain from it.

I wracked my brains a little more. I visualised that every time I asked a question she looked at Dominica Robertson to make sure that it was okay to answer. Either Amy was a very unconfident person or she was playing a game. I looked at the photo on the email again and saw the look that Amy had given during the interview with me. The look of someone who needed reassurance.

Amy had also said that she could not remember Susan Blackmore but that had clearly been another lie. She was with the person who she thought was called Susan in America. The picture was evidence of that. Unless she already knew this person as Diana King. So, what was she hiding?

Jude came back into the bedroom. She had the towel wrapped around her and was drying her hair with a matching red hand towel.

'I've left the shower running for you,, she said and, then, must have seen the look on my face. 'What is it?'

I handed her my phone so she could see the picture. 'That's Amy Dunne in the picture with Diana.'

'Amy Dunne?' Jude asked confused.

'I met with her at Ullacombe House,' I said.

'Oh, Yes. I remember you saying,' she replied. 'Didn't she tell you that she didn't know the girls? She was obviously lying.'

'Yep. But why?'

'Do you think she's involved in some way? With these secrets?'

'There must be something I'm missing. But I'm buggered if I can figure it out.'

'Go and have your shower,' Judith commanded. 'It may help you think a bit clearer.'

I had a feeling that she was probably right. I undressed and went straight in the shower. The temperature was just how I liked it, hot but not steaming. I let the stream of water cascade of my head and body. Usually I'm in and out of the shower within five minutes. This time it was so relaxing that it seemed like it was washing all my stresses and problems were being washed down the plug hole. I must have been in there for a good quarter of an hour.

I reluctantly stepped out of the shower and turned it off. I grabbed the orange bath towel from the heated rail and started drying myself. Whilst I was towelling, I toyed with the idea of shaving while I was in the bathroom but decided to leave it until the morning. I knew that that could be risky as the nerves may be a lot worse in the morning. I came to the conclusion that I would have to use my electric razor as opposed to my preferred wet shave.

By the time I got back in the bedroom, Jude had dried her hair and gotten into bed. I joined her. She handed me my phone.

'You'd better have a look at it. A message came through. It was from the same number who texted you about the secrets,' Judith said.

I picked it up and turned it around in my hand a couple of times. I opened it and saw there was a link. I clicked on it. I heard Jude's voice first.

*'Are you two having an affair?'*
*Parveen - I wish we were, Jude. Unfortunately, the real reason behind those messages is that Graham has been helping me get back into singing and writing songs. I'm hoping to perform at the memorial concert. We've been working on a couple of songs but I'm not sure if they're good enough.'*
*Jude - Oh, really.*
*Parveen - Can you get your guitar?*
*Me - Do you think you're ready?*
*Parveen - One way to find out.*

I heard some movement which must have been me leaving to fetch the guitar.

*Me - I'll just tune it.*

You could clearly hear me tuning the guitar.

*Me - Shall we start with "You"? 1, 2, 3, 4*

*Parveen singing - If everyday*
*Was like the day before*
*Would that*
*Make me love you any more?*
*You know*
*I think that it would*
*When I'm with you*
*Everything seems brighter*
*Could you hold me*
*Just a little tighter?*
*I know*
*That you could.*

*When you smile*
*I get a little warm*
*All my emotions*
*Caught up in a storm*
*When you laugh*
*I feel so dreamy*
*I just want you*
*Near me*

I clicked on the X to end it.
'How on earth?' Jude ranted. 'That was here, Graham? How did they record that conversation?'
'I'm guessing that they bugged someone's phone and recorded it whilst it was happening,' I replied.
'But surely the phone has to be switched on to be able to do that?'

'Modern day technology. Modern day criminals,' I answered. 'My phone was the only one out on that day.'

We both looked at it before I decided to turn it off.

# THE GRAHAM LONGMUIR MEMORIAL CONCERT SOUND CHECKS

Jude woke me up at seven thirty with a lovely cup of tea. We agreed to not do anything about the phone today. Today was all about the memory of Graham Longmuir. The nerves started to kick in immediately as I remembered that I would be taking to the stage with Parveen. Why did I agree to do that?

I finally decided to go for the wet shave. Thankfully I didn't cut myself. When I came back in to the bedroom, Jude had gone down to make breakfast. We had to be at the racecourse no later than eleven. It looked as though she was as nervous as me, possibly more. She was nibbling at her toast. She had made some for me with crunchy peanut butter spread on it. I didn't have any problems eating it.

'Aren't you nervous?' She asked.

'Yep,' I confirmed and carried on eating.

'I don't know if this is going to stay down,' Jude said completely giving up on her breakfast.

'Why are you nervous?' I questioned.

'My husband is setting foot on a stage with the eyes of the

world on him,' she said. 'And he's being backed by the the three remaining members of my favourite group of all time. God, I really feel sick now.'

'Are you afraid that I'm going to show you up?'

'Far from it. I know you'll do a bloody fantastic job, enjoy it so much that you'll want to do it permanently,' Judith admitted.

'No chance of that, darling,' I said. 'I like being an author too much to become a musician. You're not going to get rid of me that easy.'

'Good,' she responded and she kissed me. 'I think that Graham Longmuir will really enjoy the show today.'

We finished breakfast - well, I finished breakfast while Jude sipped her coffee before deciding to throw it away. We washed up the dishes. Jude had a quick look at our emails. There were a couple of important ones in her inbox which she quickly responded to. She let out a small sigh of relief when she looked at mine and informed me that nothing new had come in.

I looked at the cooker clock and saw that it was eight forty seven.

'Might as well go and get ready,' I said. 'Although I haven't got a clue what I'm going to wear.'

I noticed a little smirk on Jude's face. 'I'll come and help you,' she laughed.

We made love when we got upstairs. This made us a bit hot and sweaty. Jude suggested - well, more of an order really - we have another shower. She went first and I followed. I was in and out within three minutes. Jude was drying her hair and trying hard not to smile. What was going on? And then I saw it hanging on my wardrobe.

'You've got to be joking me?' I said.

Jude could no longer conceal her hysterics. 'Parveen brought it over last week. She says that it matches her costume,' she laughed hard.

The best way I could describe the costume was that it was similar to the one Dolly Parton wore at Glastonbury in two thousand and fourteen. 'I am not wearing that,' I said adamantly.

'I don't think you've got a say in the matter,' Jude continued laughing.

'Perhaps it won't fit,' I said hopefully where I was rewarded with another howl of laughter from my wonderful wife. 'Of course, I should have realised, you and Parveen would have been in communication about my sizes.'

'Of course,' Judith laughed. She tried to dry her eyes in the sleeve of her towelling dressing gown. 'But you don't have to wear it to the concert, unless you want to. You have to take it with you to change into later.'

'Great,' I said sarcastically.

We got to the racecourse at five past eleven. We were ushered straight through. A crowd was already gathering. But people always try to get to these remote places early, for these events, especially if it features one of the most famous pop groups ever. We witnessed quite a few Graham Longmuir posters but it was good to see that the other members of the group hadn't been forgotten. You could sense the outpouring of grief already. Usually there would be quite a buzz in the air, even this early before the concert. But we saw people ambling towards their destinations which would probably be to makeshift cafes that had been erected in the vicinity to cater for the influx of fans.

The supermarket car park looked busy already. They had agreed to it being used for the day and the income generated was to be donated to the Meningitis Trust. Other businesses had agreed to their areas being used, too, with the same agreement in place. Newton Abbot had pulled together in its grief for one of its favourite sons.

It was busy and chaotic inside the racecourse. The railings had been taken down so that there was more room. The stage was to the left hand side of the field as you entered. Exactly the same position as when Ladies and Gentlemen kicked off their Reunion tour. My eyes misted up when I saw it and remembered about nine months previously. How the guys had been so excited about being here after so many years of being apart. Cameras had been set up but were now controlled remotely. A few technicians were darting around the place, trying to look busy, but I couldn't really see what they were doing.

The stage looked fantastic. Olivia and Kelvin had not only done themselves proud but also the memory of Graham Longmuir. Their were five gigantic screens - one to each side and three on top. The people at the back would have no problems seeing.

We had to show our passes to get backstage. Security was tight even at this time of the day. I was taken to my dressing room which I was sharing with Tony. I hung my costume on the rail in the far corner. I was going to do the sound check in my casual, everyday wear. I took my guitar from its case and started tuning it. There's something therapeutic about doing that. There was a knock at the door. I went and opened it.

'Have you forgotten about me?' Judith was smiling.

'Sorry. I was tuning the guitar.'

She handed me a bottle of water. 'The clouds are breaking up. The sun is trying to poke through. Doesn't look like it's going to be a bad March afternoon.'

'Are they still forecasting rain for later?' I asked.

Jude nodded. 'Tony not here?'

'They're not scheduled to be here until one. They're having a sound check at half past one.'

Someone must have been approaching because Judith turned her head to her left. I saw her smile. 'Hi, Parveen.'

'Is he talking to me?' I heard Parveen ask.

'He loves the costume,' Jude laughed.

Parveen stood next to Jude in the doorway. 'It's certainly a costume to get noticed,' I said.

'Apologies, Graham, but it was my late husband's fault,' Parveen said but she still had that smile on her face. She pulled out a piece of paper and handed it too me.

I scanned it and saw that it was from Graham. It was dated September last year, just at the beginning part of the Reunion

Tour in Spain. I could tell it was from the time we were in that villa resting.

*Parveen Adams bets Graham Adams that she will get Graham Avery to wear a costume, similar to what Dolly Parton wore at Glastonbury, on stage in front of millions of people. I, Graham Adams do not believe that my friend would be such an idiot and will therefore donate one hundred thousand pounds to the Meningitis Trust if she pulls it off.*

I actually laughed out loud. 'Looks like you won the bet, Parveen.'

'I think we should match it, darling,' Judith suggested. 'What do you say?'

'Couldn't agree more,' I smiled. 'And I can't wait to prove him wrong.'

I took a sip from the bottled water Jude had brought me. 'I'd better go and get ready,' Parveen said. 'It must be nearly time for us to do the sound check.'

'You're not going to be wearing your costume now, are you?' I asked.

'No. You're safe for a few hours,' Parveen laughed.

It didn't seem to take too much longer before I was getting the five minutes call. Jude looked at me. 'How are you feeling?'

'Fine, at the moment,' I said. 'I guess it's because there won't be a crowd there.'

'There's quite a few people meandering around,' Jude said. 'They'll probably stop and listen to you and Parveen.'

'You're not really helping, darling,' I said. I grabbed my guitar and we both went and walked towards the stage.

Cat Perry was just finishing off. Jude was talking to one of the technicians as we waited in the wings. I heard him say that there had been a couple of hitches but nothing major. Cat was going to be singing "Summer Nights" and "You're The One That I Want" from their Grease film and also a Graham Longmuir solo classic "The First Time." I was just listening to her finishing off this song. She certainly was doing a fantastic version of the song.

'How can I ever compete with Cat Perry?' I hadn't noticed Parveen approach and stand next to me.

'I wouldn't look at it as a competition, Parveen,' I said. 'Your voice is different to everybody else's. I think they want to hear you. They've heard Cat Perry many times before. They haven't heard you in a very long time.'

'How do you know how to say all the right things?' Parveen asked.

'He's a writer,' Jude explained. 'He knows how to put the correct words into people's mouths. Including his own.'

Cat completed the song and got a round of applause. She was smiling as she came towards us. She hugged Parveen.

'Great performance, Cat,' I said.

She gave me me a hug next. 'Thanks, Graham.' She parted from the embraced and gave Jude a hug. 'It does seem strange, though, being on stage, singing the "Grease" tracks and Mr Longmuir not being there, in person, with me.'

That made us reflect. Yes, it was going to be strange knowing that Graham Longmuir would not be taking to the stage this evening, in person, no matter how good his hologram was going to be. I just wondered how the audience would take it.

'You're on, honey,' Jude said waking me from my daydream.

A technician handed me a wireless antenna which I plugged into my guitar as Parveen and I walked on stage. She stood centre stage, in front of the microphone, while I stood to her left. Another technician positioned a microphone in front of me. Parveen looked at me.

'Shall we start with "You"?' She asked.

I nodded and began counting the beat before playing the opening chords. I could sense the sound operators just tweaking the volume up as I played. It was weird hearing me playing the guitar through the surround speakers. And then Parveen started singing. It seemed hat everyone inside the racecourse just stopped to listen.

GRAHAM AVERY

*If everyday*
*Was like the day before*
*Would that*
*Make me love you any more?*
*You know*
*I think that it would*
*When I'm with you*
*Everything seems brighter*
*Could you hold me*
*Just a little tighter?*
*I know*
*That you could.*

*When you smile*
*I get a little warm*
*All my emotions*
*Caught up in a storm*
*When you laugh*
*I feel so dreamy*
*I just want you*
*Near me*

*Why do you*
*Always make me cry*
*Your dad jokes*
*Always made us sigh*
*But I know*
*You always loved us five*
*Now you're gone*
*Life's a little harder*
*The world is just*
*A little bit sadder*
*But somehow*
*You seem alive*

*When you smile*
*I get a little warm*
*All my emotions*
*Caught up in a storm*
*When you laugh*
*I feel so dreamy*
*I just want you*
*Near me*

*If everyday*
*Was like the day before*
*Would that*
*Make me love you any more?*
*You know*
*I think that it would*
*When I'm with you*
*Everything seems brighter*
*Could you hold me*
*Just a little tighter?*
*I know*
*That you could.*

*When you smile*
*I get a little warm*
*All my emotions*
*Caught up in a storm*
*When you laugh*
*I feel so dreamy*
*I just want you*
*Near me*

We finished the song. There had been a bit of feedback which the sound operators soon rectified. But it was the hush after we had completed the song that was eerie. I noticed that there were a few moist eyes. Then the applause started. And kept going and going. I looked around. Cat Perry and my wife were applauding where we had left them. The tears streaming down their faces. In the other wing, I noticed Samantha, Gillian, Tony, their children and Parveen's children. They had obviously gotten here early to listen. They were applauding warmly and again I could see the wetness on some of their faces. I leaned in to whisper in Parveen's ear.

'As far as I can see no one can compete with you.'

She turned to me and was beaming. 'I bloody enjoyed that.'

I signalled for her children to come and join her. 'I think this sound check is finished.'

She was embraced by her family as I walked off to join Judith. 'Wow!' She said.

'She was brilliant, wasn't she?' I said looking back at Parveen being surrounded and embraced by her family.

'Not her. You, you moron,' Jude said smiling. 'I knew you could play the guitar but you've always sang like you were tone deaf before I'm pretty impressed that you can hold a tune.'

'Hopefully I'll be able to hold it tonight when millions are watching,' I said.

'But Graham Longmuir was right,' Jude murmured. ' Parveen does have a beautiful voice.'

The rest of the afternoon flew by. They opened the gates to let the audience in. The build up was shown live on television and started at four o'clock. I was watching on a screen in the dressing room. Although billed as a memorial concert, there was to be a big drive to make as much money for the Meningitis Trust. Jude was watching with me. Tony was getting ready. The good thing about these portable, stylish, dressing rooms, when constructed there are many private compartments to change or just take some quiet time to reflect.

Before long, though, Jude had to go and take her seat. I wasn't due on until eight but I decided to watch from backstage. I started to get really nervous when I heard them call the ten minute warning. There was no going back now. I just wondered how the public would react when they realised that Graham

Longmuir would only be performing as a projected hologram. It would be strange. Very strange indeed.

# THE MEMORIAL CONCERT PART ONE

The dancers were limbering up. Five minutes to go. I had taken my place so that I could get a good view. A large, luminous, digital clock display lit up the screens. A huge roar went up from the crowd although, I thought, there was a touch of nervousness to it. I saw Samantha, Gillian and Tony enter backstage. They weren't talking to each other but that wasn't surprising as it was their collective superstition. However, they looked nervous. Not surprising really as they didn't know how the public was going to react to just the three of them. They looked a little lost without Graham. They were wearing their purple outfit. It was the one Graham liked the most. They went and got into their positions. Like the Reunion Tour opening, they were to appear, magically, on stage. The clock was showing three one four.

Tony sat at his drum kit. Samantha put the strap of her bass guitar over her head and arranged the guitar in to a comfortable playing position. Gillian stood at her keyboards. I saw her look at Samantha and smile. Samantha smiled back. She looked at Tony. The look she gave him seemed to be different than the look of encouragement she gave Samantha. I would find it hard to believe that there was something going on here after what had happened between the two over twenty five years ago.

I then heard the crowd shouting "Ten...nine...eight...seven..." This was it. I looked once more at the group. They all had their heads bowed as if in silent prayer. When the display went to zero, it went dark. The clocks actually go forward this evening but the sun was now setting. A hush descended amongst the crowd making it very eerie. A message was being displayed on the screens. I knew what it said but now, knowing that millions of people were reading it, choked me even more.

**"ON NOVEMBER 17th 2049, GRAHAM LONGMUIR, LUIGI GUSTAV AND TRACEY GEE WERE SHOT AND FATALLY WOUNDED. THIS CONCERT IS IN MEMORY OF ALL THREE OF THEM. A PROJECTED HOLOGRAM OF GRAHAM WILL BE USED FOR THE MAJORITY OF THE SHOW. IT IS BEING USED WITH THE KIND PERMISSION OF HIS FAMILY. HOWEVER, IT IS SOMETHING THAT GRAHAM REQUESTED SHOULD ANYTHING HAPPEN TO HIM. WE SINCERELY HOPE THAT IT DOES NOT CAUSE TOO MUCH DISTRESS. ALL OUR LOVE GILLIAN, SAMANTHA AND TONY."**

The caption stayed on the screen for a good couple of minutes. I could hear sobs echoing around the racecourse. And, no doubt, there would be a few wet eyes in households around the world. The screen went blank. The opening of "O Fortuna" from "Carmina Burana" blasted out. The crescendo of noise from the crowd erupted into the late afternoon air. The dancers went on and gave a spectacular performance. Many of the stars, who would be appearing in the concert, had gathered to watch the opening sequence.

"Arrival" by ABBA began. The dancers received an appreciative round of applause as they departed the set. You could feel the anticipation emanating from the audience. "Arrival" finished. Another sign came on the screen.

**"LADIES AND GENTLEMEN INVITE YOU TO JOIN THE REVOLUTION OF FUN."**

A scream erupted from the crowd, then another and, then more joined in. This seemed to galvanise the stage lighting into life. The green screens dropped through the slits in the stage. The audience saw the projected hologram of Graham Longmuir for the very first time. There were a few gasps as it/he started singing.
*We are here*
*We are now*
*And we're going to get our message through somehow.*
*Choose life*
*Not hate*
*And we'll show you where you've made your mistake.*

Gillian took over to do do her part. I know that Gillian was particular concerned about how the audience would react to her. After all it was her wife that had murdered Graham, Luigi and Tracey.

*Gillian - Ladies and Gentlemen invite you to*

The roar of approval for Gillian was deafening. I'm sure I saw her smile at the reaction.

*All - Come join the revolution*
*There's just one stipulation*
*You must put down your knife and gun.*
*No need to make a fuss*
*Just come with us*
*On the the revolution of fun.*

The audience were singing along. It actually felt like the audience had accepted the hologram. As I have said before, it did look very realistic. The tension and nervousness in Samantha, Gillian and Tony seemed to ebb away. I wanted to see how the next bit went. This was the interaction between the four and, possibly, between the hologram and the audience.

When the song finished the applause was loud - very loud. The three remaining group members left their instruments and came to the front of the stage. The hologram joined them.

'Hello, Newton Abbot our hometown,' they said in unison.

'And welcome world,' Samantha, Gillian and Tony continued. 'This is very difficult for us so we can appreciate how difficult it is for you.'

'Four months ago, my wife shot and murdered Graham, Luigi and Tracey,' Gillian took over.

'Not your fault, Gillian,' someone shouted.

This was greeted with enthusiastic applause and shots of agreements. 'Thank you,' Gillian said welling up and she couldn't continue.

'Tonight,' Tony began, finishing for Gillian, 'we shall be celebrating their memory. We're also going to ask you to dig deep to raise a lot of money for The Meningitis Trust and our cancer charity.'

'We've got a lot of surprises for you this evening which we are sure that you'll enjoy,' Samantha said.

'But I'm sure you want to hear more music from us,' Gillian said regaining her composure. This was greeted with a very warm reception. 'This is the first song we released after getting back together last year. This is "Tongue-Tied."'

A crescendo of noise in anticipation of them playing this song. I got the feeling that this was beginning to feel like a normal concert. The Graham Longmuir hologram appeared to be having problems getting his guitar strap over his head. This actually occurred and the second evening, here at the racecourse, on the Reunion Tour.

'What the hell am I doing here?' The hologram said. It sounded exactly like Graham Longmuir. I waited for the crowd's response.

'Told you that you should have played keyboards, Graham,' Gillian joked.

'Thanks, Gillian. I might just do that.'

'Looks like you're trying to put on a bra,' Tony quipped from behind his drum kit.

'Don't need your input right now, Tony,' said the hologram. Graham finally managed to sort himself out. 'That's better.'

'Are you finally ready now?' Samantha asked.

'I think so, Samantha,' Graham the hologram replied. The audience began laughing. And they laughed and laughed and laughed. This was going to be a good night. 'As Gillian said, this is "Tongue-Tied".'

Another loud cheer went up as the group struck up the opening chords to the song. The cheer went even louder as Graham started singing.

*I feel a little bit lost and a little bit lonely*
*Cos I've been sitting here thinking about you - only*
*I don't know what to do*
*And don't know what to say*
*The words are in my head*
*But my mouth gets in the way*
*I want to shout I love you*
*But all that will come out is hey*

*You've got me tongue-tied*
*I'm terrified*
*I'll get it wrong*
*Because we two belong*
*Together*
*And that's no lie*
*You make me tongue-tied.*

Kelvin and Olivia had really excelled themselves. This must have taken many hours of painful editing for them. But they had successfully created it in such a relatively short period of time. Tony, Samantha and Gillian were really starting to gel with the hologram. It must have been strange to them. I mean, I was watching the performance knowing that Graham Longmuir was dead but the image was so realistic, it was like he was actually there on stage.

The guys did four other numbers which all received fantastic reactions. It was time to introduce the first guest stars.

'Ladies and Gentlemen are pleased, and excited, to introduce to the stage our favourite pop group - Steps,' Samantha announced.

Lisa, Faye, Claire, Lee and H went onto the stage. They did the song which they both had success with "It's The Way You Make Me Feel." The audience appeared to love it. They then sang "One For Sorrow," which was Graham's favourite Steps song. They received a rapturous ovation as they left the stage.

Tony waited for a hush. When he had quiet a big poster of Graham unravelled on the screens. 'Although Graham first found fame as part of a pretty good pop group, even if I say it myself, he did go on to have numerous solo success after we split up. We're now going to play a couple of our favourite Graham Longmuir tracks while you watch a montage of Graham's solo career. The first one we're going to do is "Where We're You."'

Gillian started singing

*Where were you*
*When I started screaming?*
*You didn't wake me*
*From my dreaming*
*I don't even think you*
*Were in bed*
*Or are you messing*
*With my head?*

And then the spotlight hit the hologram as Graham shared vocals.

*I know we don't mean things we say*
*We regret in an instant*
*Try to make them go away*

*We arranged to meet up that night*
*To say things we knew were true*
*I was there waiting*
*Where were you?*

*Where were you when*
*I got a life to live?*
*You know you didn't*
*Send a gift*
*Are you watching me*
*From afar?*
*I wanted to love you*
*Not make a war*

*I know we don't mean things we say*
*We regret in an instant*
*Try to make them go away*
*We arranged to meet up that night*
*To say things we knew were true*
*I was there waiting*
*Where were you?*

And then something magical happened. The audience started singing. It has always sent a tingle down my spine when I hear concert goers singing along to the favourite tracks.

*Where were you*
*When you had your chance?*
*Standing in shadows?*
*Or at a dance?*
*What I didn't know*
*Was that something went wrong*
*The car the hit you*
*Was just too strong.*

*I know we don't mean things we say*

*We regret in an instant*
*Try to make them go away*
*We arranged to meet up that night*
*To say things we knew were true*
*I was there waiting*
*Where were you?*

*I know we don't mean things we say*
*We regret in an instant*
*Try to make them go away*
*We arranged to meet up that night*
*To say things we knew were true*
*I was there waiting*
*Where were you?*

The next song they song was the uptempo "Not Afraid To Live A Little." I sensed someone standing next to me. I turned and noticed Cat Perry. She still looked stunning. She was wearing her leather costume from Grease.

'They're rocking it, aren't they?' She said.

I knew that it was a rhetorical question but I needed to answer. 'Yes, they are.'

'The fans are lapping it up,' she said. 'It seems like they think Graham Longmuir is actually on that stage.'

'Perhaps he is,' I smiled. 'Perhaps he is.'

Cat stared at the stage. 'You know what? You could be right."

Gillian had taken the microphone. 'We are going to take a costume change break because Tony's smelling like a cesspit.'

'Oi,' Tony said who was getting up from his drum kit.

'As you know, there was no end to Graham's talent,' Gillian continued. 'Not only was he a terrific singer he was an okay actor. He kept on reminding us that he won three Academy Awards. But the film that lead him to superstardom was the remake of "Grease." The customary loud cheering greeted this. 'It's our pleasure to welcome to the stage, Cat Perry.'

There was wild applause as Cat walked onto the stage. 'Good

evening, Newton Abbot,' she yelled into the microphone. 'And hello world. I was fortunate to work with Graham Longmuir on a few occasions and, like everyone, I'm going to miss him dearly. I was fortunate to know Luigi and Tracey, too. They welcomed me into this unique family and will be remembered through their loved ones. Does everyone here remember "Grease?"

'Yes,' roared the crowd.

'With the help of modern technology, I am going to perform two songs from the movie,' Cat continued. '"Summer Nights," and "Your the one that I want". Then I'll be performing my favourite solo Graham Longmuir track "The First Time".'

The volume of the audience approval was deafening. It rose a couple more decibels as the opening bass chords introduced "Summer Nights."

The modern technology that Cat had mentioned was that, somehow, the whizz kids had managed to portray the film as though it was a wide angled hologram but had completely cut Sandy, Cat's character, from the segment. This enabled her to interact with the cast members as though they were actually there. Jude would be loving this part and, no doubt, would be singing along just like the rest of the crowd and probably even louder when Cat moved on to "Your The One That I Want."

'You'd better go and get ready, Graham. It won't be too long before you're on,' Gillian had approached unbeknown to me. I made a mental note to get my hearing checked. 'It's tough out there without him, you know.'

'I guessed it must be,' I replied.

'Do you think we're doing the right thing?' She asked. 'I mean the hologram of Graham is good but it's just not him.'

'Just listen to the reaction of the crowd, Gillian,' I said. 'I don't think they would have forgiven you if you hadn't have done this. You're keeping the memory of him alive for them. Now, I'm going to try my best not to kill that. Wish me luck.'

The fans screamed for on encore when Cat finished "The First Time", But everything had to be kept to a tight schedule. Yes, the show could run over by fifteen minutes or so but anything over that would mean explanations to the local council. Like Parveen, Cat had decided against singing the Graham

The lights dimmed again as Ladies and Gentlemen took to the stage. They had changed into casual clothes. All three members were in jeans and t-shirts. Emblazoned across the fabric were the names Tracey, Luigi and Graham followed by a heart. On the backs of the t-shirts were the words "NEVER FORGOTTEN". Those t-shirts raised a lot of revenue for the charity that evening. I watched on the screen in the dressing room. This simple gesture seemed to hit the audience a lot harder than anything previously. The camera was panning around and the tears were flowing like rivers.

Samantha introduced the next song. 'This is "Devonshire Lass".'

That was followed by "Opposites Attract". After the song the spotlight fell on Tony. 'The song that we first wrote when we first got back together was called "Close Your Eyes". It seems to have taken on a completely different meaning for this event."

The beam of light moved to the projected Graham Longmuir hologram. He was stood by Gillian's keyboard as she played the opening chords to the song. Tony and Samantha stood the other side. This was something different. It looked like it was only going to be sung with a piano accompaniment. Graham always used to sing the first verse but this time it looked like they were going to harmonise. And, sure enough, that is what they did. For me it was, and always will be, my favourite version of that song. If there wasn't a dry eye in the house before they started singing in that song, there certainly was not afterwards. The applause seemed to go on for an eternity and it deserved it. The group looked emotional. In fact, it look like it had hit them hard and they signalled that they needed to come off.

# THE MEMORIAL CONCERT PART TWO

I knew that there were contingency plans in case something like this happened. The stage went dark. 'Ladies and Gentlemen. Please welcome back to the stage, Cat Perry.'
A warm applause greeted her arrival back on stage. Someone knocked on the dressing-room door and announced that I had two minutes. Thankfully I was ready. I opened the door and walked to the wings, listening to Cat as I did. Parveen was waiting so I joined her.

'Good evening, again, Newton Abbot. Wasn't that song so poignant? And didn't they sing it so beautifully?' This raised many many cheers. 'Samantha, Gillian and Tony have asked me to introduce the next special guests. One of them has been a friend of mine for thirty years. Wow! That makes me feel really old now. She will introduce her co-guest. She was the first person I approached to do background vocals. She has such a wonderful voice. It is so angelic. I always thought that should sing lead vocals and so did someone else.' The tension of anticipation from the audience was building. I think some of them could sense who was coming on next and they couldn't hold their excitement back. 'They credit me with introducing them to each other. But I reckon they would have found each other no matter what. I asked Graham to come into the studio to play on my album in two thousand and twenty five. He was immediately drawn to the voice coming from the recording booth. He liked what he heard and saw so much that he married her. Ladies and gentlemen, I give you Parveen Parfartti, Graham Longmuir's wife.'

The crowd went completely crazy. Parveen stood transfixed next to me. I gave her a hug and whispered in her ear. 'You're going to be fantastic. They are going to love you.'

She hugged me back. 'Don't expect a build up like Cat had just given me,' she said parting from the embrace and walking onstage. She waved to the crowd which caused the volume to increase. She embraced Cat and Cat handed her the microphone.

'Hello, Newton,' she said. Oh my god, the reception back was astounding. 'I'm not surprised that Graham loved his hometown so much. You have always made me feel welcomed.'

'You will always be an honorary Newtonian, Parveen,' someone yelled.

'I'm glad to hear it,' she smiled. 'This has always been a secret of mine, to return to the stage. I wish, now, that I had had the courage to have done it when Graham was alive.' Her voice caught as she said this. The audience responded with encouragement. 'Thank you. Now, my partner tonight is not known for his musical abilities. Who here has read the Danny Williams books?' I was pleased to hear the positive response. 'Yes, that's right, my partner this evening is the most talented author and, more importantly, a great friend of mine, Graham Avery.' There was very loud applause and I was about to walk on but I was stopped by a stagehand. What the hell was going on? 'Before he comes on stage, ladies and gentlemen, he is a bit embarrassed with costume I have selected for him. You see, it all started as a bet with my late husband. He said that he would donate one hundred thousand pounds to the charity if I could get Graham Avery to wear a costume similar to what Dolly Parton wore at Glastonbury in two thousand and fourteen. Now I know that there are many people here and watching at home who are well too young to remember that so here is a picture of it. Now, do you want to see one of the world's most famous authors wearing this?' The picture of Dolly Parton was put up on the screen. I could hear the shrieks of laughter as they obviously tried to imagine me wearing it. I smiled as I realised where Parveen was taking this. 'Now, Graham's wonderful wife, Judith, as said that she will match the figure my husband bet me. Unfortunately, Graham Avery does not think this is enough for him to embarrass himself. He says that he is not setting foot on this stage until ten million pounds has been raised. The telephone number is now showing with the picture of Dolly. Please help me embarrass Graham Avery. We've got only two minutes to do it.'

'They won't do it in two minutes,' I said incredulously.

'Want to bet?' The stagehand said.

Whilst this was happening the stage crew had managed to set up what little equipment was needed. Parveen put the microphone onto its stand. She walked over to me.

'Apologies for that but Jude and me thought it would be a good idea to raise some money,' Parveen said. 'Your wife thought it better if we didn't tell you about it.'

'Don't worry, I'll deal with her later,' I smiled. 'At least it's got me out of performing tonight. There's no way we're going to raise ten million in two minutes.'

'You're up to twenty five million quid already,' the stagehand interjected.

'Looks like you're going to sing, Graham,' Parveen laughed.

'Bugger,' I responded.

Parveen walked back onstage and up to the microphone. 'Thank you everybody who donated. It appears that there is a lot more people out that who want to see Graham Avery dressed up in the Dolly Parton costume. You have increased the amount for charity by a whopping fifty million pounds. And I'm informed that it's still climbing. So, without further ado, please welcome on stage, your favourite author and mine, Mr Graham Avery.'

I walked onstage to loud applause. I got quite a few wolf whistles thrown in so I gave a grand curtsy as I approached my microphone stand, which got a large cheer and quite a few laughs.

'Give us a twirl,' someone yelled.

I duly obliged. I approached the microphone. 'I can't imagine Danny Williams wearing something like this, can you? Del Sol, on the other hand. I do believe a new plot is forming. But you haven't come to listen to an audio recording of a Danny Williams novel. These wonderful people, Parveen, have come to listen to some music. So let's not disappoint them.'

'I hope you forgive me but I didn't feel comfortable singing one of my husband's songs so the guys gave me permission to sing a couple of compositions I did with this guy. I hope you like them,' Parveen said. 'The first one is called "You".

I can see why musicians love performing live. The crowd are absolutely fantastic. They were cheering along and, even though they had never heard the song before, they started singing the chorus with us. We seemed to be only singing "You" for a few seconds when we're finishing it. The reception we received brought a tear to my eye. I shoved the guitar around to my back and gave Parveen a quick cuddle. She told me to introduce the final song. I waited for the applause to abate.

'Our second and final song is called "Without You",' I said. 'Hope you like it.'

*You've now gone your way*
*I've gone mine*
*This wasn't how it*
*Was meant to be*
*After all this time*

*What am I gonna do*
*Without you?*
*You were always there for me*
*Now I'm just lost and lonely*
*What am I gonna do*
*Without you?*

GRAHAM AVERY

*I don't know why*
*I blamed our friend*
*It wasn't her fault*
*And my love to her*
*I send*

*What am I gonna do*
*Without you?*
*You were always there for me*
*Now I'm just lost and lonely*
*What am I gonna do*
*Without you?*

*Taking you*
*Was so wrong*
*It should have been me*
*But then you'd be*
*Singing this song*

*What am I gonna do*
*Without you?*
*You were always there for me*
*Now I'm just lost and lonely*
*What am I gonna do*
*Without you?*

*You know I have*
*One secret to keep*
*I won't tell a soul*
*But for you my love*
*Still runs deep*

*What am I gonna do*
*Without you?*
*You were always there for me*

*Now I'm just lost and lonely
What am I gonna do
Without you?*

*What am I gonna do
Without you?
You were always there for me
Now I'm just lost and lonely
What am I gonna do
Without you?*

I couldn't believe the positive reaction we received when we ended "Without You". I'm sure it was their love and heartfelt sympathy for Parveen. And, boy, did she deserve it. This was another of the moist eyes moments. Unfortunately, there would be a few more to come this evening.

The audience were chanting "more, more, more". We couldn't for two reasons. Firstly, the time schedule would not allow it and secondly, we didn't know any others. We waved to the crowd as we walked to the wings. Samantha, Gillian and Tony were stood there. Gillian was in tears. This made Parveen cry.

'I'm sorry for the way I behaved at Susan's funeral,' Parveen sobbed. 'It wasn't your fault. You couldn't have known who she really was or what she was about to do.'

'Thank you for the song,' said Gillian. 'It meant such a lot.'

'Well, I don't know about you, Parveen, but I'm going to get out of this costume,' I said.

'Aren't you going to wear it for the finale, Graham?' Samantha asked innocently but with a smile on her face.

'I really don't think so,' I laughed and the others joined in. 'I think we should auction it off with the proceeds going to the highest bidder.'

The theme to 2001: A Space Odyssey began. This was their cue to come back on stage. As you know Tony is a big Elvis Presley fan and "The King" used to walk on stage to this piece of music. I quite liked it, too.

The stage had gone dark. The sky was black by now but, at least, the rain was holding off. The screens were back in place so that they would magically appear again so they went and got themselves ready.

When the music came to its climax the lights erupted on stage, the screens dropped and Ladies and Gentlemen were doing their cover version of "Substitute", which had gone down very well at the Reunion Interview. Unsurprisingly, it got yet another roar of approval. They then went on to do their tribute to ABBA. I took this time to go and change whilst listening on the backstage speakers.

After getting back into normal clothes, I went and sat next to Jude. 'Wow!' She exclaimed. 'A whole new career for you, darling.'

'I really don't think so,' I smiled. 'I just hope it gave Parveen the confidence to take to performing again.

At that precise moment, Parveen came and joined us. She gave her children a cuddle first. 'What did you think?' She asked Judith.

'Brilliant,' Jude replied. 'I was in tears during "Without You". It certainly is a very poignant song.'

'Well, I couldn't have written it without your husband,' she smiled. 'Mind you, I know what's coming next so I'll be in tears.'

'What's next?' Jude asked.

Before anyone could answer Samantha took the microphone. 'You heard the wonderful Parveen singing a few minutes ago. Doesn't she have a great voice? Well, Parveen kindly passed on a case to me recently. Inside was only what I could describe as a musical treasure trove. There were tapes inside on which graham had composed music. He had also composed melodies to my lyrics and filmed himself performing them. We probably have enough material to release two albums a year for the next twenty years.' There were audible gasps as this news sank in. Then the cheers and applause rang out in to the night. 'So what we would like to do for you now is perform some of those tracks. The first one is titled "Rebound". We think this is the last one that Graham worked on. Only because it was the last song on the very last tape.'

The projected hologram of Graham no showed him seated at a grand piano. Tony counted them in by banging his drumsticks together. Gillian opened up by playing the chords on her electric guitar. It was rare to see Gillian playing guitar. I know she prefers keyboards but I would say she's an exceptional guitarist. Possibly even better than Graham was. But, then, listening to Graham on piano, he sounded far superior to Gillian.

*You caught me on the rebound*
*My love is something*
*You've not found*
*But I thought I made it very clear*
*There's no feelings here*
*Cos I gave them to her*
*And then she went and broke my heart*
*By saying that we had to part*
*That hurt me inside*
*A piece of me died*
*And now it's just a blur.*

*She said the kid was mine*
*But I get that all*
*Of the time*
*She said he had my eyes*
*She heard me in his cries*
*I said get out of here*
*She gave me a look of hate*
*Stormed of and slammed the gate*
*But, oh, how I loved her dear*

*You caught me on the rebound*
*My love is something*
*You've not found*

*But I thought I made it very clear*
*There's no feelings here*
*Cos I gave them to her*
*And then she went and broke my heart*
*By saying that we had to part*
*That hurt me inside*
*A piece of me died*
*And now it's just a blur.*

*You caught me when I was at a low*
*I should have told you*
*To turn and go*
*But something stopped me*
*What could it be?*
*Was it the look on your face?*
*Why did I give you that kiss?*
*Was it something that I missed?*
*Perhaps I'm in the right place.*

**You caught me on the rebound**
*My love is something*
*You've not found*
*But I thought I made it very clear*
*There's no feelings here*
*Cos I gave them to her*
*And then she went and broke my heart*
*By saying that we had to part*
*That hurt me inside*
*A piece of me died*
*And now it's just a blur.*

This song just proved what a loss Graham was to the music industry. It was a beautiful song. The crowd loved it. There must have been a five to ten minute ovation. Then Gillian introduced the next one.

'This next one is called "One of Us".'

*Tonight*
*Will probably be last*
*We'll be together*
*Tonight*
*It will be a decision*
*Of whether*
*We'll go our separate ways*
*And call it a day*

*And then one of us*
*Will be sad*
*One of us*
*Will go mad*
*Being single*
*One of us*
*Will stay inside*
*One of us*
*Will enjoy the ride*
*Being single*


*Tonight*
*We will both*
*Be ready*
*Tonight*
*We will act all steady*
*Before we go our separate ways*
*And call it a day*

*And then one of us*
*Will be sad*
*One of us*
*Will go mad*
*Being single*
*One of us*

*Will stay inside
One of us
Will enjoy the ride
Being single*

*Tonight
We'll say things
We don't mean
Tonight
May not be as it seems
Before we go our separate ways
And call it a day
And then one of us
Will be sad
One of us
Will go mad
Being single
One of us
Will stay inside
One of us
Will enjoy the ride
Being single*

'Bloody hell!' Jude exclaimed. 'Is it even possible that they are getting better and better?'

'If I knew that this sort of dynamite was in that case,' Parveen said, 'then I wouldn't have passed it on to Samantha. I would have recorded the whole lot myself.'

'The crowd are loving this new material,' I said looking behind me at the audience. They were clapping and cheering and with no sign of this abating. Tony, Gillian and Samantha looked absolutely elated. Even the Graham Longmuir hologram looked ecstatic. But even better, albeit sadder, was still to come.

# THE MEMORIAL CONCERT PART THREE

'Ladies and gentlemen,' Tony began to introduce the next act as the stage hands started to move equipment which was all on wheels, 'it gives me great pleasure to welcome on stage Alyson Hannigan and Christin Milioti from that brilliant American comedy show, shown between two thousand and five and two thousand and fourteen, "How I Met Your Mother".'

Loud applause greeted the two actresses. Alyson was now in her seventies but she still had the sparkle she had when she played Lily Aldrin. Christin was in her sixties but still looked terrific.

'Don't panic. We're not here to sing,' Christin joked.

'We're not?' Alyson said as the character she played in HIMYM. 'Then what are we doing here?'

'Well, don't you remember that they asked us to take part as HIMYM was Graham Longmuir's favourite show?'

'I must have been eating a sandwich at that point,' Alyson replied which got one of the biggest laughs of the evening. You need to watch the series to get that reference. 'Did you marry Ted in the end?'

'Yes. And I died.'

'Didn't work out too well for you then,' Alyson laughed.

'Dammit! I bet Ted will end up with Robin now.'

'He did.'

'Dammit! That means I owe Marshall twenty dollars.'

'That must have been some sandwich you were eating,' Christin said.

'So why did they ask us two?' Alyson said.

'You are aware that "How I Met Your Mother" was Graham Longmuir's favourite show?' Christin asked.

'Of course,' Alyson replied. 'He was going to play me in the movie, you know.'

'No, he wasn't.'

'He would have won the Oscar for playing me.'

'I think he won enough of those,' Christin smiled.

'You can say that again,' Alyson agreed.

'Anyway,' Christin said changing the subject. 'We were invited to introduce the next special guest stars. You know that Graham was in another famous group after Ladies and Gentlemen, don't you?'

'Of course,' said Alyson. 'Another great group called "Kids Stuff". There really was no end to this guys talent, was there?'

'There certainly wasn't,' Christin agreed. 'Ladies and gentlemen, we would like you to welcome to the stage, Chris...'

'And Andy Adams,' Alyson continued. 'Here's "Kid's Stuff".'

Alyson and Christin had done an amazing performance and did get a rousing cheer but the sonic boom that greeted Andy and Chris was phenomenal. It was only confirmed at the last moment that they would be attending. After all, they were now only fifty percent of the group. They certainly looked overcome with emotion with the reaction.

Chris sat at his drum kit while Andy stood toying with his bass guitar. If it carried on like this, then it would be way after midnight the concert finished.

'We weren't going to attend this evening,' Chris said. 'Losing Steve in that crash a few years ago was heartbreaking. But losing our cousin, Graham, as well, has just made it unbearable. So, apologies if it all goes wrong. I guess we should get straight in with our first ever hit "If The Kids Are Alright" which became an anthem of ours.'

Chris hit his snare drum with eight beats signifying the tempo of the song. An image of Graham appeared at the front of the stage and a projection of Steve, playing his lead guitar, lit up to Graham's right as you watched the show.

*If the kids are alright*
*Then the future will be bright*
*If the kids choose to hate*
*Then the world they'll desecrate*

*Do you consider yourself*
*To be a good role model?*
*I don't think so*
*In fact you're very bad*
*You don't teach what's right from wrong*
*If I was black*
*I'd be feeling pretty mad*

*If the kids are alright*
*Then the future will be bright*
*If the kids choose to hate*
*Then the world they'll desecrate*

*Do you think you're*
*Quick to stereotype?*
*Why put everything*
*Into a pigeon-hole*
*It doesn't matter being black or white*
*You're a human*
*And love is the goal*

*If the kids are alright*
*Then the future will be bright*

*If the kids choose to hate*
*Then the world they'll desecrate*

*Do you reckon you've done enough*
*To save the world*
*I don't think so*
*Cos the Earth is getting warm*
*I think you now need to do what's right*
*Hold my hand*
*I'll help you through the storm*

*If the kids are alright*
*Then the future will be bright*
*If the kids choose to hate*
*Then the world they'll desecrate*

*If the kids are alright*
*Then the future will be bright*
*If the kids choose to hate*
*Then the world they'll desecrate*

    I was even on my feet at the end of the song. 'We're Kids Stuff. Thank you for watching the show. Goodnight,' Graham's image said. How the designers managed it, I have no idea. But who care. Newton Abbot Racecourse was the place to be at that particular moment in time. Apologies to those who were watching on television, I'm sure that it was very emotional. But, actually being there, you could see, feel, touch, hear and even taste the outpouring of love and grief. Strangers were hugging each other and crying and laughing in each other's arms.
    I later learnt that Kids Stuff were going to perform two songs but Chris and Andy found it so difficult performing without their two close colleagues, they just couldn't carry on. They also found the audiences' loving response to them painful to bear. Gillian told me that they came off the stage in tears. It had hit them hard. Obviously more harder than it did Gillian, Samantha and Tony. Personally, I reckon, it was only because of the

reaction the audience gave them. There was so much love but not even that could bring back their bros' Graham and Steve.

The stage went dark. I felt a light spitting of rain. The weather was only going to get worse. Parveen, Judith and I decided to continue watching the show from the dryness of the wings. We could see well from the side of the stage either by watching it live or on a sixty inch monitor. It was now time to remember Luigi and Tracey.

A big smiling picture of Luigi filled the screen. Samantha walked on stage and a single follow spot picked her out.

'My husband Luigi Gustav,' Samantha said which was greeted by applause and cheering. 'I met Luigi at a low point in my life, my divorce from Liam. He lifted me up. Not only was he a perfect gentlemen but he was a gifted designer. I would like to present, for you, a fashion show full of stunning designs by my husband. These items are available to order from the merchandise stand or from the number on the screen. All proceeds will be going to Tony's charity. Run it, guys.'

Samantha introduced each item. Friends from the music, television and film industries were recruited to be models. Hell, even I went out in a high collared salmon tee-shirt. But after my Dolly Parton inspired costume of earlier, anything would have been an improvement. Everybody seemed to enjoy this segment. Samantha had found a very fitting way to pay tribute to her husband.

The stage went dark again. Tony walked on stage and the beam of light landed on him.

A picture of Tracey was displayed.

'Tracey was my whole life,' Tony began. 'She may not have been as well known as Graham or Luigi we're to the world, but to me she was everything. She became the beloved stepmother to Harrison and Leia. And a wonderful mother to Christian. She became co-founder of our meningitis charity after what happened to our brave son. What many people did not know about her, though, was that she was a talented pianist. Here she is playing one of the most difficult pieces ever composed for the piano

- Liszt's "La Campanella".' I watched, gobsmacked, as Tracey appeared to play this piece so effortlessly. 'Not only did she enjoy playing classical but also many of the pop classics. Please listen to her as she plays one of her favourites - "I Don't Like Mondays" written by Bob Geldof and performed by The Boomtown Rats.'

Again, I could only watch speechless as Tracey tickled the keys of the piano to a song she loved. 'How long have we known Tracey?' Judith sounded equally amazed. 'Did you know that she could play the piano like that?'

'I had no idea,' I admitted.

'Neither did I,' said Parveen.

After the song had finished the spotlight fell on Tony again. Not only could she play other people's compositions but she was also talented at writing music. This is one of her pieces.' We were mesmerised by the way her hands glided over the keys. If anything this piece seemed more complex than "La Campanella" but she made it look effortless. Again, when Tracey had finished, the light shone on Tony. 'I have mixed some of Tracey's works which are available to download now. Proceeds from the sales will go to our meningitis charity. Thank you all for being so kind and listening to this part of the concert. I love you, Tracey,' he finished and looked skyward. If this didn't catch emotionally with everyone, then there must be some very callous people out there.

Tony quickly left the stage, went to the dressing and changed whilst a montage of Luigi, Tracey and Graham was being played. He then joined Samantha and Gillian on stage. Samantha started playing the opening bass melody to a very familiar Graham Longmuir solo track.

'Ladies and Gentlemen, this is Graham Longmuir's first ever solo song "Rock Me Gently".'

And then they went full swing into it. The holographic projection of Graham singing the song shone on the stage as he walked its entire length. This was followed by "Teenage Dream". The crowd were loving it. They didn't seem to care that they were getting wet, very wet. The heavens had opened. But we were now coming to end of the concert.

'We're going to let decide our future,' Tony said. 'When we visited Graham in hospital, just after the shooting, he made us promise to continue with the group if anything should happen to him. However, that decision, despite our promise, is too big a one for us to make. There are two numbers on the screen one says yes and the other says no. What we want to know is would you like us to tour with Graham's hologram? Or would you prefer that we just left it here. Press yes for us to tour or no to leave it with this concert. You've got a couple of minutes.'

It was a unanimous decision. Ninety eight percent wanted them to tour.

'Looks like we're going out on tour, then,' Samantha said.

'Ladies and gentlemen, this is "Goodbye",' Gillian said. They started the song they had ended the funeral with.

*Samantha - You closed your eyes*
*Then you were gone*
*But you'll always be remembered*
*In your songs*
*Gillian - When I hear your voice*
*It's very clear*
*It's like you're just standing here*
*Tony - But you're not*
*And We ask why*
*We never got to say goodbye*

*Samantha, Gillian and Tony*
*You may be gone*
*But you're not forgotten*
*And I thank you*
*For letting me share it with you*
*But the memories make me cry*
*Cos I never got to say goodbye.*

It was at this point everyone who contributed to the

performance; Parveen, Cat, Steps, Alyson Hannigan, Christin Milioti and yours truly came on stage to accompany Ladies and Gentlemen. Everyone, that is, apart from Chris and Andy. They had already left the racecourse.

*You were embarrassed*
*By your fame*
*You always thought*
*It was just a game*
*Your voice so tender*
*And that's no lie*
*But I never got to say goodbye*

*You may be gone*
*But you're not forgotten*
*And I thank you*
*For letting me share it with you*
*But the memories make me cry*
*Cos I never got to say goodbye*

*We were friends*
*Since first day of school*
*You were clever*
*But acted the fool*
*Now we feel*
*Tears in our eyes*
*Because we never got to say goodbye*

*You may be gone*
*But you're not forgotten*
*And I thank you*
*For letting me share it with you*
*But the memories make me cry*
*Cos I never got to say goodbye*

Gillian, Samantha and Tony took back over the lead vocals as the rest waved and departed the stage.

*You may be gone*
*But you're not forgotten*
*And I thank you*
*For letting me share it with you*
*But the memories make me cry*
*Cos we never got to say goodbye.*

'And now it's your turn to sing,' Samantha said to the world. And sing they did.

*You may be gone*
*But you're not forgotten*
*And I thank you*
*For letting me share it with you*
*But the memories make me cry*
*Cos we never got to say goodbye.*

As the audience were singing, Samantha, Gillian and Tony joined in a group hug. Then Samantha and graham shuffled sideways so that Graham's hologram could join in the embrace. It was how they had finished every concert since before the split and the Reunion tour. It seemed fitting to end it exactly the same way. Pictures of Tracey and Luigi were beamed onto the screens. And then the hologram was rising into the night sky as though Graham Longmuir was ascending to heaven. I have no idea how Olivia and Kelvin managed to achieve this illusion but it certainly made many, many people cry.

The screens, for some reason or another, decided to go all fuzzy at this point. Thankfully the technical hitch had waited until the end of the concert. Some words appeared on all the monitors.

"IF YOU'RE READING THIS, GRAHAM AVERY, THEN GO FISH".

Now what the bloody hell was happening. And then my phone sounded that I had had a message.

# EPILOGUE

The person had watched the entire concert. They had even donated to get Graham Avery to perform in the costume similar to what Dolly Parton wore at Glastonbury. The person was singing and dancing along. It had been a very go concert. The person had thoroughly enjoyed it. But, now, like most things, it was coming to an end and it was time for them to go to work.

Someone had already hacked into Newton Abbot Racecourse's software as well as the television company's. All the person had to do was type in a few things and they would have access. The person's fingers tapped away at the keys. They got the signal that they were in. The person started typing again.

**"IF YOU'RE READING THIS, GRAHAM AVERY, THEN GO FISH".**

The person smiled. They knew that that would pique Mr Avery's interest but they were not finished. They picked up the phone that was lying next to the monitor. The screen showed what they were typing.

"Congratulations, Mr Avery. Like I said before, you solved all the secrets. It's up to you now with what you do with the information. Go to the police or keep it to yourself and let them get off. Parveen won't be happy about Graham's and Samantha's little sordid affairs. But less of this triviality. I'm going to play a game with you, Mr Avery. You see, out of Samantha, Gillian, Parveen, Susan Blackmore, Chris Duncan, Tony and Graham, one of them has a bigger secret. A secret that they wouldn't want the world to know because they would be hated forever. All you need to do is work out who and what it is. Isn't this fun? Oh by the way, I'm going to give you six months to try and figure it out. Isn't that generous of me. So Mr Avery, Go Fish".

The person read it through again before pressing send. Then they stood up, went to the door and opened it. They made sure that nobody was around before exiting and moving to the last door on the left. They took a solitary key from out of their pocket, checked once again that no one was near or watching and unlocked the door.

The room was like a prison cage. It had bars everywhere. There was whimpering coming from something that was covered by a blanket.

'He's coming for you,' the person was using a voice distorter. 'He thinks you're behind it all. So, my pet it's time to play go fish.'

The blanket was thrown to another corner and the body it concealed crawled to the front bars.

'I'm ready to play go fish,' Susan Blackmore said, smiling sweetly.

The end

Copyright Graham Avery 2020.

[1]

# ACKNOWLEDGEMENT

To John, Alan, Mick, Tony, Bill and Pete - the original Rubettes. I blame you guys for making me love music so much. Sugar Baby Love is a classic but your album tracks were amazing. Teenage Dream will always be my favourite

To Faye, Lisa, Claire, Lee & Ian collectively known as Steps. You were my guilty pleasure on my ipod but now you're just a pleasure

To everyone connected with the music world. Life may have been tough in 2020 but listening to music will never go away

To Rob and Pauline at Danceworks Newton Abbot who have tried hard to sort out my two left feet. hope you had better luck with Graham Longmuir

To Jude Becca and Ian who must have by now gotten fed up with Ladies and Gentlemen but, hopefully, not with me

Finally to Alan Longmuir 20th June 1948 - 2nd July 2018. Founder member of one of the biggest bands of all time - The Bay City Rollers. If you have not heard him singing Rock 'n' Roll Honeymoon, then give it a listen. The main star of Ladies and Gentlemen owes you everything, Alan

# ABOUT THE AUTHOR

## Graham Avery

I have always been passionate about books; I love all kinds. But getting myself published last year was amazing. It got me started on a journey that I want to do again and again.

I enjoy spending time with my family and we managed to survive lockdown during the Covid-19 Pandemic without murding each other. I cannot believe that my darling wife, Jude - who is a bit like the character Judith in the novels - has put up with me for over 30 years. I am proud of my two children, Becca and Ian, who have forged their own careers quite successfully.

Music, as you've probably guessed, is a love of mine. I will listen to everything from classical through to Eminem.

I hope that you enjoy The Reunion series and - spoilers - Reunion 3 is on its way.

# PRAISE FOR AUTHOR

*Normally i read Fantasy, Sci-Fi, Horror or Historical but a friend recommended it so i gave it a go. As the blurb says it about a pop band and a mystery. This was a different speed for me but it was an enjoyable and easy read. I was amused/slightly worried about the authors obvious love of the band Steps but it was nice to see Devon represented in a story. Overall a quick, easy read with an interesting plot from someone who obviously loves pop bands!*

# BOOKS BY THIS AUTHOR

## The Reunion

s it ever a good idea for a once-huge pop band to reunite? Particularly if their split was acrimonious, surrounded by lies, challenges and complications? And especially when a quarter of a century has gone by and the group members have carved out completely different (and successful) careers? That's for you to decide. Twenty-five years on, 'Ladies and Gentlemen' are re-uniting to raise money for a certain charity close to one of the band member's hearts. Their return to notoriety begins with an explosive interview. Britain's most famous (and notoriously confrontational) political interviewer – who takes no prisoners and was the catalyst behind getting the group together in the first place – sets the scene for a future filled with fireworks and it isn't long before the proverbial can of worms is laid bare for all the world to see. But this time, the problems aren't caused by the egos of the rich and famous. Rather there's much more going on backstage… journalists with ulterior motives… heartbreak… arrests… tragedy… mental hospitals… murder… and, eventually, a band member fighting for their life. Dive into this fast-paced, chilling and evocative psychological thriller, steeped in mystery and intrigue, with compelling characters, convincing pasts, and complicated futures. And be prepare to be hooked.

Printed in Great Britain
by Amazon